I0761209

PRAISE FOR ***LOVE AND VIDEO GAMES***

"A gift of a book. Like any good video game, this love story is filled with extra heart, excellent Easter eggs, and characters you'll remember after the final level."

—*James Acker, author of the Stonewall Honor Book*
The Long Run *and* Teenage Dirtbags

"Thanks to **Love and Video Games**, *queer YA receives a buff! With a unique gaming world, swoony romance, and characters that are so easy to fall in love with and root for, Sergi has created a perfect combo."*

—*Erik J. Brown, author of*
All That's Left in the World *and* The Only Light Left Burning

"I didn't think I could be so immersed in a game that lives on the pages of a book, but Zachary Sergi got his hooks in me and didn't let go until the final boss—er, I mean, the final page. **Love and Video Games** *is an enchanting tale for gamers with secret crushes, warriors fighting hidden battles, and those of us who've escaped into a fantastical world only to end up more connected to the real one."*

—*Robbie Couch,* New York Times *bestselling author*

"A fun, fast, and fabulous read, **Love and Video Games** *has something for every reader: authentic queer teen romance, deep friendships, real-world mythology, and tons of gaming action. It's mythologically queer and nerdy—my perfect good time. I know it'll be yours, too."*

—*M. K. England, author of*
The One True Me and You *and* Roll for Love

*"***Love and Video Games** *is a gaymer's paradise! Full of worlds you could get lost in for hours, characters you root for as they level up at life, and a budding romance that deserves to be at the top of the leaderboards, Zachary Sergi's latest should not be missed!"*

—*Jason June,* New York Times *bestselling author*

"A triumphant queer romance about the unlimited potential to be the hero of your own story!"

—Adam Sass, award-winning author of The 99 Boyfriends of Micah Summers

"Love and Video Games ***will have you tearing up, staying at the very edge of your seat, laughing out loud, and feeling absolute joy. With action, swoons, S-tier levels of fun, and well-crafted characters that feel like friends, it is a warm hug of a book that will stay with readers long after the final boss (or page)."***

—Justine Pucella Winans, award-winning author of Bianca Torre Is Afraid of Everything

"Love and Video Games ***is a heartfelt, warm, hug of a book! With heart, thoughtful disability rep, found family, and a tender queer romance,*** **Love and Video Games** ***is bound to leave a lasting impression on readers. Sergi has crafted a world that's as magical as it is meaningful and will engage readers with the turn of every page!"***

—Hannah V. Sawyerr, critically acclaimed author of All the Fighting Parts *and* Truth Is

RP|TEENS
PHILADELPHIA

Running Press Teens
Hachette Book Group
1290 Avenue of the Americas, New York, NY 10104
www.runningpresskids.com
@runningpresskids

First Edition: September 2025

Published by Running Press Teens, an imprint of Hachette Book Group, Inc. The Running Press Teens name and logo are trademarks of Hachette Book Group, Inc.

Print book cover design by Mary Boyer
Print book interior design by Sara Puppala

Library of Congress Cataloging-in-Publication Data has been applied for.

ISBNs: 978-0-7624-8903-9 (hardcover), 978-0-7624-8904-6 (ebook)

Printed in Indiana, USA

LSC-C

Printing 1, 2025

To anyone who fights
to define what victory
means on their own terms.

CHAPTER ONE

WHEN I WANT TO ESCAPE AND FEEL BELOVED, THERE IS ONE place I always go. It's somewhere I can be rewarded and challenged. A space where I can belong, be strong, feel no pain, and be completely myself. I'm able to go there from the comfort of my own bedroom, yet it will still take me exploring and warring across countless realms.

Pantheonic, my favorite video game, is my happy place.

Right now I feel very far from that space—but at least I'm journeying closer with each passing second. Of course, this is a melodramatic way of saying that I'm currently riding the SEPTA Regional Rail from my job back to my house. My parents actually gave me this summer off from needing to work, after I got a partial scholarship to my dream college. "You earned a summer to just enjoy yourself with your friends," they said. It was sweet of them, but my idea of enjoying myself does happen to be working at a nearby college library. There, between my cataloging duties, I'm able to read as many rare mythology texts as I can get my greedy little hands on.

My parents also never quite seem to understand that the only friends I really feel close to are my *Pantheonic* teammates.

They don't get how I could be best friends with other teens I've never seen in person and who don't live near our Northeast Philadelphia suburb. But the truth is I've never met anyone else in real life with whom I have as much in common. Well, *almost* never. And I've certainly never met anyone in person who lives up to my epic online teammate crush.

Really, my high school life has been pretty solitary when it comes to finding peers—maybe even *because* I have such good gaming friends. They've truly gotten me through this past year. I just wish we all lived closer.

As if on cue with this thought, the muscles in my right hip area cramp up. Actually, that's not right. The pain is so hard to describe, but it feels something like a sharp throb from my hip to my tailbone. For the past ten months, whenever I sit—like right now in my seat on the train—my right ass cheek basically feels like a lightning rod.

So I do what I've always done since my "condition" started. I straighten my back, square up my shoulders, shift my weight onto my left butt cheek, and try desperately to think of anything else.

I look out the window and attempt to focus on the row houses of North Philly flying by. I try to think of myself as the Greek messenger god Hermes, traveling to deliver newly unearthed knowledge to my very own pantheon. Which is half true. During my reading today I uncovered a detail about the Japanese sun goddess Amaterasu that I think will help one of my teammates, Alix, customize his avatar. Just thinking of him turns my thoughts into little beams of light. Alix and his sun god avatar occupy my attention far more than I'd like to admit.

That's just me: avid gaymer, mythology enthusiast, aspiring Classics professor, and secret romantic, dulling the little human indignities of each day by keeping my eyes on the pantheons everywhere but here.

The walk from the train stop to my house is short, but thanks to the July humidity I'm already sweating after one block. At least the cramped knotting sensation starts to release as I stretch out my hip, stride by stride. At the library I can get away with standing most of the time, between rolling the return cart and leaning against the counter when I read. But I dread the times I have to sit or lie down. Any direct pressure on my lower right back seems to stir the pit of vipers teething in my nerves.

Once again I attempt to push this from my thoughts, not wanting to spiral into the WebMD state of mind filled with potential diagnoses. Sciatica pain? External rotator hip tightness? Lower back complications? Piriformis syndrome knotting? No orthopedist, internist, or sports masseuse has been able to figure out what's causing the pain. At least I have my weekly physical therapy appointment tomorrow, and that always helps for a day or two.

Realizing I've already failed at avoiding the worry spiral, I remind myself that soon I have a very special date with my *Pantheonic* team to escape into. Today we are playing in an invitation-only quest event for top-ranked teams, which is rumored to start with an "unprecedented" virtual announcement from the creator and CEO of *Pantheonic* herself.

I punch the code to my front door and am immediately greeted by a blast of air-conditioning and the smell of chicken pot pie cooking. It's just me and my parents in our standard three-bedroom house, but to me our place is a cozy palace. Filled with heirlooms from my parents' respective families back in Ireland, our house feels like a bed and breakfast filled with stained glass lamps, carved wood furniture, and leather-bound books. Since my parents are both tenured professors, the nerd vibes run deep in our home.

"Keegan, is that you?"

I find my mom in the kitchen, where NPR plays from an old radio beside the steaming stove. As always, she looks like the lead from a Nancy Meyers film, but only if it were set in the Shire.

"I got you a scone from that place you like, but they only had orange cranberry left." I kiss my mom on the cheek, pulling out the wrapped scone and handing it to her. I save the raspberry oat square for my own late-afternoon snack.

"Ah, the artisanal vultures got to the chocolate chips early," Mom replies. "Thanks, love. Dad will be home from his pickleball match soon, and dinner is in a couple of hours. I assume you're off to vanquish another corrupted earth realm with your fellow deities?"

"The earths aren't going to save themselves," I say, smiling and turning toward my bedroom. "See you at dinner, thanks for cooking."

I've always loved summers even more than most kids, since my parents also have time off from their schools. The three of us get to bury ourselves deep in research projects and hobbies, nestled between our curated part-time gigs. It's no wonder where I got the professor bug from. I can't wait to get out of high school and onto a college campus, where I hope to spend the rest of my days surrounded by thick books, classical pantheons, and fellow eager minds.

We usually can only afford to go on one nerdy family vacation every summer, but my parents saved our trip budget for a long weekend in Manhattan next month to help me settle into my dorm at NYU. I've been secretly happy to delay dealing with travel obstacles, since it's been challenging to make myself comfortable even at home. Of course, I've also been dreading figuring out how to manage my chronic pain in a new city, not to mention with a roommate.

Mostly I've been hoping I can kick the pain completely before leaving, because I don't want anything to interfere with my college dream. This hasn't exactly been going to plan, but for now that remains a quest for future Keegan to traverse.

Present Keegan?

He now gets to go to his happy place.

I walk into my room and throw my bag on my bed, which is tucked between my bookshelves. Both are filled with volumes and novels about world mythology, plus plenty of graphic novels. The real centerpiece of my room, however, remains my gaming setup. I have spent years' worth of summer-job income and birthday presents building this sacred shrine.

My desk holds a sleek monitor, gleaming above my precious computer tower. The rest of the desk is curated with *Pantheonic* merch and mythical knickknacks that remind me of the game. Yet the real highlight remains a present that another teammate, Mo, made for each of us a few months ago when our pantheon cracked the top 200 on the leaderboard. It's a collage of our team, the Epic Hearts, with our gaming profile photos featured beside our avatars and some luscious art from the game.

I glance at my own face staring back at me: my freckled alabaster skin under a mop of shaggy blond hair. I wear a grandpa sweater over my deeply average body, looking severely like a stereotypical Classics professor. I suppose the crescent moon tattoo I secretly got on the inside of my arm isn't particularly professorial . . . but no one has ever seen that before.

As I start powering my computer up, I admire the brand-new, silver-and-gold-themed gaming keyboard and mouse I splurged on when summer started. Both rest on a retractable tray, which rolls out at the perfect height for my gaming chair. This throne is also completely ergonomic, with a built-in lumbar support pillow and adjustable arm-, head-, and footrests.

I love my setup with all my heart, this place where I can be still and completely transported at the same time. It's also recently the one place in the world where I can sit free of the usual throbbing. I don't know if it's because my brain is always too focused on gaming to register the ache or because of the ergonomic design. Either way, I now treat this gaming altar—where I'm free of chronic pain—with even more ritualistic reverence.

Part of that ritual now means making sure that, before sitting, I stretch my lower back, then work my hip and leg muscles on a foam roller.

Thankfully, I don't need to do any of this alone.

CHAPTER TWO

AS I GET SET ON THE YOGA MAT NOW PERMANENTLY LAID out in the corner of my room, I open the Discord app on my phone. Naturally, I find Mo and Alix already chatting away in our team thread.

> **SMOTE:** You are truly delulu if you think Gambit has better fashion sense than Storm.
>
> **APOLLIX:** I'm just saying, I've never seen Miss Ororo rock a crop top the way my main Cajun man does.
>
> **SMOTE:** Oh, Keegan is here for his pregame stretch. But let's switch to voice, I have some updates.

I warm with a smile. Sure, partly because these two know me so well, but also because just seeing Alix's username makes my heart flutter online. As I start stretching, I look over at his photo in our team collage on my desk, like I do maybe a thousand times a day.

In the photo, Alix wears one of his own pieces, since he's an aspiring fashion designer. It's a structured sleeveless jacket that shows off his slim but muscled arms, perfectly capturing his designer style: future nostalgia, where alt fashion meets classic cuts. I know all this from following Alix on social media, where

I spend far too much time staring at his striking light brown face and perfectly styled black hair. All while marveling at the life he built *all by himself* after emancipating from his family in Arizona and moving to Queens.

Alix joined our team after his move and doesn't like talking about his life before. And why would he? His NYC life seems wonderful, filled with fellow trans friends and scrappy adventures. Ever since I even *applied* to NYU, we've been dreaming up all the things we want to do across the city and adding to the list of the sights Alix wants to show me. He has invited me to make the trip up from Philly to hang more than a few times, but I've always found excuses to chicken out.

The truth is, I'm a little terrified to meet Alix in person. There's no way in Norse goddess Hel someone as cool as him would think of someone basic like me as more than a friend. I've done my homework—based on all the incredibly stylish and muscled gay dudes he follows on social media, I am so not his type. I'm lucky just to have Alix as a friend, and I'm very afraid of messing that up by being around each other without the filter of our team and distance. Part of this summer has been about preparing for the move to college, but it has also been about plotting how to shift my virtual friendship with Alix into the real world as seamlessly as possible. I'm . . . still working on that part too.

"Hi, team," I say, putting my phone on speaker as I stretch out my hamstrings. "For the record, Beast is the best-dressed X-Man around, no contest."

"We get it, you like big hairy dudes in underwear," Alix snarks back.

Yeah, right. My type is way more genderqueer gay-boys in stylish clothes, but Alix doesn't need to know that. I just wish *he* liked bigger hairy dudes, then maybe I'd have a shot.

"What fun ancient sun god fact do you have for me today?" Alix finishes.

"Sun *goddess* actually," I reply, wincing at how predictable I must seem. "Did you know that most depictions of Amaterasu have her wearing a necklace made of light? In a Japanese creation myth, they lured Amaterasu out of a cave with a mirror, tricking her into reflecting sunlight across the earth. What if—"

"I try equipping a Mirrored Necklace to boost Apollix's fire casting," Alix says, finishing my thought. "It's usually used for Reaper draining spell storage . . . but it might work just as well, specifically for a sun Bender?"

"My sentiments exactly," I say, thankful Alix can't see how wide my dopey smile currently stretches. "You know the *Pantheonic* creators love a mythical reference and some secret synergy strength."

"Absolutely," Alix replies. "I'll see if I've started the quest thread to try and get one later."

"Excuse me, boys," Mo cuts in, "I *was* going to share some extra classified intel I combed from the forums once we were all assembled, but if you keep third-wheeling me, maybe I'll just keep it to myself . . ."

I can instantly picture the faux-serious look on Mo's face, doing her best impression of her own Trickster avatar. I glance over at her photo in the collage, taken at the counter of Third Eye Comics in Annapolis where she works. Mo's smile is big and bright and matches the energy of her curly hair, which frames her dark brown face like a halo. She wears an oversized T-shirt featuring a local drag queen cosplaying as Sylvie from *Loki*, which was half the inspiration for her avatar. The other half comes from Senna, the *League of Legends* character that originally got Mo into multiplayer online games.

"How dare you, Mo," Alix gasps. "You know you are our queen among queens."

"All right, let's not go overboard." Mo laughs. "The rumblings online are mostly about what CEO Dahlia Delfanti is going to announce before this invitational quest. Rumor has it the event has something to do with a new tournament."

"But *Pantheonic* already has its own esports tournaments," I reply. "We've never been in that kind of pro gamer league before."

"I know, but apparently people are thinking this event is going to be something else. There's been lots of chatter and 'signs' about shifting the game into a new story era, so people are thinking the event is about the first step."

My stomach clenches a little. The idea of my beloved game changing in some big way is not my favorite thought. But even if I don't love Mo's intel today, I'm grateful for it. I keep my gaming circle as closed as humanly possible, avoiding open chat threads, reviews, and articles so I can focus fully on the lore and my teammates. Mo is a much braver gamer than me when it comes to wading through the toxic sludge there, so I always trust her word.

"And if we're going extra deep," Mo continues, "there's another rumor going around that this era-shifting tournament might have some major in-person component."

I can hear the excitement vibrating in Mo's voice. I can't blame her—that does sound very cool. But I'm not exactly up for a last-minute gaming trip, pulling me out of my physical comfort zone before I'm ready. Especially because my friends think my pregame stretching is just a meditative thing. Aside from my parents, I haven't told anyone about my chronic pain—and I don't intend to.

I suppose the chances of us getting to go to some big tournament are pretty slim anyway. We might have made this first invitational cut, but probably just barely. We're good, but our team plays for fun, unlike the pro gamers and level grinders out there.

"That would be unbelievably awesome," Alix says. "But let's log on and find out? I just signed in and Britni is here. Let's switch to our game chat?"

"Almost done loading," Mo says.

"On my way," I add.

We end the call and I move to my gaming desk, feeling properly stretched and rolled. My computer is powered up, so I click to open *Pantheonic.* The game's mythical score begins to play, and I feel the usual wave of warm familiarity and anticipation. My computer isn't state-of-the-art, but it's still built for gaming. This ensures the best visuals while avoiding lagging and long loading times, but I have a little time to get ready before I'm logged in.

First, I set my phone timer for thirty minutes to remind future me to stand and stretch. Then I place my water thermos and oat bar on the desk so I can stay hydrated and properly blood-sugared. Feeling like one of the many cozy gamer accounts I follow, I take the final loading seconds to soak in our team collage. I do this every time I log in—a little mindful practice to remind me why I really love this game so much, mythological lore aside.

I focus on the fourth corner, which doesn't have a photo and instead shows our final teammate's purple pentagram icon. Whoever Britni Bats might be, she has opted to remain anonymous, not sharing her photo or social media and never joining us in our Discord chats. All I know about her personal life is that she lives in Los Angeles, but she always finds a way to play with us on an East Coast server.

Still, I feel like I know Britni's personality well enough from all our hours spent playing together, even if she is mostly all business. Her avatar, Chiroptera, is a brutalist bat-monster Creature with a delightful wicked streak. I've gleaned from Britni's cultural references that she is also probably in her late teens, just like the rest of us. Not all pantheon teams are necessarily made up of players the same age, but ours is—and I think it helps our synergy a ton.

Looking at Britni's mysterious icon, the idea of an in-person tournament sends a jolt of energy through me. What would it be like to meet the best friends I've ever had in person?

I suppose there's only one way to start answering that question . . .

By entering the immersive world of warring pantheons and conquered earth realms.

CHAPTER THREE

WHEN I AM K.ODYSSIA, I AM MY BEST SELF.

I become the ultimate goddess-queen, ever-defending and ever-cleaving. My elegantly muscled body is not just perfect, it is a weapon—and quite literally a temple to be worshipped. My gilded plate armor is mostly ceremonial, because my skin is tougher than any precious metal. I also wear a skirt of fringed red leather and knee-high gold boots. I always carry my sword and shield, both of which are adorned with my version of our Epic Hearts team crest: a shield that guards a heart.

I customized K.Odyssia to be a combo of some of mythology's fiercest goddesses: the visage and stature of Greece's Athena meets America's Wonder Woman, plus the red-and-gold coloring of Egypt's Sekhmet meets Hinduism's Durga. I also named K.Odyssia after the epic hero in *The Odyssey*, as a female foil to Odysseus . . .

A goddess of ushering warriors home.

Right now I enter the game with K.Odyssia falling from the sky. This is always one of my favorite parts, free-falling down into the Divine Realm's capital city, Mount Pantheonic. This is the hub where all mythical beings hang out between quests and spend time customizing our characters. As I fall I can see the entire city limits of Mount Pantheonic, a ring divided into seven sectors that represent the seven core Pantheon Pillars.

Players can customize their avatars' appearances and abilities however they choose, but all avatars must spawn from one of the seven pillars. The pillar we represent is not just about our vibe and ethos as a mythological figure, but also some of our base visuals and skills.

Just before I free-fall low enough to lose sight of the entire city sprawl, I take in the separate sectors . . .

There's Warrior Hill, with its open coliseums and banquet halls.

Trickster Alley, with its shadowy mazes and espionage dens.

Reaper Hallows, with its heavenly cemeteries and sunken graveyards.

Bender Park, with its elemental docks and winding lakes.

Traverser Lanes, with its expansive markets and secret passageways.

Then there's my own pillar's sector, Ruler Heights, with its regal palaces and fortified walls.

Finally, I fall into Creature Town, with its pocket fields and urban forests. Our team has a special spot in this sector where we always meet and hang, so that's usually my chosen drop point.

Once my gilded boots stomp onto the earth, I feel fully grounded. I pivot my view behind K.Odyssia until I spot the fountain where we Epic Hearts always gather. It's not a particularly special fountain in any way, but it's perfectly placed to watch the flight field where dragon-hybrids and other winged Creatures lift off and land.

I make the short walk across the grassy grove to find my team already gathered—and to find Chiroptera engaged in the activity that keeps this space partially protected for us: scaring off other players.

"How many times do I have to roar these newbies away?" Britni says on our team chat channel. Her voice, focused as always, is piped into the gaming headset I wear back at my desk.

Britni customized Chiroptera to be a human-bat hybrid Creature, hulking with height and coursing with brutality. Her purple fur is only clothed by a black leather harness. Its straps connect at a central amethyst chest plate, which is adorned with her version of our team crest: a broken heart being sliced by a claw.

Right now, Chiroptera finishes roaring at a centaur and a floating mermaid who tried to settle near our unofficial fountain home base. It's maybe a little overkill, but I love it. Above Chiroptera's head, beside her name and level, the Talon & Horn seal of the Creature Town Pillar gleams.

"I almost feel bad for them," Mo replies on our voice call. *"Almost."*

Mo has her avatar, sMOte, laugh, causing her battle braids to swing. sMOte is built to be the ultimate Trickster demigoddess, decked out in a sleek black bodysuit that's only one shade darker than her skin—and perfect for espionage. This suit sports two holster-sheathes for her signature dagger blasters, while her version of our team crest is just barely visible under her left collarbone: a half vanishing heart.

My favorite element of sMOte's design, however, is her regal mane of braids—which are filled with beads and adornments that hold a secret weapons arsenal. This helps make sMOte a realms-renowned mistress of whispers. Though the Dagger &

Cloak seal of the Trickster Pillar shows above her head, sMOte is best known for using the chaotic, rebellious, and mercenary tools of her pillar for nobler causes.

"While defending our honor is never a waste," Alix says, "we need to leave anyway. It's almost time for the invitational announcement."

Alix has Apollix unfurl the fiery set of wings that span from his muscled back. It took many months of solo questing to acquire this sun-drenched feature—and it was worth every sacred second. These impressive wings match Apollix's alpha male play on sun gods. Ever the fashion designer, Alix outfitted Apollix's bright brown skin with a gorgeous tunic of red, orange, gold, and silver. He also wears a ray-of-light tiara emblazoned with an open heart set aflame.

While Apollix would fit right in with me in the Ruler Pillar, his WaterWind & FireTree seal always reminds me he is actually spawned from the Bender Pillar. He wanted their elemental skills for his fire and light casting, but his Adonis appearance doesn't follow the more popular sprite, sorcerer, and monk vibe of many other Benders.

For K.Odyssia, I took full advantage of the Ruler Pillar's options for mythological iconography and wartime infamy. As I raise my sword to the sky now, my pillar's Crown & Throne seal shines proudly above my head.

"Let us commence to the Revelatory Shrine!" I battle cry.

"Aw, I love when our fearless leader goes all mythical quest on us," Mo says.

"It's inspiring enough to keep me on the ground with you earthbound wonders," Alix adds.

"Are you going to make fun of the fact that I'm a flightless bat again?" Britni groans.

"On such a momentous day?" Alix replies. "Why, I'd never!"

"Likely story." Mo laughs. "But we should probably make our grand entrance as a unified team anyway, right?"

"Right," I confirm. "Epic Hearts, let's roll out!"

As I charge forward, our eclectic gathering follows. Teams form in different ways, creating unique pantheon quartets across all pillar types. Some teams even build from scratch together to be consonant, but the Epic Hearts formed online after our avatars were already created. That's why we all adopted a heart crest of some kind, inspired by Apollix's original heart design.

Still, I sometimes like to think of us existing partially in our own *Odyssey*. Apollix fits right into the Greek sun god spot, then Chiroptera is our own beastly Scylla or Cyclops, while sMOte is like a deadly combination of Circe and Siren female force.

That said, over time we *have* synergized our builds to cover a complementary range of strengths and abilities. Even though our team falls into the gaming-for-fun category, we've still worked hard to rank among the best casual players. So getting invited to this ceremony feels like a real honor.

That feeling doubles as I gaze up at the Revelatory Shrine. Looking like an architectural mash-up between a Gothic cathedral and an ancient pyramid, the Revelatory Shrine is reserved for the most special *Pantheonic* occasions. I've only ever been up there a few times myself.

This sacred space sits atop seven literal pillars rising out of the city sectors. Avatars that can't fly or portal jump directly there must take one of the transport tubes built into the seven pillars. It's a short walk over a bubbling river and through some thorny woods to reach the Creature Town Pillar. At the entryway in its base, a metallic centurion checks invitations.

As we approach, we watch a team of Reapers get turned away, their Scythe & Angelwing seals glowing in deathly unison. I'm not surprised—having a team of four healers and health-drainers from the same pillar doesn't necessarily spell a recipe for success.

"Hey, have you heard the one where an angel, a demon, a ghost, and a grim walk into a Revelatory Shrine?" Mo asks.

"Can't say I have," I reply.

"Ha, neither have those guys," Mo finishes, laughing at herself quite heartily.

"You're lucky no one else can hear your bad jokes, Mo," Alix says, laughing a little himself. "It would totally undercut sMOte's reputation for badassery."

"Everyone have their invitations pulled up?" Britni asks as Chiroptera's eyes roll. The rest of us, her party of beloved knuckleheads, nod along.

Once our team is cleared, the centurion ushers us into an elevator-like transport. Soon enough we're rising out of Creature Town high enough that the rest of the sectors become visible again. Looking at my team, I'm so proud of all we represent.

It always fascinates me the way humans can endlessly mythologize ourselves—and how video games are an especially potent form of that. I bet if we compared our everyday selves to our *Pantheonic* personas, we'd find our avatars are vessels to reach for our ideal selves—but also perhaps safe spaces to process our . . . lesser instincts. It's one of the most insightful and illuminating parts of playing an online action role-playing game.

And that's all before we even get to the most *fun* part, full of combat and adventure.

Before long, the cityscape view vanishes as our transport reaches the Revelatory Shrine. As the doors open again, light from this hallowed hall bathes us in a warm glow.

And we step forth to take our place among the mightiest pantheons to ever assemble.

CHAPTER FOUR

FROM THE INSIDE, THE REVELATORY SHRINE IS A LARGE HALL with a ceiling full of skylights. The entire space feels open to a bright blue sky, one filled with glittering rainbow stars that remain eternally visible. The hall is scattered with stone statues that memorialize iconic *Pantheonic* lore figures, but the space's true focal point is a large stage with a pulpit in its center. Behind this, several banners display the pillared *Pantheonic* logo.

There have to be a couple hundred teams between those here and those still arriving. Seeing all the unique riffs on world mythology embodied in the other avatars, I get momentarily lost soaking in all the bright, brutalist details.

"Cary says their team is near the Bender statue," Mo says, pulling me out of my stupor. "Can we go meet them?"

Mo's partner, Cary, is also an avid *Pantheonic* player and had formed a team with local Annapolis friends before they met Mo. We don't get to game with their team very often because they tend to be late-night players, but we do try to hang whenever we can.

"Of course," I reply, spotting the statue toward the back of the hall. It'll take some jostling through the crowd to get there, so I start leading the way.

The first team we walk by grabs my attention. While one of them is a rather tough-looking unicorn-hybrid Creature, the other three—an elf, a faerie, and a dwarf—all sport the Portal & Chariot seal of the Traverser Pillar. If they're ranked high enough to be here, it obviously disproves my theory that single-pillar teams are at a disadvantage.

Then again, the Traverser Pillar boasts one of the more original bits of *Pantheonic* lore, giving these typical fantasy-genre species abilities that are focused on travel. I've always wondered what elves and faeries and all have to do specifically with traversing, but many mysteries of the original *Pantheonic* mythology have yet to be fully revealed.

Really, any composition of pillar types within a pantheon can become competitive, as long as a team diversifies their secondary abilities enough. Of course, there are still popular compositions that players *believe* to be the best or the strongest . . .

And no one exemplifies that type of thinking more than the "best" team in all of *Pantheonic*. I spot them front and center, right in front of the pulpit.

"The Mythic Goats are exactly where you'd expect them to be," I say.

"I spend way more time than I'd like to admit watching their streaming channel," Mo replies with a sigh.

"Yeah, but who would want to go pro like them?" I counter. "I mean, they're all about grinding. Do they even have any fun when they game anymore?"

"Can I get an omen?" Alix utters his signature catchphrase and snaps along through our headset call.

"Sure, but who needs fun when you're drowning in sponsorships?" Britni replies, sounding uncharacteristically wistful—though her undercurrent of bite sounds more familiar.

The Mythic Goats designed their team from scratch not only to feature the most popular Ruler-Trickster-Warrior-Bender pillar composition, but also to combine some of the most famous Greek and Norse deities. This visual theme for their avatars is hammered home by the names floating above their heads: Odinzeus, Lokihermes, Freyjathena, and Thorares.

When I see Freyjathena in particular, I always focus on the Sword & Shield seal of the Warrior Pillar above her. I like to think that she is a kind of sister deity to K.Odyssia, one who even more fully embodies the epic hero, arena contender, and battlefield traits of the Warrior Pillar. I always wonder if that's the pillar where K.Odyssia should have spawned from instead of opting for the courtly vibes of the Ruler Pillar. This classifies me instead with the Goats' sole Ruler, Odinzeus, which doesn't feel totally correct.

"Wait, I think it's starting," Britni says.

Indeed, a countdown sequence begins above the stage.

"It's okay, we can just watch from here," Mo offers. "Maybe we'll get to see Cary's team in the quest event instead."

I'm about to reply, but I fall silent as a cutscene sequence begins to play across my computer screen. I can tell from the first few musical notes that this is the opening animation for *Pantheonic*. I've seen it hundreds of times by now, but somehow it never really gets old.

For centuries upon centuries, the Source Wing's pure light has fueled life across the endless multiverse of earth realms. No beings are more empowered by this light than the countless *Pantheonic* deities, who watch over the human worshippers of every earth from the Divine Realm.

A great phoenixlike bird then spreads its full wingspan. These wings shine light over an endless row of earth spheres scrolling horizontally. From these earth realms, seven pillars rise up to support the city of Mount Pantheonic.

That is, until an unknown and unprecedented evil descended upon the realms: the dreaded Stoneruned Horde. No one knows where this relentless foreign force came from, but it nonetheless found a way to do the unthinkable. The Stoneruned Horde kidnapped the Source Wing and harnessed its endless energy to propel their own armies across the multiverse realms. Operating from its still-hidden Nerve Center, the Stoneruned Horde continues to conquer countless earth realms and force their peoples to live under their reign of monotheistic tyranny.

The gray and brown bleakness of the Stoneruned Horde begins to spread, threatening to soak the entire screen. Each Stoneruned automaton is a cloud of hivemind energy trapped inside a stone-stacked body, bound by alien-looking runes. Their endless numbers march over the Source Wing and the earth realms, threatening to conquer all.

Just as the Stoneruned Horde is about to completely overrun everything, the pillars suddenly crack open. This unleashes the seven archetypal *Pantheonic* deities, who hold back the tide of the Horde: The Ruler, The Trickster, The Warrior, The Creature, The Bender, The Reaper, and The Traverser.

In order to free the Source Wing, uncover where the Stoneruned Horde came from, and discover how they trapped this sacred source, an unprecedented alliance was forged. To match this endlessly replenishable enemy, pantheons from across every earth realm united. Their shared goal? To save the Source Wing by reclaiming conquered realms, one by one. This polytheistic alliance of pantheons vowed to put aside their considerable egos and rivalries . . . But that is no simple task, especially when engaged in an ultimate quest for glory. And so the dire and wondrous age of the Pantheonic Stoneruned War began.

As the cutscene ends, we are returned to the hall. Then a spotlight falls on the pulpit, shining down upon the avatar of the game's chief creator and CEO, Dahlia Delfanti.

Her avatar, Queen Trinidy, wears a simple, flowy suit made of a luminous white fabric and a leafy crown carved from gemstones. In interviews, Dahlia has said she took inspiration from world-spanning variations on goddesses of love, creativity, and conflict to create her avatar. Just like her real-life self, this avatar drips with casual cool and courses with the charisma of a video game icon. In the game, Queen Trinidy is also the head of the Pantheonic War Council that plots all quests to reclaim earth realms.

"Oh, mightiest teams of the Pantheonic Pillars, I thank you for gathering here today," Queen Trinidy begins, her voice reverberating through the hall. "For we have a proclamation to deliver that only the worthiest pantheons will be strong enough to hear.

"Throughout time immemorial, humans and deities alike have always loved games. We can find beings playing, watching, or judging games in every single culture, in every corner of every version of earth. Billions of souls spending even more trillions in resources on sporting, reality, board, mobile, and video games. But why are all living beings so drawn to the gauntlet of gaming?

"While the answer to this question might ultimately impact our own endgame, we first must solve the four core mysteries of the Pantheonic Stoneruned War: Where exactly is the Source Wing being held? How is this vital force being contained and tapped by the Stoneruned Horde? What weapon will ultimately defeat the strongest Stoneruned automatons? And finally, what will happen to our competing pantheons should peace be restored—and what unknown home will the Stoneruned Horde be banished to?

"Together, we here have spent years chasing the answers to these questions while battling the Stoneruned Horde. Today, we have gathered our boldest and brightest to announce that the Pantheonic War Council has finally plotted a course to solving these fundamental mysteries—and to ending this great war. That end-quest will begin this very summer. But be warned: claiming victory will require unprecedented efforts from the very best pantheons among us.

"To usher in a new era from this endgame, *Pantheonic* will hold a brand-new in-person tournament in New York City. The pantheon teams who have earned places here today will soon enter a raid quest event—where seven tournament team invitations will be up for grabs. This event will begin shortly.

"Prepare thyselves. And good luck."

Queen Trinidy finishes her speech with a regal nod and vanishes from the stage. Once she does, I feel like I exhale for the first time in many minutes.

"Uh, we have to win one of those invites," Britni says, sounding pumped.

"I mean, does anyone else have chills?" Alix asks.

"Right now I have more questions than chills," I respond, my mind spinning.

"A list of rules and terms just got uploaded to the *Pantheonic* website," Mo says, ever perched on the online pulse. "I'm skimming it now . . . Okay. Invitations to this announcement were only extended to American-based teams to begin with. Next, contingent on event performance, seven teams will be further invited on an all-expenses-paid trip to NYC to compete in . . . a fully streamed augmented reality tournament!"

"Augmented reality?" I reply first. "That's . . . new. But . . . maybe very cool?"

I mean, I do also happen to love watching reality TV competitions when I'm not reading or gaming. Could that be the vibe of this new tournament, merging physical challenges with *Pokémon Go*–style gameplay for *Pantheonic*?

"Agreed," Mo says. "And . . . oh my goddess."

"What?" Britni asks as Mo's pause lingers.

I don't blame her. All this has me on the edge of my seat as well.

"The winning tournament team will receive a prize of $800,000."

"No way," Alix gasps. "That'd be $200K each."

"That's life-changing—no, that's life-*starting* money," Mo agrees, her voice rising. "Not to mention the free trip for a once-in-a-lifetime, cutting-edge gaming tournament. Incorporating augmented reality? I mean, has that been done in an MMORPG or an action RPG?"

"I don't know," Britni replies. "But something like this will probably make influencers out of all its gamers—everyone is going to be watching for the lore reveals alone."

It's obvious my team is breathlessly excited. I am too . . . well, half excited at least.

"Not to ruin the mood," I start, "but what happens to the game if the war ends and the mysteries are solved?"

"That's got to be the answer to the fourth and final question," Britni says. "What happens to the Stoneruned Horde once they are dethroned and peace is restored?"

Mo jumps back in. "So whoever secures an invite in this upcoming event gets the trip of a lifetime to compete in a groundbreaking tournament, close one chapter of our favorite game, help define a new *Pantheonic* narrative, and potentially win money and fame?"

When Mo puts it that way . . . how can I not be 100 percent excited?

Still, a small stone of dread also lodges in my chest. I hate thinking this way, but I can't help wondering how my chronic pain could ever handle trains and hotels and hours of displaced gaming. The promise of discomfort would be huge—and that struggle is not how I want anyone to define me, least of all these safe-space friends.

Then again, attending this tournament would mean meeting my friends in person for the first time. It would be so cool to finally get to hang with Mo and to reveal a mystery of our own: learning who Britni is beyond Chiroptera. My heart also starts to ache at the idea of meeting Alix ahead of my NYU schedule. What will he be like? Smell like? Look like, outside of a screen? Will we click in person as much as we do online? Will doing so with the buffer of our team be even better than just one-on-one?

The four of us meeting in person could be the coolest gathering ever . . .

Unless being together in real life somehow ruins our dynamic. Would lifting us out of our safe virtual space and dropping us into the physical world change everything . . . for the worse?

"It sounds incredible," I blurt out, not wanting to fall too behind in the conversation. "But should we get our hopes up? What are the chances we'll be able to win over hundreds of the best teams in the game?"

"We gamed our butts off to be good enough to get invited to an event like this," Alix says. "And Keegan, you know better than anyone most event types aren't about brute-level strength. Queen Trinidy said this is a raid quest, so we just have to think on our feet fast enough and maybe get a little lucky."

"Very that," Mo adds. "If they wanted only pro gamers, they'd never have set things up this way. They must want a mix of casual players in there too. And if this whole thing has to do with revealing more of the game's own mythology, having Professor Keegan on our team might be the ultimate secret weapon."

"Well, flattery will get you everywhere . . ." I reply, starting to feel converted.

"Plus, they need to find seven teams who can come to NYC for a week on short notice," Britni says. "Even if we're not among the first group of seven, we might still make some alternate list. And I am definitely making this trip work."

I am slightly surprised to hear Britni say this, since we obviously know the least about her life outside the game. But we learned a while back not to push Britni's privacy boundaries.

"I already live here, so I'm sure I could move my hours around at the tailor shop to make it work," Alix says.

"My friends would happily cover my comic store shifts for something like this," Mo squeals.

Everyone knows I'm off this summer and that I'm due to go to NYU in a month. Everyone also knows I'm obsessed with *Pantheonic*. There'd be no excuse for me not to go . . . Save for the gripping panic over how to manage my chronic pain before I'm fully healed and ready. But I'm not about to say that out loud.

"The quest to find our seven prime pantheons will now begin," Queen Trinidy's voice proclaims from all around, like a divine message. "May you be deemed ever worthy of the quests we face."

Hearing this, I make a quick decision. I must ignore my frail human Keegan brain. Instead, I must focus only on what the goddess K.Odyssia would do: cast aside all doubts to dive headfirst into battle and lead her team to resounding victory.

CHAPTER FIVE

NEXT THING WE KNOW, THE EPIC HEARTS ARE TRANSPORTED to a realm gate. Gathered in the small marble vestibule, our team faces two columns that pulse with portal energy in the space between. This also puts us face-to-face with UnderTee, *Pantheonic*'s non-playable-character event quest guide.

"Oh, my body is so not ready," Mo cries. "I am still traumatized by UnderTee's last briefing—and that one wasn't even for a special event."

"At least they gave her a better outfit for this quest," Alix offers.

UnderTee's character draws from many mythological underworld figures, all rolled into a dark-humored, werewolf-hybrid drag queen who always "spills the Tee." She has two roles as our NPC usher: First, to debrief pantheon teams for event quests. And second, to respawn our fallen deity avatars from the UndeRealm. Today UnderTee wears a deep crimson sheathe dress and a ruby tiara that matches her scepter. Both really bring out the redness in her sharp eyes and the matching streaks in her werewolf fur.

"Oh, you lot again? I assume you're here to try to rise as one of the sacred seven pantheons? Or at least to attempt to? Honestly, I don't see the point.

"But if you're determined to embarrass yourselves, here's what you need to do. In this Mythic Volcano earth realm elite raid, you must expel the Stoneruned Horde by dismantling their stronghold. This base of operations is held above a lavascape by dozens of gilded pillars. Your objective is to seek and destroy these pillars of gold, which will require all four members of a pantheon to strike at once. Oh, and pro tip? How quickly teams crack gilded pillars will count toward your final existential grade.

"Wow, you're still going on, even after all that? Well, I won't say 'I told you so' when I'm dispatched to river raft you all the way back from the UndeRealm. Oh, who am I kidding? Of course I'll say 'I told you so!'"

As UnderTee's signature howling cackles reverberate through the entrance gate hall, the portal changes colors. We only have a few seconds to gather our thoughts—and that's usually my strength as team leader.

"Obviously our goal is to stay alive to find a gold pillar as quickly as possible," I begin. "And there will be lots of teams with higher levels than us. But like you all said, this event type isn't just about brute strength. We know the big teams are gonna go for the most visible pillars, so we're better off sneaking away to find a hidden pillar from the start. Which is perfect, since it happens to vibe with our Epic Hearts code . . .

"Battle efficiency and Horde kills always win the day. We don't aggravate our fellow deities, but we will defend ourselves to the death should any seek provocation!"

"Copy, oh fearless leader!" Mo shouts. She is the one who insists I find some way to speak our mission statement at the start of every gaming session—and I am most happy to oblige.

As Alix and Britni both offer cheers of support, we are ushered into the column portal . . .

And begin loading into the base of a very active volcano.

The Divine Realm has access to the entire multiverse of earths, so while some realms look much like the earth we know, others are vastly different. New earth realm maps are released in expansions, but many events are reskins of existing maps—like this one.

Except I've never seen the Mythic Volcano map look quite this . . . apocalyptic. Twice as many rivers of lava flow from the peak, which also spews fireballs and ashen rain randomly. The Stoneruned base stretches in a rune shield-protected ring around the middle of the mountain, which is barely visible through the smoky haze.

This means we're not just going to have to battle the hundreds of Stoneruned automatons defending the stronghold—we're also going to have to contend with the environment. That's normal, it's just that the environment isn't usually *this* treacherous. Clearly they're using this map to convey some serious End of Days energy, maybe signaling our own Ragnarök or Fall of Rome.

"Any ideas where to start looking for a more hidden golden pillar?" Mo asks as we all begin running.

"I vote for heading around and up the mountain ASAP," Britni says. "Things are about to get seriously heated."

Britni is very right. Our third and final threat presents itself as dozens of other pantheon teams also finish emerging through our randomly assigned gate point, of which there are always seven. Technically pantheons should all be fighting on the same side, but we're definitely always in competition—especially now for the glory of claiming these golden pillars.

We keep sprinting through the chaos that erupts all around us. The smoke shifts from a new downpour of lava rain, and I suddenly see two massive gold pillars stretching under either side of the stronghold ring. These pillars are set high enough to be equidistant from all entrance gates, so there's obviously going to be a rush toward them.

"There's no way we'll win that king of the hill battle," I say.

"I'll get us a little farther away from the fray," Mo replies.

sMOte reaches to pull a glowing short-portal crystal off one of her braids. Tricksters are strongest at the "rogue" trait, stealthing through the shadows and stockpiling arsenals or inventories. This also means Tricksters can be best at filling the pillar traits that are inevitably missing from any team, with rosters limited to four. In this case, sMOte covers some of the skills we lack by not having a Traverser.

"Have a nice trip . . ." Mo says as sMOte throws the crystal down to create a portal. "See you next fall!"

Our team appears just a little way down and around the base of the volcano, on the other side of a bubbling lava river.

"I don't know what's more lethal," Alix says, "sMOte's smiting or Mo's corny jokes."

"Definitely the jokes," Britni replies. "We've gotta start climbing the volcano if we're gonna find a golden pillar fast enough. I'll start plowing through that Stoneruned battalion blocking our way."

Chiroptera charges up the mountain and we follow behind. As our resident Creature "tank," Chiroptera is built to take damage—which she does beautifully as several Stoneruned begin bashing her with their rocky fists. She executes a block, wrapping her flightless bat wings around her body as a padded layer. Then she begins slashing away with her Elemental Talons—a feature even harder to quest for than Apollix's fire wings.

Right now, Chiroptera shifts her talons to ice mode, making them sharp, frosty tools for evisceration. She uses these ice talons to slash through the standard Stoneruned troopers all around. These automatons are made of strong and durable gray rocks animated by glowing runes, but Chiroptera is able to cut through several troopers at the same time.

Once the Stoneruned automatons are destroyed, the energy trapped in their spellbound bodies floats away in a cloud. This energy returns to the Horde's "One True" RunedGod—a terrifying boss we sometimes have to defeat expressions of in other quest events.

While the standard battalions Chiroptera just reduced to pebbles are tough, it's the brown-rocked, environment-siphoning Stoneruned that can be especially deadly. Right now a troop of them come barreling down the mountain straight at us. These magma Stoneruned glow with lava-lit runes, enabling them to blow fire from their split-stone seams and wield giant molten maces. Luckily, we happen to have a fire-wielding force all our own . . .

"I can take them apart," Alix jumps in.

Apollix flies by Chiroptera, his fiery wings looking right at home in this hellscape. Then Apollix engages what I know is one of his favorite Bender abilities, *Landscape Casting.* He reaches out his hands to summon any nearby fire or light to him—which, in this case, pulls fire *directly* out of the magma Stoneruned automatons. They blast apart as Apollix powers up with all their firepower . . .

Which he gathers like a giant sun bomb and redirects to blow apart another Stoneruned battalion approaching from our left. As his *Landscape Casting* cools down to recharge, Apollix flies back closer to our team.

Apollix's "long-range DPS" melee clears enough space that I don't have to worry about any attacks for the next few seconds.

"I'm going to use my *Over Sight* ability to see if I can spot anything," I say.

Activating the move, I jump K.Odyssia up high into the air. For a few moments, I will become invulnerable and time will slow so that I can survey the battlefield.

Then I see it—a tiny glimmer of gold where the stronghold meets the mountain. It's maybe the realm's smallest pillar, but it will still count. My heart swells. We knew we needed some strategy and skill for this event, but we also knew we needed some *luck* to be in the right place at the right time. Now we just need to take full advantage of that luck.

"I spotted a tiny gold pillar, upward to our northeast," I say as K.Odyssia lands back beside the team. "Follow me."

This elicits a various array of gasps and whoops over our voice call, but then we all lock into focus. Any nearby team with a Ruler or a sight-enhancing item will have pulled the same maneuver, so even this tiny pillar is sure to be overrun if we don't get there as quickly as possible.

We rush up the volcano as a unit, dodging a fireball that craters to the ground and jumping over a gushing molten stream. I take point as we battle up through another Stoneruned battalion in our path. We all use our standard combat moves, which for me means employing my equipped sword for attacking and my shield for blocking.

We manage to make it to the tiny pillar first, but just barely. Several other teams are right on our tails—and one other arrives from the opposite direction at the same time.

"Are they going to race to the pillar or—"

Britni cuts herself off as this rival team's Bender hits us with a focused tidal wave. Chiroptera takes less damage than sMOte and me, but Apollix takes *more* being fire-based. Okay, so they're taking the attack option. Which tracks, since they only need to down one of us for our entire team to fall out of this event. Our deities are immortal, but if they take too much damage they still need to be reborn by UnderTee from the UndeRealm. That process takes enough time that, for any timed event requiring a full team, you're done.

But two can play that game now that we've been provoked.

"We need to knock them back long enough to destroy the pillar together," I say, speaking as fast as I can. "But other teams are close. I'll use my ultimate, then we hit the pillar."

We're already moving as I hear a flurry of confirmations. Turning all my focus on this rival team, I only have a moment to register their name: the Crescent Kilyas. Their avatars all sport matching symbols: a crescent moon chomped by fang bites. My mythology brain clocks the Incan moon goddess Mama Killa as their inspiration—but the rest of my body has a different reaction. Crescent moons mean quite a lot to me . . . for reasons I don't usually dwell on for too long. So I do what I always do when I see this symbol in *Pantheonic*:

I unleash holy Hel upon my enemies.

I trigger my Ruler ultimate ability, *Battle Cry.* I leap into the air and scream a mighty rousing cry with so much force, it creates an enhancement bubble around our immediate battlefield. This "intimidates" our opponents and slows them down for several seconds—an edge we need as the Crescent Kilyas launch their own attacks. But thanks to my ultimate, we're just a little faster.

Chiroptera charges at the other team, successfully knocking their Bender tide sprite and Reaper retrograde demon into the air. Apollix then uses his *Sun Beam* ability to blast both of them and deal tons of damage.

From the side, sMOte stealth-approaches to use her dagger blasters on their remaining two grounded members: a Ruler moon goddess and a Creature vampire. Both of them still have health bars too high to try sending them to the UndeRealm, but sMOte manages to stun the vampire by adding a poison-drip item to her daggers. Which means if I can temporarily KO their rival Ruler, we'll have the window we need.

And K.Odyssia is happy to deliver this justice. We might not start fights, but we always aim to finish them.

Running at their Ruler with one final boost of speed, I opt to use my shield as a battering ram. This won't deal much damage, but it does succeed at knocking the moon goddess farther back down the volcano.

"Hit the pillar, now!" I cry, smashing my keyboard to pull a fast pivot.

Within seconds, we're gathered around the tiny gold pillar. Other teams have managed to reach us, and we can see their spells and weapons being hurtled at our backs. We won't survive for long.

But we don't need to.

Chiroptera talon slashes. Apollix slings a fireball. sMOte blasts energy from her daggers. And I hack with my sword. As the Epic Hearts all strike at the same moment, the golden pillar cracks apart.

Our world is swallowed by continued rival team attacks, but they don't land anymore. Instead, we are encircled in a protective bubble as the pillar breaks open, revealing an especially potent cloud of energy. It's sort of like when the Stoneruned automatons are destroyed, but instead this energy transforms into something precious: a crystalline energy bird. This achievement represents a freed fraction of Source Wing light required to reclaim the realm. Dozens or sometimes hundreds of these winged fragments are needed to end an event.

We don't know how many are needed today, but we did manage to be one of the teams to reclaim one.

"Holy Hel, we did it!" I shout.

"Can I get an omen?" Alix cheers.

"That was deeply epic of us!" Mo chants.

"How fast do you think we were compared to—"

Britni cuts herself off, because her screen must be filling with the same thing as the rest of us—a message scroll from the Pantheonic War Council.

THE EPIC HEARTS

Apollix. Chiroptera. K.Odyssia. sMOte.

Congratulations!

Your team was the sixth pantheon to destroy a golden pillar. You have been deemed worthy of our mythical tournament. Details to follow. For now, rejoice and revel!

Oh my goddess . . .

We did it? We got invited to the tournament?

So many emotions begin to flood my body, I don't even know where to begin.

CHAPTER SIX

A BEAD OF SWEAT DRIPS DOWN MY FOREHEAD AS I COMplete a set of reps at my weekly physical therapy appointment. As much as I look forward to how I feel afterward, I always magically forget how tough these sessions are.

"Good job, Keegan. Go get yourself some water," Chris says, patting me on the back.

I try not to let it, but the gesture sends a little jolt through my body. I'm not sure if all physical therapists are six-foot-tall hunks with muscle curving around every inch of their flawless porcelain skin, but mine certainly is. It helps that Chris is in his thirties and most definitely straight, otherwise my basic-boy attraction to him would be unbearable. Not that a guy who looks like him would go for a thick, femme-leaning nerd like me, even if he were queer.

I grab my water bottle and breathe through the burning in my stomach muscles. Part of our chronic-pain easing protocol is strengthening my core, so our now-familiar sessions have a similar flow. We start with targeted massage for blood flow, move into leg and back stretches, then finish with various core-building exercises. It's all strenuous work, but it does help soothe the inexplicable ache in my lower right hip area. For a day or two, anyway.

"I know you're having doubts, but I really think you need to go to this tournament," Chris says as he sets up my next exercise, a hip extension with big thick rubber bands. "We can do our usual session mostly over video chat, if it helps."

Something I didn't necessarily expect when I started PT earlier this winter? The relationships I'd build here in this clinic, along with Chris feeling a bit like an older-brother therapist. He's pretty much the only person beside my parents who I can talk to about my pain without judgment, so it has created a foundation of trust for other life realms.

Like the decision I've delayed making about accepting our coveted tournament invite. I celebrated with the team as long as possible last night before logging out. We felt incredible—we were *worthy*. But this morning, when the formal details arrived, the real-world logistics started closing in.

"I know, it sounds silly when I doubt it out loud." I sigh. "But in my head, the spiral goes even deeper. To start, sitting for the train ride would probably be painful, but at least I could stand and walk whenever I needed to. As for packing, I'd somehow have to find ways to carry my ergonomic neck pillow and the full body pillow for between my legs. Plus my smaller foam roller, massage gun, and heat pad. I could easily fit ibuprofen, Aleve, Icy Hot, and an ice pack, but would it fit in a mini fridge freezer? Then how would I sleep in a different bed on a new mattress, maybe even with a roommate? I also would have to figure out clothes comfortable enough to game in that don't look like my usual sad sweatpants. Then would I even be able to sit and play comfortably without my specially set-up chair? Even if I do pull off a miracle and manage to avoid being in pain, how could I do so without making it a big deal to everyone else?"

I sigh again, shallower this time.

"I was just hoping to get the pain under control this summer so I could have a fresh start when I move to New York. A totally clean slate, you know? I'm afraid if I go now, too soon, I won't be ready and will fall off course."

"Okay, first of all, deep breaths, Keegan," Chris says, smiling to try and soothe me.

I didn't even realize it, but I had started taking increasingly short breaths through my little rant. So I inhale deep once, feeling the tension rattle out as I exhale.

"Listen, in my experience, if you always wait for the absolute perfect timing to do something, you usually just spend all your time waiting," Chris offers. "I know we haven't figured out why your pain is persisting yet, but letting it rule your entire life and your decisions probably won't help it heal any faster."

I smile back at Chris, but I can't say I feel fully convinced. I'm not sure he understands just how much *Pantheonic* means to me as an outlet, in every way. The same terrible questions leap back into my mind. What if going to this tournament and experiencing nothing but panic and pain somehow ruins my favorite game for me? Or even worse, ruins things with my precious team friends?

"Of course, I don't want you to put yourself in a situation you're uncomfortable with," Chris pivots. "But this invitation sounds pretty once-in-a-lifetime, on every level. It's always better to try and fail than to live with regret for letting fear win. Besides, what do you think Annie would say to you?"

I don't know how it's possible, but I feel like I smile and frown at the same time. I could be mad at Chris for pulling the dead friend card, but he knew Annie way longer and better than I ultimately did. If he's invoking her name, it's for a good reason. Especially since this clinic is the place we all met.

What can I imagine Annie saying to me if she were still here? *Keegan, quit whining and do the damn thing.*

"Okay, I hear you." I sigh. "Can we do the next exercise?"

"Damn, if you're asking for the dreaded banded work, you really don't want to have this conversation." Chris laughs. "Just promise me you'll think about it? We're going to get this pain sorted, I promise. But . . ."

Chris pauses and I know why. It's the same worry I've carried for nearly a year now: *but this pain might be something you have to learn to live with, maybe for the rest of your life.* It reminds me how much I've learned since this all started—and how little anyone knows for sure.

The pain came seemingly out of nowhere last October, right when I was in the middle of completing my college applications. I was doing my usual workout of sit-ups—my ever-futile attempt to slim out my belly fat and get six-pack abs—when I tweaked something in my lower back. The next day it felt entirely seized up. And whenever I sat I experienced blinding pain radiating from both of my hips, through my butt cheeks extending down my legs. The only way to feel comfortable at all that first week was to lie down flat on the floor and not move.

Once that initial back spasm loosened, the pain in my right hip and butt persisted down that leg. So my parents helped me find an orthopedist. At that first appointment I had a very hard time explaining or pinpointing the pain—it just felt all over my lower right half. So he ordered imaging, including an MRI.

That's the delightfully fun way I learned how claustrophobic I also am. Being slid into that tiny tube, with the loud banging of the machine all around me, I panicked. I convinced myself the power would go out and I'd get stuck inside that cramped space, where it felt impossible to breathe. To get me to stay inside the thirty minutes required to complete the MRI, it took three more tries and wearing special mirrored glasses angled to give a view outside. To add insult to injury—literally, because the pain in my ass and legs was on fire the entire time—the very cold MRI technician treated me like an irrational mess. Not just for my "dramatic" reaction, but also the idea that I could possibly be in any pain without some specific traumatic injury to explain it.

That was my first dose of a very fun trend: amorphous chronic pain is very easily invalidated by others. Especially since the MRI came back clean, with my spine perfectly healthy. The orthopedist said there was no reason I should be in pain, so it must be sciatica from sitting too much and having a weak core. Now, telling a teenage gay boy—one who does cardio and works out pretty regularly, mind you—that he is in pain because he is too flabby and weak is not a real boon to his mental health. I don't have a flat stomach or toned arms and I probably never will, no matter how fit I am underneath the flab. And to doctors, that's been an easy target to blame for my pain: being an unathletic nerd who doesn't move enough.

Still, I took the orthopedist's physical therapy prescription and attacked the problem over the holiday break. I also upgraded my desk and gaming chair to be fully ergonomic, enforced habits to stand and walk whenever I could, and set timers to keep myself in motion every thirty minutes when doing the things I love the most: reading and gaming. Of course, perhaps most important of all, I started PT with Chris.

As I learned to more effectively stretch and work out my muscles, the all-over pain definitely improved. However, the pain in my right hip-to-butt has persisted. Chris was actually impressed with how fit I was when we first began, despite the softer appearance of my body. Still, we both started researching what could be causing this unusual pain, especially at such a young age and without any specific physical trauma. Maybe it was piriformis syndrome? Maybe a joint issue? Or a nerve condition like fibromyalgia? Nothing has really hit the nail on the head yet, in terms of a targeted diagnosis or treatment.

As I start the next banded exercise with Chris, I try to push this history from my mind. Because the one lesson I learned in the many months since? Doctors don't have all the answers, even if they pretend to. And when you tell most people about pain they can't understand, they dismiss you as overdramatic or oversensitive.

And Chris wonders why I don't want to further expose this chronic pain to new people?

CHAPTER SEVEN

ONCE I'M HOME, I DO THE THING I ALWAYS TURN TO WHEN I need to feel better: some solo *Pantheonic* play. Team events like the one we crushed last night are where we get to display our deities, but we need to also spend a lot of time running around and questing to *build* our characters.

Right now I have K.Odyssia on a fetch-quest chain to recover the last artifact needed to forge a new weapon. I've been working to gather the resources and save enough Worship Points to equip this upgrade for months. Other people might find this sort of thing monotonous, but I love it. I read in some ancient parable once that true happiness doesn't lie in the moment of achieving a goal, but rather in making steady progress toward it. I don't know if this definition of happiness applies to everyone, but it certainly does for me. Perhaps that's why I also don't dabble in building alt avatars like most other players. I like to devote all my effort toward making K.Odyssia as spectacular as possible.

Solo play has us either entering earth realms still occupied by the Stoneruned Horde or serving our "home realms" as deities. We can always reach these maps from Mount Pantheonic, where we can also hang, explore, shop, and modify. The open-world solo quests are usually about deities swooping in to save someone, deliver something, or acquire a resource. Tales of our epic pursuits are written into the mythology back on our home earth realms, which inspires Worship Points—the currency used for upgrading our avatars.

The weapons and items that are up for grabs can also add abilities that help our deities flex toward unfilled pillar traits. Smart teams coordinate their efforts to build well-balanced rosters—and the Epic Hearts are most definitely a smart team.

sMOte, demigoddess mistress of whispers to many godly courts, moves between earth realms as silently as smoke. Her Trickster quests usually have her gathering intelligence or delivering messages, which she uses as an opportunity to gather more abilities and items that give her Traverser and Reaper powers.

Chiroptera, mythical Creature of savagery feared even by the most barbaric earth realms, is known for quests that focus on avenging wrongful deaths and unleashing righteous fury. Chiroptera fought hard to equip her Elemental Talons to shore up our team's shortcoming in not having a Warrior's combat versatility.

Apollix, sun god beloved by many realm-spanning pantheons, runs quests that allow him to spread light to the darkest places. This also lets him level up his Bender fire- and light-casting to the highest levels possible.

And of course, K.Odyssia is a Ruler deity worshipped by several realms as a goddess of ushering warriors home. Her quests usually have to do with returning lost people and things to their proper homes. Currently, I have her built toward Warrior stats for battling, but I always have a few healing items to make up for our lack of a Reaper. Lately, my primary focus has been completing this quest chain so I can forge a Gravity Stone to equip to my sword.

Right now, K.Odyssia runs through an Enchanted Wilderness map, which feels very classic high fantasy *Lord of the Rings*, with huge stretches of forests and grassy plains dotted with villages and fortresses. The last quest pointed me toward a specific cave somewhere to the south to unearth the final rare resource I seek. This cave is guarded by battalions of environmental Stoneruned covered in moss and spewing venomous dew.

In the game as K.Odyssia, I feel strong and powerful and purposeful. I can take out all my frustration and anxiety and anger by cleaving through the predictable-yet-challenging enemy hordes that stand between me and my ever-just objective. I am not crippled with doubt and indecision or riddled with pain and caution. Here, I know exactly who I am and what I need to do. I feel at one with K.Odyssia as my fingers tap the keyboard like an instrument. The epic soundtrack and clangs of battle boom through the gaming headset I wear like a crown. I just feel *good*.

Then on the bottom of the screen I see a chat notification pop up. But it's not just any notification—it's a private chat from Alix. As usual, my heart leaps into my throat seeing him reach out to me. Although this time, it's not just because of my big crush. It's also because I know Alix must want my answer about accepting the tournament invitation.

Finding a quiet place for K.Odyssia to rest and open the menu, back at my desk I stand and shake out any tightness in my right hip. Then, with my heart still thudding in my chest, I sit to answer Alix's chat.

APOLLIX: How close are you to finally forging that gravity sword?

K.ODYSSIA: Close! How's your day been?

APOLLIX: Way too much alterations work and not nearly enough *Pantheonic* play.

APOLLIX: Though I've been riding high about making the tournament cut. It still feels too good to be true!

K.ODYSSIA: I know, right? It still hasn't sunken all the way in yet.

APOLLIX: Have you talked to Mo or Britni much since last night?

K.ODYSSIA: No, it's been a weirdly busy day.

APOLLIX: Well, they're both all the way in on the tournament. Between the free trip, this new augmented reality twist, solving the ultimate game mysteries, and that prize money, they don't need any convincing.

K.ODYSSIA: I know I haven't said yes yet.

K.ODYSSIA: I'm still figuring it out with my parents.

I hate lying, especially to Alix. But I suppose this is technically true—there *are* lots of logistics to consider.

APOLLIX: I get it. It's easier for me, I already live here. But if it helps, tell your parents I'd be the best city host ever!

APOLLIX: Also, I'm so excited to meet you and Mo in person. And to see who Britni really is beneath the bat berserker.

APOLLIX: Plus, you'll be moving here soon anyway. We could kick-start all our IRL hang plans while our game literally comes to life all around us!

As usual, Alix is right on all accounts. Meeting Mo and learning who Britni is would be so damn cool. Plus, finally getting to meet Alix in the flesh? Despite my worries, I'd be lying if I said I didn't do a little . . . okay, a *lot* of daydreaming about all the magical ways Alix and I might click in person. Emotionally—and definitely physically. It's all a fantasy, I know—which is maybe why I'm still scared of potentially ruining it with reality.

So I return to thinking about how much I'd also love to be a part of forging the next mythological chapter for *Pantheonic*. Invitations to the tournament have remained private, so no one knows exactly which teams will be going. We can't be sure how we'd stack up against the competition yet, but if we did somehow beat all the odds to win, the money could help with the tuition and college costs that my scholarship doesn't cover. Not to mention the medical copay costs my parents have picked up this past year.

K.ODYSSIA: I know. Everything about this feels too cool to process.

Why can't I just say yes? I wish I could take a pill and make the pain go away so I could live like a "normal" teenager. Then I remember there *are* pills that will do that—but that's a path I'll never walk down. Ever.

K.ODYSSIA: Hey, I should finish this quest part before I get called away for dinner. But I promise I'll get back to everyone tonight.

APOLLIX: Okay! Fingers and toes crossed you can make it!

I close the chat with a pang of guilt. Because what Alix doesn't say? If all four of us don't agree to attend, they'll move on to the next alternate team who destroyed a pillar. If that happens, then my chronic pain wouldn't be just holding me back—it would be holding back three people I care a ton about, my realest friends. I wasn't bullied or anything in high school, which is lucky for an out gay geek like me. Instead, I was mostly invisible in my huge public school. I had casual friends in classes and stuff, but I just didn't meet anyone I really clicked or connected with outside of school.

At least, not until I met Annie. She didn't go to my school, but she did have PT appointments after me with Chris every week. I would always spot her walking in like a runway model as I was wrapping up, looking like the epitome of effortless cool with her short platinum blonde hair and silver crescent moon necklace. I remember feeling more intrigued by her than anyone else I'd met my own age, so I eventually worked up the courage to ask Chris to introduce us.

It turned out she was a fellow senior at another school, a star volleyball player who got a bad knee injury—hence the need for PT. We got smoothies one day after our appointments and had an unexpected blast. We both loved the same reality TV competitions and pop culture nerd nonsense and ended up talking for hours. It felt like I had met my first new friend in real life, someone I just clicked with automatically.

But because we were new friends, I had no way of knowing Annie had gotten addicted to the painkillers the doctors prescribed after her knee surgery. When those ran out, Annie—like so many others—turned to cheaper and more dangerous substitutes. When Chris, with tears welling in his eyes, told me that Annie had overdosed, I didn't understand.

I guess I still don't.

I mean, I understand it logically. Someone dealt her the wrong batch and . . . yeah, I know the story. What I don't understand is the emotion. How can someone so vibrant and successful and with so much promise be just . . . robbed of a future? And how could I be robbed of getting to know the first potential friend I'd ever really liked enough to make in person?

The very next day, I got my tattoo: a crescent moon, in honor of Annie. I had never even contemplated getting a tattoo before, but something in me felt the need to memorialize this loss. That first day Annie told me all about her signature necklace and her love of crescent moons. She thought they were aesthetically beautiful, but also a deeper reminder that sometimes we only glimpse a sliver of the whole in our shifting perspectives. The moon is a universal thing that everyone sees, but it's always changing its shape depending on the angle you're viewing it from.

I'd been lucky, having never experienced someone dying unexpectedly like this before. But I had also just met Annie, so one thought kept repeating: *What right did I really have to grieve her?* Surely that was reserved for the people who had already been in her life, not someone brand-new like me.

So I shut down my misplaced grief this past winter. Just like I do now as I lean back in my gaming chair. I feel very overwhelmed by the massive choice in front of me, by all I stand to gain or lose either way. It feels way easier to slay some more Stoneruned with K.Odyssia at my fingertips.

Before I know it, I've battled my way into the cave where my precious final resource is being guarded. The interior of this hidden cavern looks like the brilliant inside of a geode, all dark amethyst glinting off the ambient light from a shimmering sapphire pond. Knowing I need to dive into that water to uncover the coveted artifact of this side quest, I feel a sense of wonder and awe wash over me.

It's the same feeling I get when I'm reading about world mythology—where the fantastical meets the practical, where fiction meets faith, where lore meets history. My passion in life is researching and sharing the sacred mysteries of ancient mythology, elaborating on how timeless myths can teach us lessons about modern humanity. How lucky am I that a game like *Pantheonic* exists to capture that very same magic?

And how could I ever turn down the chance to explore this mythological game's greatest mysteries? To uncover the answers to core questions I've pondered for years. To maybe even meet and interact with the brilliant minds who have so lovingly crafted this modern mythical experience. What lessons and epiphanies would the answers at the center of my favorite game teach me about my own life?

Then again, the consonance of pondering these questions with K.Odyssia in a cave is not lost on me, locked here in my own bedroom cave. It always feels safer in my enclosed world—yet I'm also always seeking portals to take me away. As I face the magical waters onscreen as K.Odyssia, I know I won't hesitate to make this leap headfirst, even if it could be filled with unseen dangers.

And if K.Odyssia is an extension of me, why can't I be more like her in real life?

These questions swirl in my mind as I dive into the sacred cave waters. After swimming for a bit, I reach an ornate dais. Floating in front of it, I press a seal in the center—and finally unlock my coveted quest-chain prize. A power-sourcing relic rises out of the dais before me, floating like a beacon of light.

The sight takes my breath away.

Not just because of the satisfaction I feel at finally completing this difficult task. Or because of the anticipation I feel at seriously upgrading my signature sword. Or even just because of the strikingly beautiful nature of the relic.

Mostly I lose my breath because it turns out to be imbued by a moon goddess. A depiction of her hovers above the relic like a spirit, wearing an ornately tiered crown that glows with moonlight. My best guess is this deity is inspired by Chandra, the Hindu moon goddess—but the depiction is general enough that it could be inspired by many others. Below this goddess, the relic is carved in the shining shape of a *crescent moon*.

I suppose I shouldn't be too surprised by this. After all, it follows that the gravity upgrade I sought would naturally have to do with the pull of the moon and the tides in some way. And in a game built upon world mythology, sun and moon symbolism is highly common.

Still, seeing crescent moons obviously means a lot to me. And ever since Annie died, I come across them specifically in *Pantheonic* all the time. Sure, it could just be that I am on the lookout for them now. But after reading about many global traditions of the departed sending signs to the living, it always feels meaningful when a crescent moon appears to me.

So I rub my secret tattoo as a little reminder, a small way to keep Annie's memory alive. But in this case, it almost feels like I can hear her voice in my mind, delivering a very clear message with this specific relic:

You can battle through pain. Suck it up and go to the tournament, you silly boy.

Registering this, it becomes clear that deep down I've always known what I want to do about this tournament. I guess I just needed to let my worrying head catch up with my epic heart. Because sure, the crescent moon is a reminder of what was lost. But it's also a reminder of how lucky I am to be alive, every day I get to be here—in pain or otherwise. I need to swallow my fear, block out that pain, and dive headfirst into this unprecedented adventure. Really, I need to think of this as my very own real-life *Odyssey*.

After all, I've always fought hard to make K.Odyssia stronger.

It's about time she returned the favor.

CHAPTER EIGHT

THE TRAIN RIDE TURNS OUT TO BE WAY LESS TRAUMATIC than I had imagined. Then again, I made sure I was prepared. The moment I decided to attend the tournament, I also chose to spend some of the savings I was planning to use for college clothes shopping a bit early. I ended up making out big at an outlet mall, buying a bunch of sleek hoodies and tapered joggers to replace my tattered, oversized at-home sweats. That covered my indoors air-conditioned gaming wardrobe, but I also got several athletic T-shirts and pairs of five-inch shorts to show off my best feature: my legs. The name of the game was comfort, but make it cute.

Right now I walk west on Thirty-Third Street rolling a truly embarrassing amount of luggage. I am most thankful for one purchase: the specially ergonomic gel inserts for my brand-new sneakers. The walk from Penn Station to the hotel didn't look very far on Maps, but I guess I didn't properly account for my baggage and the July humidity. Still, as sweaty and overpacked as I might be, nothing can touch the euphoria I currently feel. Once I finally resolved to be here, my usual spiral of worry started swirling with a new feeling: racing excitement.

That's also why I purchased a blank journal, one themed with stone columns and laurel wreaths. If I really want this tournament adventure to be like my own *Odyssey*, I should probably chronicle its trials. I hope to have some fun not just capturing this experience, but also maybe using what I learn in the tournament to craft a new chapter of personal mythology. If *Pantheonic* can do it for the game, why shouldn't I do it for my life? That's my mission as a future professor, after all.

Barreling through the streets of Manhattan, I already decide my opening journal entry will be about this first walk. Because it occurs to me that I am getting sponsored to be here with generous travel stipends so I can play a pivotal part in the story of my favorite game—while finally meeting my best virtual friends. How could I ever have thought missing this was even a remote possibility?

I suppress the urge to physically skip as I enter Hudson Yards. My whole body hurts from lugging my suitcases and backpack here, but I don't seem to care knowing I'm about to meet my beloved teammates for the first time. Britni's flight was scheduled to land an hour before the respective trains carrying Mo and me, so Alix suggested we plan to meet near the sculpture-like Vessel building. The idea was to make our very first in-person meeting feel super special, which we all agreed was worth the extra effort. The tournament is taking place in a section of the Javits Center, so *Pantheonic* decided to put us all up within walking distance at the very fancy Zenith Hotel. At least, it certainly looks fancy from all my online previewing. It's like a sleek slate and warm wood palace in the sky, fit for us weary warring gamers.

As I drag my way toward the Vessel, I am in awe of its complexity in person. It looks like a multistory alien honeycomb, a massive and metallic architectural wonder. Of course Alix would be drawn to this landmark—it screams alien superstar fashion and modern mythical shrine all at once. I still can't quite process that I'm about to meet Alix especially in person. I really hope I don't make a total fool of myself in front of the cutest and most stylish boy I know.

As I approach, I begin to worry instead that Alix might not have accounted for how crowded this courtyard would be with tourists and pedestrians. We didn't choose a specific spot, so it might be difficult to pick each other out in the crowd. I scan the perimeter of the Vessel barricades to find a place to rest and text our group chain. Butterflies flutter through my stomach, reminding me of how nervous I actually am. Nervous, but also thrilled.

Perhaps these nerves are why I don't see a little break in the pavement as I walk. My foot catches and I stumble to catch my balance. Unfortunately, my two roller bag handles proceed to fall in opposite directions. I let them go, trying instead to steady myself. But the heavy backpack strapped to me makes that very hard to do. Impossibly, I feel myself falling forward. In a last-ditch corrective effort, I throw all of my weight backward instead. This actually works—except now I'm going to fall on my ass instead of my face. Which, for someone with chronic lower back pain, is a remarkably stupid instinct.

Until suddenly I feel two hands grabbing my shoulders and holding me in place. I reach out to brace myself on this mystery savior's chest. In that same moment, my roller bags hit the pavement with an echoing snap. The people around us all gasp and turn to the source of the sound . . .

And that is how I first meet Alix Cornejo—saving me from tripping over my own feet, in a little bubble of stopped time.

Two seconds later the crowd clocks what happened and moves back into their blurred rush. But I only catch that in my peripheral vision, as all my focus tunnels in on Alix. His face looks so familiar, yet it's still a revelation this close. The slope of his nose, the fullness of his lips, and the brightness in his brown eyes catch me off guard. Paired with the stubble carefully sculpted along his jaw and the scent of minty pine mixed with sweat coming off him . . .

I am awestruck from the drop.

Literally.

"Keegan! Are you okay?" Alix asks, stepping back and letting go once I'm steady on my feet. That's when I see he only carries a weekender duffel bag and a leather backpack, making my expansive luggage display feel extra embarrassing.

I feel my sweaty cheeks flush even redder, if that's physically possible.

"I have no idea how that happened," I reply, breathless.

"I saw you walk through the courtyard and was trying to catch you to say hello," Alix explains. "But you move fast for someone with so much luggage. I'm glad I was behind you for that little tumble."

"Trust me, I am too," I say. "Though this is not exactly the epic meeting I was picturing."

"I don't know, that felt pretty epic to me." Alix hits me with a dazzling smile, and I swear there's a literal twinkle in his eye.

It melts me into even more of a puddle.

Uh-oh.

I was expecting to have some reaction to meeting Alix in person, but I was *not* expecting a steamroller of emotions and hormones to hit within the first few seconds. Maybe it's the heat or the adrenaline from the fall, but it feels like the air around us charges and crystallizes somehow. We smile at each other like that for a few seconds . . .

Then I see the T-shirt Alix has on.

"Holy Hel, is that a custom *Pantheonic* shirt?"

"Printed, pressed, and cropped by yours truly," Alix answers.

He moves his hands to frame the image of our four Epic Hearts avatars posing on his chest. Despite this awesome sight, my eyes can't help but drop to the spot where the shirt ends and Alix's stomach is exposed. It's flat as a board, and out peeks a happy trail.

I snap my eyes back up to his face before I get even more ahead of myself.

"I was saving all my merch clothes for the tournament," I say. "But your shirt is so much cooler than anything I brought."

"Then it's a good thing I made three more," Alix replies, beaming. "I marked you for a size large, if that's okay?"

Before I can process the magnitude of Alix's thoughtfulness—or the idea that he considered my body for any reason—a joyous scream rips across the courtyard. More pedestrians turn, their attention grabbed for a second time. Alix and I both spin to find none other than Mo Lyon in the flesh, running at us like a smiling cannonball.

Mo scoops Alix and me up into a crushing hug.

"Epic Hearts unite!" Mo cries, squeezing us tight.

I can't help but smile from ear to ear. Mo's exuberant energy is certainly infectious over our gaming calls, but it feels exponentially uplifting in person.

"You boys are even cuter in real life!" Mo says, letting go and stepping back to look us over.

I do the same, drinking in Mo's outfit: an oversized *X-Men* Rogue T-shirt, green biker shorts, and bright yellow sneakers.

"Did you not bring any bags?" I ask, realizing Mo isn't carrying anything except a Loungefly backpack.

"Well, I have this," Mo answers as she spins, revealing her backpack is themed after *Pantheonic*'s pillared logo. "But the rest of my bags are over there with Cary."

Mo points across the crowded courtyard to a fellow teen with brown skin, dressed all in powder blue and sporting an asymmetrical buzz-to-bob haircut dyed lavender purple. Mo then starts motioning sign language as she speaks to Cary.

"Sorry, babe, I didn't mean to leave you with all the bags. I just got so excited when I spotted Keegan and Alix!"

Cary's team managed to snag the fourth invitation by finding a unique suspension pillar at the peak of the volcano. Their team is the only other we know for sure is attending the tournament, since *Pantheonic* still hasn't released the official roster. Still, it's nice to have some familiar allies along for the ride—especially another skilled non-pro team like ours.

"No worries," Cary speaks as they sign in return. They also wear hearing aids in both ears, since they have partial hearing. "Come over here so I can finally meet the famous Epic Hearts!"

Mo grabs the handle of one of my bags to help as we make our way over.

"It's so nice to meet you both," Cary speaks and signs. "We know the rest of my team from around Annapolis, so we've been so excited for Mo to get to do the same."

"Nice to meet you too!" Alix says. "I'm sorry, I don't know sign language."

"I can hear a little, thanks to these," Cary replies, motioning toward their in-ear implants.

"I always thought your avatar was the coolest," I say, picturing Cary's Traverser, a brown-skinned elf styled between Link from *Zelda* and Robin Hood. "But you're even cooler."

I immediately register how nerdy and awkward I must sound, but Cary laughs.

"Thank you," they reply. "So are you both as curious to meet the mysterious Britni as we are?"

"Um, well, I think the wait is over. It's me, hi."

We all turn toward this new voice, prompting Cary to turn as well.

And I can most definitely say I am stunned to see Britni Bats for the first time.

CHAPTER NINE

A HALF HOUR LATER, THE EPIC HEARTS SIT AROUND A lunch table. We were a little early to officially check in, so the concierge held our bags for us. While Cary went to meet their own team, we decided to head up to the restaurant in the Zenith Hotel. Nestled on a high floor, it has gorgeous skyline views. Inside, as expected from the website, it feels like a curved mahogany and gleaming chrome wonder. Thankfully, Delfanti Games provided a stipend for meals placed on our room tabs, otherwise I doubt any of us could afford to eat here.

Despite the splendor of our surroundings, I've barely been able to take my eyes off Britni. I keep stealing glances, trying not to be rude and stare. She is the tallest out of us all and has her shiny blonde hair up in a ponytail. Her delicate face and full lips are dusted expertly with dewy makeup. Every other part of her appearance is equally manicured, from her baby pink nails to her crème and caramel jogger set and starched white sneakers.

I know it's wrong of me to make assumptions, but this is definitely *not* who I expected Britni to be. Especially given her monstrous avatar. Britni would almost remind me of

Annie—but Annie was all warmth and extroverted energy, while Britni seems way more guarded upon first impression.

"I guess I could kick us off by addressing the elephant in the room," Britni says, looking nervous. "Or I guess, the bat monster in the room."

We all laugh, and I'm thankful for the break, especially in Britni's demeanor. As I feared, it's been a little awkward as we find our in-person footing. But I try to tell myself it's a normal adjustment and things will ease, given how much time we've spent with one another's voices in our ears. Thankfully the tournament orientation doesn't start until tomorrow morning, so we have the rest of today to break any lingering ice. I suppose there's no better place to start than with Britni.

"I'm really nervous, but also excited to finally tell you all who I really am. And I guess why I've kept that private in the game," Britni begins. Her voice sounds so familiar, but it's still weird attaching it to this modelesque person in front of us instead of the bat-hybrid bruiser we've all come to know and love.

"My parents are both Albanian, and they moved to Michigan when my mom got pregnant with me," she continues. "I started doing some modeling stuff on social media when I was in high school, and my accounts kind of took off. I have a pretty big following under my real name, Britni Kola. So I graduated early and moved to LA right after I turned eighteen to give the whole influencer-model thing a real go. My 'brand' is about fashion products and lifestyle experience. I had this whole vision for who I wanted to be in LA, but . . ."

Britni's face falls for just a moment, but then it's like she thinks better of it and pivots.

"Anyway, it's all a bit of a grind. But gaming has always been my escape. That's why I made my *Pantheonic* account anonymous and separate from my social presence. I didn't want to deal with the pressure of who I'm *supposed* to be in the game. There, I can be wicked and brutal and angry and calculating and ugly, and it's all celebrated. Plus I see how most female avatars can get treated in games—I deal with enough of that in real life.

"Even though I had my reasons, I know it probably felt to you all like I was hiding myself. Especially given how transparent you've all been about your real selves outside the game. But I want you to know, the version of me you all get to experience—that feels so much more like the *real* me. Not the perfectly curated social media model everyone else wants to see. Deep down, I have always felt far more like Britni Bats and Chiroptera."

"I believe you 100 percent," Mo replies first, placing a comforting hand on Britni's. "The Epic Hearts is a safe space for all of us, and we all need it in different ways. But let me just say, I'm very happy to match a face to the voice we've heard all this time—one that doesn't constantly have purple drool hanging from its fangs."

We all laugh, Britni most of all. Clearly, keeping this secret identity must have been weighing on her. It looks like a huge relief to have it off her chest.

"And I totally hear you on the female avatar thing," I follow up. "K.Odyssia gets all kinds of lude and aggressive comments directed at her. I guess I don't internalize it because I'm a dude in real life. A queeny dude, but still."

"K.Odyssia *is* a stone-cold babe," Britni replies, smiling a bit easier now. "But she's also a goddess. She doesn't have to work quite as hard at it as the rest of us."

"I mean, that's part of the fun of gaming—we all get to craft idealized fantasy personas for our avatars," Alix says next. "I know Apollix definitely helped me figure out a few things as I started transitioning."

"Oh, that reminds me," Britni replies, frowning a little. "I hope this doesn't ruin the team vibe . . . but despite my best efforts, I'm not queer."

Alix, Mo, and I share a glance—then burst out laughing.

"Not the straights needing to come out of the closet now!" Mo howls.

"Of course it's okay," Alix adds. "Happy to have an ally on board, always."

Britni smiles, looking relieved again. "Well, I don't know if it counts, but I did realize recently that I'm probably on the Ace Spectrum as demisexual. I think I'm only comfortable being physical in very trusting, long-term relationships. And honestly, I've never had the right one. Guys our age are . . . not any better than older guys in LA. But those are stories for another day."

"I can't wait to hear all the Britni stories, good, bad, and ugly," I reply, giving Britni the warmest smile I can.

"For the record, demisexual counts as being queer," Mo adds. "But don't worry about 'counting.' I always thought I was purely into other girls until I met Cary, who is nonbinary. Static identities are a little silly, and everyone is welcome in the queer community."

"Can I get an omen?" Alix snaps along, beaming.

Hearing this in person melts my entire heart, once again. How the hell am I ever going to focus on building an in-person friendship with Alix when all I can think about is asking him to be my lawfully wedded husband? I was hoping my crush might shift to something more friendly once we met, but the opposite is very rapidly becoming true.

Maybe I'll have to find the courage to actually . . . *tell* Alix how I feel? Right now, the thought of taking that leap makes me want to hurl, especially given the odds Alix doesn't see me that way. But if my feelings keep trending in this direction, I might not have a choice.

We are interrupted as our server appears to set down the food we ordered. It's a well-timed break, giving us all a moment to gather ourselves.

It also gives me a moment to process how I've been sitting at this table and haven't felt one pulse of pain in my usual hip-area muscles. I wish I understood why sometimes the ache decides not to plague me, but I do notice I tend not to feel it when I'm socially engaged. Is that because my brain is distracted elsewhere, or is there some reason the pain doesn't even start? It's mystifying, but I just try to be thankful for this pain-free meal.

"So there's a hot topic I was saving for us to go over in person," Mo begins after taking a sip. "We don't know the rules of this tournament or most of the other teams we'll be facing yet, so there's no way to know what our odds of winning are. But I think if we don't at least *believe* that we can win, we never will. I figured it'd be good motivation to go over why winning that money would be a big deal for each of us?"

"I love that idea," Alix agrees. "Who wants to go first?"

"I can," I offer. "From what I know, I'm the only one of us starting college next month. I'm proud to say I got a nice scholarship, but it doesn't cover everything. If we win I could use my portion of the money to help with the extra loans and stuff."

It's all true, but I don't feel like mentioning the desire to pay my parents back for the annoying medical and physical therapy copay costs that have piled up. We have decent health insurance, but it's still been a bit of a strain.

"And the world deserves Keegan's brilliant mythological mind to start his academic journey debt-free!" Alix proclaims. "Britni, want to go next? I'm dying to hear about your influencer accounts, since you know I'm a fashion girlie myself."

"I know, I love your stuff," Britni replies, smiling.

But then, whatever she is about to say next, her whole face falls.

"I haven't lived in Los Angeles very long yet, but I'm pretty . . . miserable there. Business stuff has been going better than ever, and I got signed to IMG Models. But everyone I meet is . . . well, I guess everyone I know is an influencer or a model. I couldn't wait to get out of Michigan, but now I miss the warmth of the people there. But it took a lot of my savings to move to LA, so I have to stay and do the model thing to build back up. I'm just realizing how much I kind of . . . hate all of it.

"But I also don't really know what I'd do instead, or where I'd go. That's why I was dying to come here for the tournament. A change of scenery, around people I actually like, doing something I genuinely love. I hoped it might inspire me to figure out how to get out of the influencer trap I set for myself in

LA. Obviously money would help that fresh start, but that's not all I'm looking for here."

"We got you, girl," Mo replies. "Helping other people discover the things they love is my favorite passion in life. It's why I love working at Third Eye Comics—getting to talk to people and figure out what they enjoy. Especially because the store sells comics and toys and books and vinyl and costumes and games. Nothing makes me happier than when someone thanks me after loving a recommendation I gave them. I mean, I'm like the biggest pop culture lover of all time, so I'm glad to spread the joy.

"My dream is to open a store and be a proper small business owner. Especially because, as you all know, I love drawing and writing my own comics and games. I've done a lot of practice work on interactive storytelling apps . . . anyway, I'm rambling. I see the vision for the store I'd want to open, curating nerd culture for customers like a personal stylist at a department store: games, music, comics, books. Plus hosting events to promote queer artists like myself. But all I need to get that started is money. So, hello big prize!"

"Um, I need this store to exist ASAP," Britni gushes. "Hell, I'd come work for you in a heartbeat. It would be nice to use my social media powers for something I care about instead of riding the trend wave of what's already popular."

"Well, I'll be your very first and most loyal customer," I add.

"Same. Though I'm in a similar boat to Mo," Alix picks up. "I mean, you all know I'm an aspiring fashion designer. I moved here to New York to start my transition and to make my way as a designer. When I first arrived, I got my GED and started working as a tailor's assistant at a local dry cleaner. Actually, the owner is also the landlord of my tiny studio apartment above the shop, and he's become like my surrogate uncle here in the city.

"Anyway, I've gotten by thanks to his generosity, and I've made a nice little alterations business for myself in the neighborhood. I've gotten wildly good at sewing, but it doesn't leave me with much time or energy to design. And all my focus has been on making ends meet while affording the steps of my transition, so it hasn't exactly given me lots of time to network. I could never really afford fashion school, and I don't have any connections to make it in the industry. Plus, I don't have the extra money to make a collection to start promoting my brand. Anyway, obviously the prize could help finish paying for my transition and finally start my own label, whatever that looks like."

"Okay, that's it," Britni says, banging both of her fists on the table like she is channeling Chiroptera in real life. "We 100 percent need to win. Not just because I want everyone's dreams to come true, because *duh*. But because selfishly I want to move east and work as the social media brand manager for the two coolest, most creative people I know!"

I smile from ear to ear, just like the rest of my teammates seated here. What a dream—the Epic Hearts not just winning this unprecedented tournament, but somehow finding a way to be creative forces together? It's certainly a vision worth fighting for, attainable or not.

"Well, I don't know if we really can win," I begin, "but I do know this much—just getting to be here and meet you all in person and get along? To me, that's already a big win."

"Here, here!" Mo cries, raising her water glass. "To us!"

"To the Epic Hearts!" Alix adds, raising his glass.

"And to winning *Pantheonic*'s brand-new tournament!" Britni joins in.

As I raise my glass to cheers, I can only think one thing:

This really is starting to feel like our very own creation myth in the making.

CHAPTER TEN

OUR LONG LUNCH TURNED INTO DINNER, WHICH TURNED into a much later check-in than anyone anticipated. The good news? To my relief, the Epic Hearts started to get along just as well in person as we do online as teammates.

The less good news? By the time we checked in, there was only one two-queen-bed room left. The remaining option was a room with only one king bed. We all stood at the desk a little frozen. Given what Britni shared about her physical intimacy boundaries, I could tell she'd prefer her own bed. Plus Mo has a partner. Cary has their own team reservation, but they'll still be bouncing around rooms—and probably wouldn't love their girlfriend sharing a bed with a literal model. So we decided Alix and I should take the room with one king bed.

I smiled and nodded along with Alix's suggestion, but like a duck my mental legs were churning under this smooth surface. Sleeping comfortably is obviously a huge concern for me, but I also resolved to not give my chronic pain any more attention by letting my team know about it. So I couldn't vocalize my sleeping anxiety any more than I could vocalize the other reason blaring in my mind:

How am I supposed to share a bed with a gay boy I have a fast-evolving, unrequited crush on?

If there was any chance of me telling Alix about my feelings before, that has certainly been obliterated now. I'd never want to make him feel uncomfortable in our shared space.

Cut to me making the tiny fold-up cot bed they rolled into our room. Since I was the one with so much internal drama surrounding the solo king bed, I thought it was better to opt for a cot. It's a control freak move and a kind gesture all in one lumpy package.

"Can I help you with that?" Alix asks from the big bed, where he has his bag open for unpacking.

"No, I find making a bed weirdly soothing," I reply, fiddling with a fitted sheet.

"And you're absolutely sure you don't want to share?" Alix tries again. "I sleep on a twin in my studio apartment. There's no way I'd even know someone else is in this enormous bed."

But what if I want you to know I'm in the bed . . . ?

The thought slips loose and I force it away before my cheeks flush red.

"Trust me, I'm a restless sleeper," I try instead. "We'll both sleep better if I have some space."

Alix forces a smile, but I can tell he isn't buying the excuses I'm selling. It's not that they're lies . . . it's just that they're just not the whole truth. Regardless, Alix appears slightly offended by my insistence on sleeping separately.

"Well, I'm at least leaving you more of the closet space," he offers, trying to mask his reaction.

"Now that would be a crime against fashion," I reply with a smile. "My athleisure stuff can be shoved anywhere. But your clothes deserve to be in a showroom. Actually, they kind of match this whole room."

Looking from the shirts Alix has hung up and across the rest of our room, it's true. The décor is all soothing suede and warm paneling, along with a view of the city skyline. Alix's clothes, whether sewn himself or purchased, look like curated museum pieces, each one sleeker and more interesting than the last. I am deeply dazzled and impressed, but that also makes me embarrassed to show my own basic-boy clothes to him.

"You're welcome to borrow anything you want," Alix offers.

I laugh in response. It's sweet that he thinks I can fit into his small to extra-small shirts. Or that anyone would want to see my hairy belly exposed. I am not a hairless Irish muscle twunk, despite my deepest aspirations—or the way I can sometimes make myself look in the right clothes. Sort of.

But then I watch Alix's face fall, and I suddenly want to die. He must think I'm making fun of his clothes, finding the idea of wearing them laughable.

"Oh, no!" I blurt. "I'd be honored to, but I doubt I'd fit into anything. I wish I had a body like yours to show off your designs."

Or a body not riddled with mystery pain—which, speaking of, flares to life right now as I squat to tuck in the top sheet. It was behaving itself all afternoon . . . so why is it suddenly rearing its ugly head now?

"I hate being so thin," Alix says. "I feel scrawny. You look so sturdy, to me."

Well, now I can't help my cheeks flushing red. *Sturdy.* That's not exactly the top adjective I'd love to elicit from a cute guy I'm crushing on.

"I mean, like, strong," Alix fumbles, clearly catching my reaction. "I can't put on weight no matter what I do."

"I do work out a bit, but I can't lose weight no matter what *I* do."

Alix and I both give each other tight smiles, but now an awkward tension has sunk into the room—the exact kind I was dreading so much. I try not to panic, because that'll only make things worse.

"Should I put on some music for us to settle in to?" Alix tries instead. "I forget, do you like Beyoncé? Or Bad Bunny?"

"I mostly listen to country pop, believe it or not. I know, it makes me a bad gay. Do you like Taylor Swift?"

"Oh. Talk about being a bad gay—I don't really love Taylor Swift," Alix replies. "But if you repeat that in public, I will vehemently deny it."

"Yes, the Swifties are no joke," I say, forcing a laugh.

But I can't fight the pit that starts to form in my stomach.

Screw my potential crush—what would really *crush* me is if Alix and I aren't easy friends. Is it me? Am I incapable of making friends like everyone else the "normal" way? This makes me think of Annie, the only person my age I've ever had easy chemistry with. Though that doesn't exactly make me feel any better. Not just because she's gone . . .

But also because I now wonder, as time passed, would we really have bonded like I hoped?

"Keegan, can I ask you a . . ." Alix starts, pulling me out of my spiral. "Never mind."

"You can ask me anything," I reply, not sure I really mean it.

Or, I do. I'm just not sure I'd *answer* every question.

"It's just . . . well . . ." Alix stammers, which seems really unlike him.

It's like a war rages behind his eyes, deciding whether he wants to say out loud what's on his mind.

"I know I'm maybe being paranoid, but . . ."

Alix exhales, summoning all his courage.

"The reason you don't want to share a bed isn't because I'm trans, right?"

My entire brain feels like it explodes. It turns out while I've been directing the dramas in my own head, Alix has been doing exactly the same thing.

And he couldn't be more wrong.

"No!" I nearly yelp, my response seeming too forceful.

But I take a quick breath, because *this* we need to get right.

"I think you being trans is deeply wonderful," I continue. "If anything, I want to know more about your experience. We don't talk much about it, and I know you don't like dwelling on your life before New York. But I don't want to pry or make you feel different. I promise, my bed stuff is . . . purely a me thing."

I leave it there, because as much as I'm tempted to match Alix's honesty, I certainly don't want to make this about me and my chronic pain all of a sudden. Nor can I tell Alix the ways I'd like to *get to know* him if we did share a bed . . .

I just pray he really believes me this time.

"Thank you," Alix says, exhaling again. "I figured I was probably making things up, but I've never had to share a room with a friend this way before. And you're right, I would like to just be treated like any other guy. For lots of trans people, leading with our identity is an important part of representation. And it is for me too. But right now, more than anything, I just want to be considered one of the guys."

Alix looks like sharing this has drained him of every ounce of social energy he has left. I can't say I blame him. I certainly know the feeling after this big travel day and spending all afternoon together.

"I can't exactly say I have much experience being one of the guys. Or even being one of the gay guys," I reply. "But you don't have to worry about me judging that part of you. Ever."

Alix smiles and I can see the tension leave his body, thank goddess. It makes me feel good . . .

But it also makes me wish I would be brave enough to share about my own private anxieties too. I don't know what feels louder in my body, the stabs of pain or the pangs of attraction I feel being this close to Alix.

"Thank you, Keegan. I'm going to go shower, if you don't mind. I have a fairly exhaustive skincare routine, if you want to head in there to pee or something first."

"Bladder all good," I say, trying not to cringe over my word choice. "I take the shortest showers and use zero special products."

No, all my self-care time goes toward stretching and rolling. And all my products include cooling and heating pain relief—all of which I can do while Alix showers, come to think of it.

Then I see Alix's face falter again. I realize I've said yet another thing signaling that we might have less in common than we thought.

"But maybe you can teach me your skincare ways one of these nights?" I try again.

"Absolutely," Alix responds, already moving toward the bathroom.

It's like he can't get in there—and away from our flailing conversation—fast enough.

Then the pain in my right side suddenly shoots down my thigh to my foot, quite literally taking my breath away.

CHAPTER ELEVEN

A FEW HOURS LATER, I LIE ON THE COT I MADE FOR MYSELF in silent agony. Alix and I both went about our separate night routines, then spent time scrolling on our phones until it felt like time for lights out.

Now I lie in the darkness flat on my back, trying not to squirm from the pain rocketing between my right hip and butt. I also feel soaked in my least favorite emotions, the ones I was most afraid of experiencing here: feeling trapped and helpless, both in this shared hotel room and in my own body.

I try to breathe and focus on anything else, but the pain just feels so *pressing*. It started out okay when I got into the cot, but I could immediately tell the lumpy mattress and metal crossbars were going to be an extra challenge. I began in a position Chris taught me: on my left side to avoid pressure on my right, with a special neck-contoured pillow and a foam body pillow between my legs for proper support. But before long, the pain started worsening from a background ache to a blaring alarm.

So I tried my backup position, lying flat on my back with both of my legs extended. This eased the pain a bit, but I can never really fall asleep in this corpse-like pose. I miss sleeping on my stomach or in the fetal position the way I used to, but those both intensify the pain a ton.

As usually happens when I can't sleep, my mind scrolls through the medical and therapeutic advice I've gotten to try to find a remedy. I think back to my work with a Pilates instructor, who taught me exercises to strengthen my lower back and pelvic floor. These were important tools to add to my arsenal, but the most important thing she ended up teaching me was what the piriformis is: the band of muscle between our lower backs and butts that connects the hip bone to the tail bone. A muscle that also sits on the sciatic nerve.

Learning about the piriformis was like a light bulb going off. It felt like it described *exactly* the kind of muscle that pained me most on my right side. It would also explain the leg pain if my muscle was knotting up and affecting the sciatic nerve. Everything is so interconnected in that area of the body, I had previously struggled to articulate the acute pain I was experiencing. But after that, I could be more specific:

The pain felt like a permanent cramped knot in my right piriformis muscle.

Armed with this new knowledge, I returned to the orthopedist. If my right piriformis muscle knotting was indeed the exact symptom, then why was it cramping up to begin with? The orthopedist performed more standard motion and pain tests, which led him to settle on my sacroiliac joint. With a condition called sacroiliitis, this joint that links the pelvis to the spine becomes loose and can cause all kinds of tension and pain. This usually happens to older or pregnant patients, but my orthopedist said it was possible in anyone. So we scheduled a bilateral SI joint injection of a steroid cocktail to hopefully retighten the joint and cure the issue. It was an outpatient procedure that required a surgical team, since they needed a laparoscopic camera to guide the ultra-long needle to my joints.

Obviously I was terrified by all this. Even more so when I got to the appointment and was separated from my parents to put on a medical gown and cap. I had never been in a hospital or surgical space before, so I definitely wasn't expecting this big a production for what sounded like a simple shot. I almost bolted, but my desire to cure this pain outweighed my fear.

When I was rolled into the operating suite, I counted eight people aside from the surgeon in the room, and countless beeping or whirring machines. This was clearly a room where serious spinal procedures were performed. In my case, I was meant to stay awake during the injections, which simplified things. Still, this required two giant local numbing shots to be administered. I remember lying face down on the table wondering how I got there and just yelling at myself to be brave. The doctor, rather sweetly, offered to play a song that might calm me down. I instinctively chose "Trustfall" by P!nk. After all, that's what this was—letting a team of strangers inject my joints with huge needles.

After it was all over, I was so proud and hopeful. This experience had been like an in-person boss battle, and I had fought my way through it.

Then the steroids hit my system once I was home. Those amped me up for an entire week like some kind of never-ending caffeine drip, making me feel like the un-incredible Hulk.

And the pain in my piriformis promptly returned the very same night.

It seemed . . . impossible.

I resolved to give it a few days, but the pain persisted as if the injection had never happened. Clearly, my joints weren't the source of the chronic muscle knotting.

Finally, my parents got a copay bill they still refuse to show me to this day.

That's when I started minimizing the pain I experience to my parents. It was devastating to spend all that energy and time and money on a remedy that ultimately did nothing, save for giving me roid rage for a whole week.

After this, I became convinced I had a tumor on my piriformis. If my spine and joints were healthy, what was causing this seemingly permanent knot on the muscle there? I could feel the deep knot and so could Chris, but only if I lay on my back and crossed my leg over my body like a yoga master. I ultimately tried to report all this to my general physician, but he was skeptical. He didn't do more than poke at my hip a few times and say he felt nothing. He did rather reluctantly order an ultrasound, then practically laughed at my paranoia when it came back clean.

That was the last time I saw a medical doctor for this issue too.

Right now, back on this torturous cot, I shift my leg and press my thumb against the howling knot in my upper butt muscle, looking for some relief. I try to repeat the lyrics to "Trustfall" in my mind to distract myself from the perpetual ache. I even try to think of how excited I am for tomorrow, for the *Pantheonic* tournament to begin. But it's hard to focus on anything other than the pain, especially when I'm trying to sleep. This is usually the point at home when I get up and walk around my room a bit, but . . .

"Keegan."

I hear Alix's voice and freeze. I must have been squirming more than I thought. Damn.

"I can hear you squeaking over there," he continues. "That cot cannot be comfortable."

"It's . . . um . . ."

I don't want to lie, but I don't want to get into the truth for so many reasons.

"There are enough pillows on this bed, we could build a little wall," Alix tries. "It'll be like having our own separate beds. And before you try to be polite and refuse, think of it as a favor to me. Those cot squeaks are going to be hard to ignore."

I exhale. Alix has me there. I might be willing to isolate myself for my own discomfort, but I refuse to make him uncomfortable too.

"You win," I reply, rolling out of the mercilessly noisy cot. "My back thanks you in advance."

Once again, that statement is close enough to the truth. It's not like I'm going to thank Alix on behalf of my ass.

Minutes later we have built a very cozy pillow wall between us. As I settle into my half of the bed, turned onto my left side and nestled properly with all my support pillows, I actually feel some blissful, cloudy relief. I don't have the energy to process how charged it is to have my body this close to Alix's. All I focus on is how lovely and warm and safe I feel lying beside him, even through a wall of pillows.

"Good night, Keegan."

"Good night, Alix."

I don't know how, but I fall asleep quickly after that.

CHAPTER TWELVE

WALKING INTO THE JAVITS CENTER THE NEXT MORNING I feel like an entirely different person. I can't say I got the most restful night of sleep ever, but I'm just grateful I slept at all this first night. Every time I woke up to switch positions, I could sense Alix across the bed. Smelling the fresh shower products wafting off his skin, it made me feel less alone. It also made me feel lots of other things, but at least that helped me stay distracted enough to fall back asleep.

Alix and I both woke up buzzing with anticipation, so I let the bright light of day erase my bleak night of anxious aching. Speaking of light, it feels like the Javits Center was built specifically to capture it. Beams of late morning sunshine streak into the lobby from the towering glass ceiling. The effect is *dazzling*. It only serves to hype up our collective excitement.

"I still cannot believe we're here," Mo exclaims, her usual volume as high as her spirits.

She wears a bright yellow jumpsuit and a matching dagger-like pin in her halo of hair. We were all told tournament events would be filmed for social media and website platforms, so they requested no visible brands or logos on our clothes—save for *Pantheonic* merch, of course. We all also agreed to save the team T-shirts Alix made for tomorrow when gameplay begins, since today is just orientation. That's why I wear my beloved gray Pantheon Pillar hoodie and a new pair of maroon sweat-shorts. And why I'm extra grateful when we finally enter an air-conditioned space on this July day.

"This feels like the best day of my life," Britni adds, stars in her currently wide eyes.

I would have expected an LA influencer like her to be harder to impress, especially after stalking her socials last night. Britni's life in LA looks so curated and glamorous, I thought she might consider all this nerdy stuff basic. But now I remind myself that here today, *this* is probably the real Britni, not the version of herself she presents on social media.

Perhaps accordingly, today she wears a fitted purple baseball cap tight over her face, an oversized lavender sweater, and black yoga shorts. It all looks very expensive and comfortable-chic, but it also feels a bit like a disguise. Britni mentioned she scheduled a week of LA posts and isn't planning to feature this trip on her main feeds—but she swore it's because she wants to do this tournament for herself and for us, not for anyone else.

At first I was skeptical, but judging from the way Britni reaches to clutch Mo's hand, it's clear she is genuinely excited. It's also clear these two must have bonded even closer sharing a room last night. I hate to admit it, but I'm a little jealous. I wish I could say the same for Alix and me. Despite our semi-peaceful slumber, we were definitely more about awkwardly fumbling conversation, probably thanks to me.

"We're supposed to report to the Level Four meeting rooms," Alix says.

He looks painfully sexy in a rust-colored sleeveless shirt and brown cargo pants, seeming like a hot extra from *Dune*.

"Renting out meeting rooms must cost a fortune," Alix continues, his jaw dropping a little. "Adding in the prize money, how is this tournament remotely cost-effective for Delfanti Games? I mean, I know monthly subscription revenue keeps climbing, but . . ."

"I was thinking the same thing," Mo replies. "So I did some more digging last night. Rumor has it this entire event is Dahlia's pet project. She wants to push *Pantheonic* into a new era while it's still growing. Most are thinking this augmented reality tournament experiment is her big shot—a flashy event to transition into a future vision for the game. If it works, she has proof of concept. But if it flops, a lot of people think maybe she'll be asked to step down."

Part of me wants to judge this company—one that Dahlia started—for stifling her innovative creativity. But another part of me understands: Why fix something that's not broken, something that's in fact *beloved*? Then again, Dahlia has never steered this game wrong. Don't she and her team deserve some benefit of the doubt?

"That means this maybe isn't just about us winning anymore," I say, letting this new pressure sink in a bit. "Maybe this is about making *Pantheonic* and its founder look good? About setting the future course of the entire game?"

"Then we'd better put on one damn good show," Britni finishes for us all.

It takes another hour for us all to get checked in and sign some additional paperwork. My parents and Mo's parents helped read all the contracts and waivers ahead of time for us, so we all feel comfortable signing. It's pretty standard for a contest like this.

Now the twenty-eight players from all seven teams wait to enter the next meeting room for orientation. We don't know what pantheons everyone belongs to yet—except for two pro teams I recognize from their streaming channels, the Mythic Goats and the Heroic Heirs. Seeing them here isn't surprising, but it is intimidating as Hel. Aside from Cary's team, the Ann Apolis, and us Epic Hearts, that leaves three additional teams. I'm hoping they're also experienced casual gamers like us.

Though really, I'm way more focused on the camera operators that have begun to follow us. Some carry shoulder cams while others carry phones for social media coverage. We were also told they installed plenty of wall cameras in the gaming rooms. The production team will be posting packages all day every day, but apparently these will be edited on the fly instead of live-streamed.

This means we also surrendered our phones, officially agreeing that all tournament content will be funneled through the *Pantheonic* platforms. We can post the rest of the time while here, just not specifically during the gaming events. That's fine by me—it's not like I want to be an influencer. And just by posting a bit about my arrival yesterday, I have a ton of new followers. The interest surrounding this mysterious new tournament format remains high.

As the double doors in front of us swing open, I feel my whole body tense up. Thankfully not with pain since I'm standing, but instead with a new sensation. I've never been an athlete or a performer, so the rush of nerves and fear and adrenaline I feel right now is quite new. It's almost . . . paralyzing.

Then I feel a warm hand on my shoulder.

"Just breathe," Alix whispers in my ear. "Remember, it's basically still the four of us playing together. Everything else is just very fun noise."

I turn to Alix and smile, forcing out an exhale.

"How did you know that's exactly what I needed to hear?"

In response, Alix just winks at me: *Duh, because we talk almost every day.* It makes my heart melt all over again.

But I quickly mop up that emotional mess.

I do not want to add breaking my own heart to this already pulse-pounding experience.

We all walk into another expansive meeting room and collectively gasp. While the last one was full of sign-up tables and chairs, this space has been fully transformed into a futuristic, arcade-like hub. It feels somewhere between the hull of a spaceship and a godly banquet hall.

Around the room stand seven impressive pillars, each one surrounded by four cubicle walls. I assume these must be semi-private gaming stations. Each pillar also features a banner hanging from its top, listing a different team name. Even cooler? The outer walls of the gaming cubicles feature the images and names of our individual avatars—including Chiroptera, sMOte, Apollix, and K.Odyssia.

It's a sight that takes my breath away. This is all *real.*

"Our babies have never looked so epic," Mo proclaims, courting the attention of a nearby camera phone.

Everyone seems appropriately awed by this converted space, scanning the impeccable details of the coliseum we'll be competing in. Taking in all twenty-eight avatars displayed on the walls, they feel as varied and diverse as their human gamers. It's an intimidating and overwhelming presentation—one I can see impacting my fellow teammates as well.

"Don't worry," I whisper, "we'll make a war board in our rooms later to study our opponents. Right now let's focus on enjoying the moment and learning all we can?"

This elicits relieved nods from my teammates.

"Though maybe we should also size up our human opponents while we're here?" Britni recommends. "Since part of this tournament is going to somehow be augmented reality in person?"

"An introductory recon mission," Mo replies, channeling some sMOte energy. "Got it."

A new voice then pipes through the speakers mounted throughout the room—one I instantly recognize.

"Please take a seat at your designated stations," says the realm-portal NPC character from *Pantheonic*.

Approaching our Epic Hearts station, we each walk through a door in the cubicle walls designated by our avatars. Stepping inside, we find ourselves in a little private gaming room with the central pillar at its center. Four enormous flat-screen monitors are mounted in a circle, each connected to a humming, state-of-the-art computer tower on the floor. These are matched with brand-new gaming keyboards and mouses.

Eyeing the chairs, I'm relieved to find they're sleek and ergonomic office-style seats. It won't exactly match my setup at home, but it should be supportive enough for pain-free gaming . . . I hope.

Settling into my chair, I notice we all also have a *Pantheonic* water thermos and a branded gaming headset. I bet the general announcements will be piped through the room speakers, but our team communication will take place between closed calls as usual. Except these calls will be recorded for public consumption. And instead of being in different states, now Alix sits to my right, Mo to my left, and Britni only half obscured across the pillar. We'll be able to see each other while we game, which I hope only works in our favor.

I lean back into my chair as the game loads, somehow feeling both relaxed and surged with adrenaline at the same time. Mercifully, the usual pain in my right piriformis from sitting doesn't seize up.

I expect K.Odyssia to drop into Mount Pantheonic as usual, to maybe meet the others at our Epic Hearts fountain before being summoned to the Revelatory Shrine again. Instead, we all populate directly into a columned portal hall—a gilded one I've never seen before.

"Special event, special portal gate," Mo says out loud for all of us—or maybe for the cameras. Yeah, that's going to take some getting used to.

And apparently so will this gaming setup. The graphics quality is crystal clear, and I'm amazed at how K.Odyssia looks as her idle animations play, but the keyboard and mouse are extra sensitive. I go to walk forward and suddenly I am running.

I spend a second getting used to the new equipment and testing out my hot keys—making K.Odyssia jump, attack, and use a few abilities next to a wall. Once I feel comfortable, I realize it's not just our team in here—it's all seven teams gathered. This gate hall is much larger than usual and filled with golden pillars and statues—of *us*.

Spotting K.Odyssia rendered in virtual stone makes my heart skip a beat.

Before I can nerd out on this with the others, our realm-portal NPC arrives: TravelGee. They monitor and power all the portals across the Divine Realm to the earth realms—and they only meet us instead of UnderTee when we need special portals to the hardest-to-reach realms.

"Thank you for joining me at this critical juncture," TravelGee says in their soothing voice. They are a small, child-like immortal being with brown skin. They also sport a large set of rainbow-swirling portal-energy wings—once again an amalgam inspired by many mythological child and travel figures.

"I have been ordered by the Pantheonic War Council to transport you seven pantheons. Are you ready?"

Even though we have no idea where we're going, we all click accept. This causes TravelGee to unfurl their brilliant, shining wingspan. As they do, a swirling light portal opens up between the columns in front of us. Our avatars all step through . . .

And it feels like stepping somewhere over the rainbow bridge.

CHAPTER THIRTEEN

WE ARE TRANSPORTED AGAIN, BUT AGAINST EXPECTATIONS TravelGee teleports us across the Divine Realm. I can tell because beyond a sprawling wall of windows, I see the skyline of Mount Pantheonic. The city looks almost suspended in space, rising in the distance beyond a lush orchard right outside.

I've never been here before. I don't know that anyone in *Pantheonic* has.

"Anyone know where we are?" I ask.

"If you don't know, Keegan, there's no hope for the rest of us," Alix replies.

"We're in the castle headquarters of the Pantheonic War Council," Mo says. "Everyone turn around."

We swing around and probably all feel a little silly to find ourselves in a round stone tower—with the words *Pantheonic War Council* hanging across a grand banner.

"I don't think you get any extra spy points for that one, Mo," Britni teases.

"Oh, I always get extra spy points."

We go quiet as Queen Trinidy emerges from a set of stairs to address us. She walks up behind a small pulpit dressed in a deep green regal dress, wearing a matching emerald headpiece.

"It was once written that any good game is a balance between the cost of frustration and the joy of satisfaction," Queen Trinidy begins. "I believe the same balance applies beyond our war games to the very nature of life, mortal and immortal. Thus, to reclaim the unknown realms where the Stoneruned Horde Nerve Center is hidden and where the Source Wing is held, you all must transcend your current states of being. To succeed, we must converge at the place where virtual reality and physical reality meet, where human and artificial intelligence merge into a bold new augmented existence.

"As such, I now invite you to evolve your understanding of this holy game of life. I invite you to leave your virtual selves and become deities as your physical selves. I invite you to traverse earth realms by joining me in our Revelatory Shrine."

As Queen Trinidy finishes, the lights in the gaming hub shift to a warm blue. Looking to my teammates, we agree it's an indication to stand up. Exiting our cubicle, we find the rest of the teams doing the same, all moving toward a set of double doors that lead into the next meeting room. As we are all ushered through these doors, I begin to hear gasps ahead of us.

Once I see this new space, I understand why.

The next meeting room is made to look like a recreation of the Revelatory Shrine from Mount Pantheonic, with the same statues and stage layout. But instead of the skylight, there are massive screens behind the stage to appear like a window to the usual rainbow-starred sky. And instead of Queen Trinidy standing on this stage . . .

Dahlia Delfanti stands in the flesh. The founder and CEO of *Pantheonic* looks resplendent wearing a crisp white suit and layers of chic gold jewelry.

This set of sights sends chills running through my entire body. They've brought our game to life. I'm standing in an actual Revelatory Shrine. All I can do is turn to Alix, Mo, and Britni to share silent beams of excitement.

The sensation only intensifies as the final players enter—and the double doors to the gaming hub lock with a loud click. A keypad lights up with the words *Code Required.*

"Please, gather around," Dahlia speaks into a microphone, smiling warmly. "First, I'd like to thank you all for pressing pause on your busy lives to be here. This tournament has been a dream of mine for many years, but it would mean nothing without your physical presence. To me, *Pantheonic* has always been about bringing people together in real time. About fostering teams and found families. So it has also been my vision to bring teams even further together in this grand way. Hopefully this is only the first bold step . . . But now I'm getting ahead of myself. For before we usher in any future ages of tomorrow, we all face a seemingly impossible war to win.

"This endgame will be battled across four grand stages. The Stoneruned Horde is ever clever, so for each final earth realm we advance across, our access will become more limited. Every round is also designed to answer one of the core four mysteries at the center of the Pantheonic Stoneruned War. In round one, we aim to learn: *Where exactly is the Source Wing being held?* Once this question is answered, we only have enough portal energy to transport the mightiest five teams to this hidden earth realm chain.

"In round two, we aim to learn: *How is the Source Wing's vital force being contained and tapped by the Stoneruned Horde?* TravelGee will then only have the energy to carry four teams forward into round three, where we hope to answer: *What weapon will ultimately defeat the strongest Stoneruned automatons?* Finally, round four will see three final teams fighting to end our great war and answer the most precious question of all: *What will happen to our competing pantheons should peace be restored—and what unknown home will the Stoneruned Horde be banished to?* Of course, here one team will be named our grand victors."

Dahlia pauses for a moment, letting the scope of this tournament structure sink in with all of us. Though really, all I can focus on is one stark reality:

Two teams are going home in round one.

And then another team every round until the final three.

That's . . . terrifying.

"As for how these war rounds will be fought, perhaps that is the most exciting part," Dahlia continues. "Here in our own physical earth realm, we have tasks that must be solved to regain entry to the gaming hub—your portal back to the virtual earth realms. These tasks will range from augmented reality scavenger hunts to escape rooms to puzzling maze races, as the Stoneruned Horde has set up challenges here in our own realm to protect their most vital wartime intelligence.

"Your goal will be to uncover the entry code unique to your pantheon team. Each round the code for every team will change and remain unique, so there will be no way to copy another pantheon. As always, you must forge your own paths forward. Once you have obtained your code, you will then complete a team quest event in the virtual realm, as you are accustomed to . . . mostly.

"Rest assured, like our invitational event, these quests are designed to reward skill, ingenuity, and teamwork. Your avatar levels will perhaps provide an edge for some, but this factor will not be essential for winning.

"I'd like to be the first to welcome you all to the future of gaming. Tomorrow, our journey together officially begins with round one—even as it will quickly end for two mighty teams. Heed this call and spend this day preparing for battle. Tonight, we will gather for a send-off banquet fit for the divine beings you all are."

I can't help it—I look to Alix, Mo, and Britni. I see the same joy reflected across all their faces . . .

This sounds so. Freaking. Fun.

And it sounds like the gaming spirit that got us here might hopefully help *keep* us here. With a little more luck, we might make it all the way to the final three. But we should focus first on surviving round one—which means spending some time today studying our newly revealed opponents.

It's time for the Epic Hearts to plan for war.

CHAPTER FOURTEEN

IT IS A POOR PLAYER WHO PLAYS THE GAME AND NOT THEIR *opponent.*

I've written this ancient wisdom in thick black marker at the top of our brand-new war board. It's a thing of beauty, currently resting against the window in Mo and Britni's room. Behind it, golden hour casts warm light across the bustling Hudson River.

Earlier this afternoon we took one very satisfying trip to an office supply store to buy a whiteboard and marker set. Since then we've been assembling this war board to familiarize ourselves with the other teams. Well, with their avatars at least. We'll get to know the players behind the pantheons more at tonight's inaugural banquet.

For the board, we used our laptops to look up the six other competing teams now that they've been officially announced after orientation. Aside from the two pro teams, the rest of us are pretty evenly matched level-wise. After lots of transcribing, we now have a decent understanding of the other pantheons' compositions.

The two pro teams have identical compositions: Ruler, Trickster, Warrior, Bender. It's a more flexible take on the classic defender/healer/fighter/ranger team build, given that Rulers and Tricksters can sometimes be more versatile than Creatures and Reapers.

Cary's team has taken a more unique approach, building from the "less popular" opposite pillars entirely. As for the three teams totally new to us, one has the more classic pro composition, one is built from Traversers and Creatures only, while the final team is *all* Benders. The fact that so many compositions can thrive in *Pantheonic* is one of my favorite parts of the game. Single-pillar teams shouldn't be able to compete, but if pantheons customize and balance their avatars with enough coordination, anything is possible.

I pry my eyes off our war board and turn to Mo. She sits on her bed with her own eyes glued to her laptop. Britni and Alix took the first bathroom-getting-ready shifts, leaving Mo and me extra prep time. We aren't the only ones who seem obsessed with studying and books, though. More than a few times my eyes have fallen on the stack of novels Britni flew across the country. Britni hasn't volunteered this information herself to me yet, but Mo shared that she is a veritable speed-reader. She thinks Britni should use her platform to become a bookfluencer, but Britni insists no one would take someone who looks like her seriously as a reader—or as a gamer, for that matter.

I wish I could tell Britni how wrong she is, but I always second-guess myself. I mean, I still feel intimidated just being around her, and I've already seen how other people treat her differently when we walk through rooms. It's a reminder that everyone suffers when we stereotype each other.

This is also a reminder of the progress I made with my journal today. I stole a little time away to break it in. After recording the vibes of my opening day journey, I decided to capture the spirit of the upcoming tournament rounds by generating four core questions for my own life. I found they came to me pretty easily: *How can I conquer my chronic pain? How should I handle my feelings for Alix? How do I build equally genuine friendships IRL? And how can I lead my teammates to victory?*

Perhaps by naming these questions, I'll find some answers from our mythological gaming experience. If nothing else, it definitely helps me set some intentions for the tournament: live bravely, embrace new emotions, expand my social circle, and help friends win.

Obviously, I need to find a way to apply some of these goals to my relationship with Britni. But right now, I can focus on doing so with Mo. I see she has *Pantheonic* open on her laptop—with sMOte shopping in her favorite Trickster Alley store.

"Whoa, someone is going on a spending spree," I say.

"I've been saving up lots of Worship Points," Mo responds. "I was waiting to see if there was anything specific I should spend them on. Since we still don't really know what's coming, I'm stocking up on portal and healing items."

"It will be good to have your braid arsenal fully loaded. I spent all my Worship Points forging and equipping the Gravity Stone for my sword."

"I cannot wait to see that in action. Smart, saving it to debut here at the tournament."

Mo's words seem cheery, but her expression and tone signal otherwise.

"Hey, is something up?" I ask.

"No. Well, sort of," Mo answers. "I guess I'm just nervous about all the attention we're about to start getting from this tournament."

"I know, but we have to remember we're doing this for ourselves, not anyone else," I say. "And for better or worse, *Pantheonic* is editing the coverage for round one instead of live-streaming. I think that's to give everyone some grace in case anything goes wrong."

Mo does brighten, hearing this.

"You're right. No use worrying about the stuff we can't control," she says. "Much better to worry about sizing up our competition."

"Indeed," I agree, grinning. "We all need to channel your mistress of whispers energy tonight."

The banquet turns out to be more of a buffet, but that makes sense trying to feed twenty-eight ravenous teen and twenty-something gamers. The meeting room where we gather is the same Revelatory Shrine from earlier, only partially reset to feel more like a grand mess hall. Our team sits at an eight-top table with Cary's team, the Ann Apolis.

"I'm glad we're all on the same page about teaming up," Cary speaks and signs.

"I know we can't be sure if we'll even be able to work together event-wise, but you know the other teams will be making alliances too," says Laura, a transfem gamer who plays a Reaper on Cary's team.

I know all these details because everyone filled out nametags with our names, teams, pronouns, and any other details we opted to share about ourselves. Laura sits next to her girlfriend, Natalie, who is also a Japanese American queer teen who plays a Creature. In general, the vibe of Cary's team is easy and breezy. Which makes sense, given that they're all real-world friends in Mo's own extended circle.

"Do you think we should try to go mingle, now that we're done eating?" Mo asks. "Not that I don't love you all tremendously."

"Probably," Alix agrees. "We don't need to confirm everyone else's suspicions that our teams have linked up."

Alix looks painfully cute as ever, wearing a fresh outfit. Tonight he sports a structured vest that reveals some chest hair . . . which I most definitely haven't already fantasized about.

"I think that ship has already sailed," Britni adds. "But you're right. We should get to know the other teams as much as possible before tomorrow."

It doesn't take us very long to decide which pantheon sits at the top of our team's need-to-meet list. Nor does it take us long to find the Mythic Goats, since they set up court at a central table like gaming royalty. As anyone who follows their streaming channel knows, their team met in a local disability chat room. Of course, we learned during orientation that all events will be completely accessible.

The Mythic Goats sit, perhaps predictably, with the only other pro team—the Heroic Heirs. Both teams' members also appear to be among the oldest here, being in their mid-twenties.

"Ah, the final team to come meet us," Jim, the Goats' Odin-Zeus leader, says as he greets us.

He uses a wheelchair, and a quick scan of him and his nametag tells me he is German American, cis-male, and straight. He is dressed in a plaid button-down and jeans, looking nondescript in a way that you'd never know he is the leader of *Pantheonic*'s top-ranked team.

"It's been wild, we've had visitations like we're actual deities or something." The next to speak is Hanna. Ignoring their humble brag, I scan to see they're an Australian immigrant, nonbinary, and wearing a prosthetic leg. Unlike Jim, Hanna is dressed like they are about to attend a cosplay rave as their Loki-Hermes avatar.

"I know your pantheon isn't technically Greek mythology-based, but we clocked the *Odyssey* references," Jim jumps back in. "We're the only two Euro-Classical mythology-based teams in the tournament."

"I like to imagine my teammates' avatars are *Odyssey*-adjacent too," I share, happy to nerd out. "But we had already designed our avatars before we formed our team in the game chats, so the theme doesn't apply globally."

"We recruited for our team the same way," Joey, the leader of the Heroic Heirs, interjects. "Though we only interviewed elite local players who leaned into our superhero theme."

A quick glance at the Heroic Heirs tells me they're all cisgender, straight, and European American. Their team is made up of three guys and one woman, all wearing pantheon-branded T-shirts. Their team has taken their "superhero as modern myth" inspiration literally, customizing their avatars to look as much like costumed heroes as the game allows.

"Though I wish I let you onto our team," Joey adds, his eyes looking Britni up and down like an elevator. "Ever think of switching to a pro team?"

"Never," Britni responds through gritted teeth. "And not interested."

"I like a girl with attitude." This voice belongs to Cain, another of the Heirs. "Ignore my teammates, they don't know how to treat a beautiful girl."

"And you do?" Mo responds, her voice full of fire. "We all just barely turned eighteen, for the record."

Instead of putting the so-called "heroes" off, this only seems to increase their interest. All three of their dudes keep leering at Britni, while their sole female member quite literally looks the other way.

It turns my stomach.

"I think we've learned everything we need to," I reply, setting my eyes on Jim, the supposed-mightiest player of the Mythic Goats.

The fact that they sat together all night with the Heirs—and still sit together now—is a pretty clear sign the two top teams have aligned themselves. Unfortunately, there's no apology or concession on Jim's face. Perhaps he doesn't mind a bit of mind-gaming intimidation, earnest or otherwise.

"Agreed," Alix backs me up.

"Aw, we've offended the snowflakes." Joey laughs. "No surprises there. See you in the tournament arena."

Mo looks like she is about to explode at him, and I don't blame her one bit. But before she can, Britni places a hand on her shoulder and shakes her head. The message is clear—*they aren't worth it.*

So, taking our cue from her, we all turn and walk away.

Britni is the first to speak once we're safely out of earshot: "I'd much rather kick their asses in the tournament."

Direct and brutal—and graceful—as ever.

"Can I get an omen?" Alix replies.

"Oh, it is so game on," Mo says, looking every bit as angry and motivated as I feel.

After all, it's guys like those who make gaming feel unsafe for women like Britni—and for the rest of us, to varying degrees. And that was just the tiniest tip of the troll iceberg.

"I know our team doesn't believe in directly attacking other pantheons," I add, "but I think we just found an enemy as vile as the Stoneruned Horde."

The part I don't say out loud? This is also a potential enemy teamed up with the best of the best. So if we're taking them on, we'll have to play this smart.

Thankfully, that's our specialty.

CHAPTER FIFTEEN

BACK IN OUR ROOM AFTER DINNER, I'M SOMEWHAT relieved Alix looks as worn out as I feel. I can't remember the last time I was this social for an entire day. Meeting all these new people has me feeling drained to the last drop. Luckily our entire team agreed to return to our rooms early to rest up before the start of round one tomorrow.

Despite all this, I'm still tempted to talk to Alix about our experience briefly meeting the remaining three tournament teams. Did he feel the same pull of excitement to be sharing this once-in-a-lifetime experience with fellow gamers? But also the clear undercurrent of intense competition? The Goats and the Heirs aside, we all want to be friends and have a blast together. But no one wants to lose—especially if it means cutting this adventure short. It's like the rivalry war from *Pantheonic* has bled from the game into real life. Except in the real world, there's no automaton horde for us all to rally together against.

So while yes, I'm tempted to talk to Alix about the other teams, I also know what I *need* right now is to unplug and unwind. Usually I do that at home by lying on the floor on my stomach—to avoid piriformis pain—and watching a reality TV competition show. But there's only one TV in here, and I don't want Alix to think I'm some weirdo, sprawling out on the floor alone with my laptop. Then again, it might be better than asking Alix what he wants to watch and learning this is yet another awkward area where we have nothing in common.

Right now I stand at the window weighing my options as I stare out at the city lights. But my time to decide arrives as Alix emerges from the bathroom, freshly scrubbed. He only wears a pair of joggers with a towel around his shoulders as he walks toward the closet for a shirt. My breath catches in my throat at the sight of all that exposed skin. Alix might be thin, but he is fit as hell. And the top-surgery scars curved under his pecs only make them look even more defined. I feel a current of attraction jolt through my entire body like a lightning bolt. Still, I do my best not to physically react. In several ways.

"Hey, would you mind if I found something to watch?" Alix asks before I can say anything. "I seriously need to turn off my brain for a while."

"I was just thinking the same thing," I reply, pleased to remain capable of normal human conversation while Alix is shirtless. "What kind of stuff do you usually watch?"

"Nothing religiously, honestly. Well, except for *Project Runway*. I've seen every episode."

Suddenly a light bulb brightens up inside me.

Ding ding ding, we finally have a winner!

"I don't know how we never talked about this before," I reply. "But that happens to be one of my favorite shows."

"No way! I didn't think you were that into fashion."

"Ouch," I gasp, fake pouting. "How dare you!"

Alix is about to explain himself until he realizes I'm joking. Indeed, fashion isn't my gig. I'm happy to leave that to Alix, who has mercifully put on an oversized Beyoncé concert sweater.

"It's not about the fashion specifically," I explain. "I just love watching talented and creative people compete. *Top Chef, The Voice, Project Runway, The Great British Bake Off*—I love all shows like that."

"And yet you hesitated to enter this tournament, which is basically like a reality talent comp?" Alix says next, sliding effortlessly once again past my defenses.

I mean, I did think of the potential competition part, but . . .

"Oh jeez, I don't mean to keep insulting you," Alix says, spotting the look on my face. "I just always tease the friends I like most."

First, my brain buzzes at the phrase *like most* being how Alix thinks of me.

Then it fizzles over the word *friend.*

"Not insulted," I recover. "I just didn't think of gaming as that kind of creative talent. But you keep helping me surprise myself."

I can't be sure, but I swear I see Alix blush for a second. At least until he quickly moves toward his bag.

"I can pull up an episode on my laptop," he says.

"Perfect. Hey, have you ever thought of applying to *Project Runway* as a designer?"

"I have," Alix answers. "I've been too young until this year. And I've been working so many alterations hours, I haven't had enough sewing time to put together a proper womenswear presentation. Or the money, obviously."

All of this is a blaring reminder of how privileged my life has been so far, while Alix has been forced to fend for himself in every way. I know his early independence had a lot to do with affirming his trans identity, but I already promised not to pry there.

"Anyway, why do you think you like talent competitions so much?" Alix pivots as he climbs up onto the bed.

I immediately know it's going to hurt like hell sitting upright on the soft bed. My piriformis area pings with fresh pain, almost like a warning alarm. But the promise of being close enough to Alix again to smell his shampoo and skin feels worth the potential discomfort.

"Honestly, the answer is kind of cosmic, if that doesn't make you cringe," I say, arranging some pillows against the headboard for back support. "Or bore you."

"Are you kidding? Now I'm dying to hear."

"Okay. We're all academics in my family, and we're not particularly religious," I begin, settling into a seat on the bed. "But we all study some form of mythology or history or sociology. I guess that has made us all agree on a kind of . . . spiritual understanding."

"I don't think you mentioned that both your parents are teachers. That explains why you sometimes sound like a textbook when you speak," Alix interrupts, smirking.

I groan. Because *that's* deeply sexy, I'm sure.

"No! It's cute!" Alix insists.

I feel myself blush. Does he mean cute, like attractive? Or cute like your favorite teddy bear? Assuming the disappointing latter, I carry on.

"If you say so. Anyway, if there's one thing most world religions seem to have in common, it's the idea that we're really energetic or spiritual beings that are dropped into these physical bodies to experience life. I don't know if it's to learn something, or to teach something, or to grow, or to accomplish something specific. Who knows, maybe the reasons are different for everyone.

"But it seems to me that life here on earth is like one big school. And all of it is designed to bring out the best and worst of us. To *test* us. So I think that's why I'm drawn to competitions. It reminds some deep part in us of the meaning of life, the one we don't ever get to really know while we're here. It goes back to Queen Trinidy's announcement speech about why all humans are so drawn to games."

Alix stares at me with his mouth open.

"Have you always been like this?"

"Like what?" I laugh, a little more than nervously.

"Like this deep, wise old soul comes over you out of nowhere?"

"I guess?" I sigh. "I honestly haven't had many friends in person I can really be myself around."

I don't know if I meant to say that out loud, but I'm too tired to edit myself. I expect Alix to look at me with pity, but instead he gazes at me with understanding.

"The only person in my family who accepted me for who I am was my abuela, Rosie," Alix shares. "No one else understood what it meant for me to be trans, especially if I was also attracted to men. To be honest, I'm not sure my abuela understood either. But she only cared about protecting me, because I was her favorite. It probably wasn't right of her to say so out loud, but she knew I needed her protection. She . . . she died when I was fifteen. Without her . . .

"Well, there was no way I could stay home. As soon as I could after that, I emancipated myself and moved here. What I'm trying to say is that, until then, I knew what it was like not to have many people you could be yourself around."

"Alix, I'm so sorry," I say. "I can't imagine how hard that was."

"Losing my abuela was hard," Alix replies. "But moving here turned out to be less difficult than most other young queer people seem to have it. I found my chosen family really quickly, including the people who gave me a place to live and a job. I found the way to start affirming who I truly am. And if we're really talking cosmic stuff . . ."

Alix hesitates, like he second-guesses wanting to share more. But I just nod, hoping he'll feel comfortable enough to go on.

"Obviously no one knows for sure what happens when we die. But I have always felt Abuela Rosie *with* me, ever since she passed. Like she is . . . looking out for me, especially moving to New York. And I know this sounds bonkers, but I swear she is always sending me little signs to remind me."

I feel chills roll over my arms.

"That doesn't sound bonkers at all," I say. "Have you ever heard of a book called *Signs* by Laura Lynne Jackson?"

Alix looks like he experiences some chills of his own.

He doesn't answer. Instead, he stands up from the bed and reaches back into his bag. And he pulls out that exact book.

"I kept seeing people recommending it on social media when I moved here," Alix explains. "It was weirdly relentless. I swore it felt like my abuela wanted me to read it."

"My mom gave me that same book this past year. After a new friend of mine died. She thought it would help and . . . honestly, it really did."

"Oh, I'm so sorry to hear about your friend," Alix says. "If you ever want to talk about it, I'm here."

I smile halfheartedly—and Alix can tell I really don't want to. Instead he sits back down with this well-worn copy of *Signs*, which has been dog-eared and highlighted over and over.

"I don't mention the book to most people because they think it's silly," he continues. "But the way the author writes the stories of how people who have crossed can send us signs . . ."

"I always see crescent moons when I play *Pantheonic*," I say out loud.

And it's the first time I ever have.

"Crescent moons were my friend Annie's favorite."

"Wow. I never notice that in the game personally," Alix says, smiling warmly. "Who knows if it's all just coincidence. But when you're open to the idea, too many signs come for them not to mean *something*. My abuela loved playing cards, and her favorite suit was always hearts. She favored them over the other suits when she could because she said nothing mattered more than playing to the heart."

Hearing this, something clicks in my own mind.

"Wait, is that why you chose hearts as a crest for Apollix?"

"Bingo," Alix says with a smile. "I don't know if all this signs stuff is just a self-fulfilling prophecy. But I do know choosing hearts to honor my abuela led me to our team, and to this experience. She'd be so proud to see our team partially inspired by her. And you wouldn't believe how often I come across stray hearts playing cards in the street, walking in the city. I have a shoebox full of them at home."

"I believe you," I say. "And I mean, if life is like some game, our passed loved ones are kind of like cosmic NPCs. They can only speak in a few set ways, but those limited messages guide our journeys all the same."

"Wow. I've never thought of it that way before."

Alix stares at me, a little in awe. Honestly, I must be doing the same to him. Whatever awkward start we had yesterday suddenly feels like a distant memory. Because right here, sitting beside Alix, I've never felt closer to anyone.

Or more seen by anyone.

Or more attracted to anyone.

"Thanks for sharing, Keegan. I don't open up to many people about this stuff."

"Me neither," I reply. "Ever, really."

"Well, I'm honored."

For a moment, I swear Alix might put his hand on mine. For a moment, it's like I can even feel his warm skin. Like he might lean in and kiss me right here in this bed we've been brought together on . . .

But instead he turns and opens his laptop to turn on *Project Runway*.

Which, despite my swimming head and tingling body, is probably for the best.

CHAPTER SIXTEEN

EVERYONE INVOLVED IN THE TOURNAMENT HAS GATHered in another large meeting room late this morning for round one. Soaking in our surroundings, we're all a bit awed.

That's because this space has been transformed into another replica, this time of the Pantheonic War Council castle from the Divine Realm revealed yesterday. Except we now stand in the orchard outside this mini castle replica's walls, unable to see inside. This already feels like one of my beloved reality TV challenge sets—and that feeling is only enhanced by the various camera operators circling around. Dahlia stands at another central pulpit, dressed in a lilac suit.

Every bit of this makes my heart beat double time.

This sensation at least clears away the cobwebs from my somewhat-less-than-restful night. My chronic pain came back with a vengeance as I tried to fall asleep. In an attempt to ignore it, I instead focused on the magical notion of Alix rolling over and wrapping his arms around me. We didn't bother putting up the pillow wall between us last night before turning the lights out. I couldn't help but wonder: Was it possible Alix also wanted to find me under the covers in our big, warm bed? The whole time we watched *Project Runway*, I kept wishing we could be closer, that our arms would touch. Then once we were in bed, I kept thinking—what if I just crept closer, inch by inch? What if I reached out my hand in the dark and . . .

Well, the pain might not have been top of mind anymore. But this train of thought didn't exactly help my body calm down enough to sleep, either.

Right now, I suppress a yawn as I stand with our team. We all wear the custom T-shirts Alix made for us, proudly displaying the Epic Hearts avatars on our chests. Now knowing what hearts mean to Alix, I'm even prouder of our team's shared iconography. We all give each other excited glances as Dahlia begins her next speech.

"Prime pantheons of this earth realm! Thank you for gathering here to embark upon this most sacred quest, the centerpiece to the endgame of the Pantheonic Stoneruned War. To begin the first rounds of our quest, the War Council believes we must go back to our own beginning—the place where *Pantheonic* mythology started. To our very own creation myth."

My jaw drops. Aside from the opening animation sequence and some bits revealed in quests, the origins of how the Divine Realm and our NPCs came to be have never been revealed. I grab Mo's hand to stop it from shaking with excitement. She gives me a little squeeze and a wink back.

Mounted on the exterior castle wall above Dahlia is a flatscreen TV, which lights up as she finishes speaking. She pivots and we all look up to find a new animation playing, rendered in the usual *Pantheonic* cutscene style.

We first see the War Council castle in the Divine Realm, situated once again outside in the lush apple orchard. The focus zooms in on one tree in particular. It is luminous, its branches bearing golden apples. Though not nearly as luminous as a gorgeous firebird child who appears, with golden skin and wings of colorful flaming feathers. This being snatches several of the gilded apples. Then the usual text style starts scrolling.

Once upon a time there lived a King whose pride and power was his golden apple tree. His one thorn, however, was the mysterious bird child—the only being capable of stealing his prized youth- and strength-giving apples. The King tasked his eldest Heir with capturing the bird child to prove himself worthy of his inheritance.

Unable to catch the magically swift bird child, the Heir fell into despair. Until he was advised by a wolf woman he came across in the orchard. The wolf woman told the Heir to soak some apples in wine, to slow the bird child by getting them secretly drunk. This plan worked. And so the King kept the bird child in a gilded cage, naming his Heir truly worthy.

Soon the King sent his Heir on a journey to a remote island, to escort the King's chosen Princess bride from her island home. On this journey, the Heir and the Princess fell in love. So the wolf woman once again appeared to intervene. Revealing herself to be a shapeshifter, she offered to turn into an even more beautiful princess for the King to marry as a replacement.

Accustomed to coveting the most beautiful things, the King indeed took this shiny new princess for his bride instead. But at their wedding, this false princess revealed her true nature as the wolf woman. Upon seeing this, the King died from shock.

Freed from his rule, the Heir and the Princess were soon married as the new Heir King and Queen. Knowing it was the just thing to do, the Heir King set the bird child free—and thus never heard from the wolf woman again.

The interventions of the bird child and the wolf woman caught the all-seeing eye of the Source Wing. Struck by a new idea, the Source Wing was inspired to change the way of all things. First, it used its light to create the Divine Realm, at the nexus of all earth realms. Second, it called the bird child and the wolf woman to live in a castle of their own, surrounded by a life-giving orchard. Making the bird child and the wolf woman the very first deities, the Source Wing left them to use the orchard's gilded apples to harvest a new divine species . . .

One meant to watch over the humans of all earth realms.

I feel lightheaded. I cannot believe we've finally learned the creation myth for *Pantheonic*. We now know where our key NPCs and divine home really come from.

As the animation depicting this myth ends, my Classics brain buzzes. This must be inspired by the Slavic creation myth of the Firebird. Except in *Pantheonic,* the Firebird is clearly our "bird child," TravelGee. And the classic gray wolf is clearly our "wolf woman," UnderTee. But this also shares aspects with so many other creation myths: the snake and the apple with Adam and Eve in the Garden of Eden from Biblical mythology, or the Zoroastrian myth of the worthy heir Ahura Mazda versus the trickster heir Ahriman.

This list could go on and on, but I focus on the fact that all the creation myths I can think of have to do with balance, inheritance, and temptation. Will this connection help us navigate the upcoming challenge?

I feel my adrenaline pump even higher. These are *exactly* the kind of insights I was hoping to glean by being here. And I can't wait to tell my team about this, if they haven't already figured it out themselves.

It's time to put all this knowledge to good use in round one.

CHAPTER SEVENTEEN

I EYE THE ENTRIES TO THE REAL-WORLD PANTHEONIC WAR Council castle, both of which read *Labyrinth Entrance.* It looks like they are identical, except the left one has three starting slots and the right has four. If this is going to be a maze, I bet the first fork will be identical for fairness. Choosing these start slots must be more about potential alliance lines—and potential rivalries.

One glance at Mo, Alix, and Britni makes it clear we are all feeling pulled to the left entrance, where Cary and the Ann Apolis already move. I wish I had a moment to tell the others about the mythological background, but as we walk we're joined by another team, the Effing Divas. We haven't had much time to interact with them past surface exchanges—but the same goes for the One4All Seasons and the WeReap WhatYouSows, who head for the right entrance to join the Mythic Goats and the Heroic Heirs. Seeing this last team makes my skin crawl all over again.

"This is perfect, we were hoping to find a second to chat with your two teams alone before we got started," a heavyset guy with dark brown skin and twists in his hair whispers.

His nametag reads Damien, and his avatar immediately pops into my head from our war board. The Effing Divas were one of the easier teams to memorize because all of their avatars resemble iconic pop stars. Damien's avatar, ItsTime!, is a Traverser elf modeled after the queen of Christmas.

"We heard those dudes on the Heroic Heirs were total sleazes to Britni last night," says Davi, a guy with light brown skin and wearing a little monster T-shirt. This tracks, since his avatar, LadyChromatica, is an armored Traverser dwarf. "Those morons told us to go back to our countries, even though we're all American."

"You can imagine what they thought of us all being queer dudes of color with female pop star avatars," Damien adds. "Anyway, want to team up to take the Heirs down?"

We don't have much time to process this offer as a countdown clock begins on the central flat-screen. I only have time to turn to Mo and Cary as the most obvious connection between our two teams. But I find them both with their eyes focused on only one person . . .

Britni.

"Let's smoke those clowns together," she says, a determined smirk on her face.

Just then, a start buzzer sounds. Round one has officially begun.

But are we now starting with an alliance advantage . . .

Or are we in the minority against the other four teams?

There's no time to worry as we all run into the labyrinth. We have to break into groups of three past the initial entrance to fit through the castle corridor. One brush against a wall makes it clear this castle labyrinth is made of some cheaper imitation material, but it's still painted perfectly to appear like real stone—probably especially to the cameras that chase after us.

After winding through this opening path, we come to our first maze fork. There are three doors, each with a letter written on it. Looking up, I see a prompt scratched on a chalkboard. There are then three multiple-choice answers, all written in a speech bubble coming from the wolf-woman version of UnderTee we just saw.

> Your first code coordinate awaits with the heroes of our juicy creation myth . . .
>
> A. The Heir
>
> B. The King
>
> C. The wolf woman
>
> Once you enter a doorway, you must strut until you reach the next question. Or until you reach a dead end and must turn back like a total booger.

"Obviously the answer is the Heir," Damien says first.

"But couldn't the real hero be the wolf woman?" Britni immediately counters.

"The prompt reads 'heroes,'" I jump in. "That implies there's two correct answers. I say we split up between those two doors."

"I think Keegan is right," Cary confirms. "We'll go Heir, y'all go wolf woman?"

"We're going Heir too, just to be safe," Damien replies.

"I'm fine with us going wolf woman solo," I say, turning to my team.

Everyone nods back at me. Good, this will give me a chance to fill everyone in on the Slavic Firebird myth connection . . .

Which I do, rather breathlessly, as we run through our chosen door and down another corridor. By the time I've covered the basics, we reach another chalkboard.

You're a winner, baby!

Each pantheon requires a unique three-number code.

Find your pantheon's first number and keep grooving.

Scanning a little grid, I spot a list of seven numbers written in different colors. There's a line for each team, and our first number is listed as nine.

"I'm also memorizing the Ann Apolis code, two for the price of one style!" Mo adds, scanning the grid. "Let's move!"

We keep winding down this path, which feels like it leads us toward the center of the castle labyrinth. Although honestly, by now it's already hard to tell. Jogging along, I feel a burst of joy shine through my rattling nerves. Because I mean . . .

How awesome is this?

Instinctively, I turn to Alix to see how he is doing. But instead of finding an equally bright smile on his face, he just looks stressed.

"Alix, you okay?" I ask.

Alix just nods back at me, forcing a smile. That doesn't seem like him . . . but maybe he's just in the zone. I mean, none of us have ever done anything like this before. Still, I make a mental note to check in with him when we can catch our breath.

After this, we encounter two more simple forks in the path. Each one has a more fact-based question about the myth, making our directional choices even easier. I just hope our other two aligned teams were also put on correct paths from the jump. I'd hate to think we somehow led either one astray.

We then all spot another three-door chalkboard intersection ahead. Before we get there, the Heroic Heirs come down a different path to reach it first. They're all dressed in identical tracksuits with their team name on their chests.

Trying to ignore them entirely, I listen as Mo recites the next wolf woman prompt, reading along.

Your second code coordinate awaits with the most valuable possession in all the realms.

A. The golden apple tree

B. The kingdom

C. The bird child

This question is definitely a little trickier—and it's not like we want to discuss our theories in the open to help the Heroic Heirs. Processing silently, I first consider the moral of the original myth: that taking sole possession of the Firebird—which represents spiritual truth—only invites ruin, while good fortune is granted to those who share its feathers freely. I quickly deduce that the bird child must be the wrong answer here. Then I have a second thought.

I mean, if we want to sabotage the Heirs . . .

"The myth is about valuing the divine over the materialistic," I whisper to my team, quite loudly. "So the physical options are obvious fake-outs. Oh, crap."

I pretend to look upset with myself for letting the Heirs overhear my whispers. Without hesitating, their leader turns and opens the door marked C for the bird child. I instantly feel a flash of guilt for the Heirs falling right into my trap, not thinking for themselves.

But then I see the smile on Britni's face, and that guilt washes away pretty quickly.

"We're going golden apple, right? As the first fruit of the Divine Realm?" she asks. "And Keegan, did you just do what I think you did?"

I only smile in return, confirming Britni's suspicions. And also confirming this bit of intrigue for the cameras that still follow us, I suppose. I just hope the dead end that the Heirs will eventually reach will slow them down enough for us to get ahead, so they can't somehow return the favor.

We all head for door A, and a few turns later we come across our second coordinate. After that, we make our way through another couple of trivia forks in the maze . . .

Then, winding around one last turn, we finally emerge into a back "courtyard" of sorts. Which means we did it—we escaped the maze without making any wrong turns. We all turn to give each other high-fives as we keep running, celebrating our team effort.

Then in the center of this courtyard I see a gilded cage. Behind that is the locked entrance to the gaming hub—and there I spot the Mythic Goats already punching in their entry code. Damn, they are *fast*.

Turning back to the gilded cage, I realize the WeReap WhatYouSows are already there as well. Though not for long, as they seem to come up with a wrong answer. They all curse and turn around to retrieve something from back inside the labyrinth. A wave of relief washes over me, knowing we're definitely not in last place. But then I remind myself we have to focus on not making whatever mistake the WhatYouSows just did to obtain our own final code number.

Mo announces the final prompt out loud as we read along.

> For your final coordinate, pluck a feather with the number of my dazzling wolf woman forms.

Looking inside the gilded cage, we see a beautiful, puppet-like replica of the bird child, a.k.a. TravelGee. The wings have many feathers for plucking, each with a number on it.

"Okay, the obvious trap answer is two, since those are the forms the wolf woman took in the story," Britni says. "Though really, if she is a shapeshifter, the answer would be infinity. Is that an option?"

"Yes, it is!" I reply, brimming with pride to see one of my teammates even more engaged with the lore than me.

"Pluck away!" Mo cheers.

Britni reaches down to snatch an infinity feather from the bird child. Turning it over, we indeed find a correct answer coordinate grid.

"Flawless victory!" Mo cries, jumping up and down.

I don't blame her. But with our code now complete, we run to the gaming entrance door.

Alix is the one to punch our unique team code into the keypad. It takes a few seconds to process—seconds that feel like a lifetime. Alix looks more serious than I've ever seen him. I understand. If we somehow get this wrong, will we have to go back to the very beginning?

Thankfully we don't have to find out.

The keypad lights up green, unlocking the door and granting us entry to the gaming hub.

I breathe a sigh of relief. We're ahead of at least one—and most likely two—other teams entering the second phase of this quest.

I just hope that gives us all the edge we need as we enter the virtual world of *Pantheonic.*

CHAPTER EIGHTEEN

SEATED IN OUR EPIC HEARTS COMPUTER CUBICLE, I'VE LOST all sense of space and time as we battle through a familiar map.

When we first arrived, UnderTee—returned to her modern wolf queen form—briefed us that this event would be a boss quest. All teams must battle across an earth realm to defeat a RunedGod-imbued boss. Not just to reclaim the realm, but also to uncover the intel this high-level leader possesses: the earth realm location of the Stoneruned Horde Nerve Center.

We then found ourselves gated into the Shrine Gardens earth realm map. It's one of my favorites, loosely inspired by Japanese mythology. The setting features a series of sacred shrines surrounded by tranquil gardens. Every organic item is home to spirits that unleash if we engage them, but it's impossible to predict whether these spirits will help or hurt us. And the tournament twist on this map? An increased environmental hazard in the form of *double* the amount of spirits.

I'm delighted the game designers chose this map, since it always reminded me of another Japanese creation myth. It tells of a trinity of forces that spawned generations of deities, the seventh of which created the earth and filled every natural phenomenon with godly spirits of ancestral deities. That connection to *Pantheonic* feels even stronger now, given the way that energy imbuing things is central to the game's lore.

"The boss gate is just beyond this shrine," Mo speaks quietly into her headset, since we can also hear her inside our gaming cube. "Time to show everyone who's the boss!"

sMOte has just returned from scouting ahead. The rest of us have been battling through the Stoneruned still blocking our path. The environmental automatons in this Shrine Gardens realm are even harder to kill, because when they unleash a spirit, it usually imbues them with twice the strength, speed, and durability. We try to stop these environmental Stoneruned from doing so in the first place, but engaging the spirits ourselves is always risky. They're just as likely to attack us as they are to assist us.

"Okay, let's make one big push to clear this garden," I say as we keep battling. "I'm sure Mo's puns have already weakened our foes' will to live."

Mo sticks her tongue out at me as sMOte fights her way back to our ranks. Meanwhile, Chiroptera takes point. She has equipped her tornado talons, since they are quite effective at dispelling any rogue spirits.

Above her, Apollix swoops back and forth on his fiery wings, hurling fireballs and blasting beams of light from on high. He also managed to equip the Mirrored Necklace before the tournament, which has indeed helped boost his fire casting. It's delightful—almost as delightful as the idea of Alix actually taking my nerdy mythology suggestions to heart.

Though again, Alix has been unusually silent and serious. I thought getting into the game might break him out of this mode, but doing so has only seemed to make him more intense.

"There's just one more battalion blocking our way," Britni reports as she slashes through some Stoneruned.

"I can handle them," I reply.

"Oh, boys and their new toys," Mo jokes.

"Please, my new precious is nothing to toy with," I poke back, in my best mythical voice.

Because I've got a brand-new gravity sword and I know how to use it. When it comes to standard combat, the sword is lighter and moves faster thanks to a lessened gravity effect. It also hits twice as hard by redirecting that gravity.

Deciding to put on a little show, I activate my newly customized weapon ability. I jump into the air, lifted by the displaced gravity I've collected in the equipped stone. I then slam back down, driving my sword into the ground tip-first. This emits a pulse of released gravity that clears the surrounding area. It's not strong enough to KO the Stoneruned automatons in our path, but it creates a passage for us to move through. Unfortunately, this attack also engages a ton of nearby nature spirits—but Apollix and Chiroptera are behind me quickly to quell any spirits that turn hostile.

"Okay, that was seriously awesome," Mo gushes. "I want a gravity sword now too!"

"You don't need one when you've got me," I reply, smiling. "Let's move to that boss gate while we have a brief window."

sMOte takes the lead, winding us out of the garden and onto a path that cuts into an open clearing. Turning left and passing over another swath of rolling, grassy hills, we see a wooden footbridge extending over a pond. There waits UnderTee, who always appears to usher us into boss battles. These showdowns take place in cathedral-steepled spires, one of which looms in the distance beyond UnderTee.

"Wait, everyone see that over there?" Alix asks, speaking some of his first words this entire round. Whatever he spotted, it must be important.

I swing around to see what Apollix is facing . . .

And I suddenly understand why he wanted us to stop.

In the valley below, another fierce battle takes place—but this one doesn't involve any Stoneruned legions. Instead, it appears the Effing Divas and the Heroic Heirs are engaged in a direct conflict.

This is the first glimpse we've gotten of other teams in the gaming realm. Since there are only seven teams for this event, we all entered through seven separate gates. Usually when there are hundreds of teams, encountering other pantheons is inevitable as we all battle toward the middle. But today it feels like you'd really have to actively work to find and ambush another team.

Mini wars are being waged between the members of each team, but my eye is first drawn to a black unicorn-hybrid swooping through the sky. That's Whitneigh from the Effing Divas, taking one of the most popular Creature forms. She shoots sonic waves from her horn at a star-spangled superheroine I recognize as Republica4, the Bender from the Heroic Heirs. Republica4 shrugs off Whitneigh's direct blast like a gust of wind. Clearly, these deities will be tough to down. It's definitely gutsy of the Divas to take on the Heirs this way.

My eye is then drawn to a battle playing out on the ground below. LadyChromatica, the dwarf, shrugs off blasts from giant cannons wielded by SliverStreet3, a grinning jester supervillain Trickster. SliverStreet3 decides to use an ability, swinging his silver cape and unleashing a cache of crescent blades . . .

Crescent *moon* blades.

It's not exactly how I'd choose to see my beloved sign in-game, but my heart is momentarily warmed nonetheless. In our gaming cubicle, I turn to Alix to find him already smiling at me, finally looking like his cheerful self. To have someone else understand this moment for the first time is more meaningful than I can express. Not to mention that it seemed to lift Alix's spirits as much as mine.

So I wink at him, then get back to business.

"If I was a betting woman, I'd put money on the Divas attacking the Heirs to settle their score," Mo says. "The Heirs are gross, but they're a pro team—they're too calculating to waste time being petty in an event like this."

"I agree. Especially because it doesn't look like it's working," I add. "So do we help the Divas out?"

"Keegan, we were in such a hurry to get gaming, you never spoke our team battle cry," Britni says. "Can you say it now?"

I smile. Because of course.

"We don't aggravate our fellow deities," I say, cutting to the core to speed us along.

"Correct," Britni replies. "We don't have time to mess around."

"True colors, Epic Hearts!" Mo cries. "To the boss gate we charge!"

I breathe a little sigh of relief. As Britni reminded us, fighting dirty isn't the reputation we want to establish for our team. So our pantheon moves up to the boss gate without looking back.

Today, UnderTee has taken on a green goddess look, in a flowing flowery dress and jade jewelry. Now knowing her true origins, it's hard not to see her as the ultimate mother. A mean mommy dearest, but still.

"Wow. I did not bet my Worship Points on you lot making it here. Anyway, this RunedGod-powered boss is so gnarly, I'm sure I'll be fishing most of you out of the UndeRealm soon. That is, assuming you're sharp enough to even gain access. This rare boss gate requires a color-coded entry. I believe you were given three colors in the castle labyrinth that corresponded to your unique coordinates?"

My mouth goes dry.

Yes, each of our numbers was written in color, but I just assumed it was our assigned team color. I didn't pay attention at all to the colors changing, or what they were. Panic seizes me. We're going to have to run back through the whole maze, aren't we?

I lose my breath at the thought. Surely that would put us in the bottom two. Unless other teams made the same mistake? Thinking this, suddenly the knot in my right piriformis area cramps up.

No.

The chronic pain doesn't bother me when I game. That's been the rule.

None of this can be happening.

"Green, blue, yellow," Mo rattles off without hesitation. "Oh, hey, my shining 'true colors' pun really works double time here!"

I exhale. Of course Mo has us covered. I want to run across the cubicle and hug her.

"I wasn't paying attention to that at all," Britni says. "I trust Mo."

"Me too," Alix adds.

"Mistress of whispers for the win," I say, smiling over at Mo.

She beams as she has sMOte push the color sequence in a color wheel presented by UnderTee. Once she finishes, we all hold our breath another few seconds . . .

Until UnderTee smiles a row of fangs. Then two gate doors swing open behind her, revealing a path leading to the boss spire.

"Best of luck, my dashing deities. Trust me, you are going to need it."

CHAPTER NINETEEN

"THE SECRET LOCATION OF OUR SACRED NERVE CENTER shall never be revealed. You will fall under our singular might, false gods."

The boss speaks its usual threats, reminding us that whatever mysterious place the Stoneruned Horde came from, they always find our polytheistic pantheons insulting. Almost as insulting as we find their monotheistic, single-minded focus on spreading and conquering.

Right now, getting conquered feels inevitable, since we've been battling this RunedGod-imbued boss for what feels like forever. The StoneTower boss has a body four times the usual size, with a level that just appears as an infinity sign instead of an actual number.

We've hit the StoneTower with everything we have, but its health bar hasn't taken nearly as much damage as we'd hoped. Obviously, this boss has been made even more gnarly for the tournament. Right now the name of our game has just been trying to stay alive while our ultimate abilities finish replenishing.

We almost already lost Chiroptera—sMOte had to use the last of her healing items to keep her from being killed.

Unfortunately, my piriformis area feels like one big knot of pain. Facing this foe, my muscles seem to be tensing alongside my racing nerves. But I don't have time to spiral into worrying about why this pain is activating during *Pantheonic* play for the first time. Instead, I cross my right leg over my left knee, lean further to that side, and get ready to rumble.

I execute a tumbling dodge as the StoneTower pounds two rocky fists into the ground where I just was.

"Okay, my ultimate is almost off cooldown," I say. "How's everyone else looking?"

"I'm good to go when you all are," Britni answers first. "Plan still to use everyone's in succession, in our usual sequence?"

"Assuming we stay alive long enough," Mo replies. "My health is dangerously low and I'm all out of items."

"Same," I add, wishing one of us was a Reaper right about now. Looking at the StoneTower's health bar I can see we have managed to bring it down, but this boss could have a second phase that we'll need to defeat. Hel, I hope not, otherwise we might be done for.

"Ready when everyone else is," Alix says, sounding just as tense as the rest of us.

Apollix blocks and absorbs a wave of spirit blast that the StoneTower directs at him. Oh yeah, this enhanced boss also has an amped-up spirit-channeling environmental ability. Apollix holds on, but his health drops dangerously low as well.

Mercifully, my ultimate ability finally comes off cooldown.

"I'm good," Mo says at the same moment. "Let's get ultimate with it."

"Epic Hearts, you know what to do," I say.

I start us off by triggering my Ruler ultimate. The usual *Battle Cry* effect takes hold, temporarily slowing the StoneTower and boosting my teammates. sMOte triggers her Trickster ultimate next, *Knifed Back*. She has customized it to charge her dagger blasters with stun force. sMOte darts under the StoneTower's massive legs like a lightning-fast shadow. Then she leaps up to dig both her daggers in its back, emitting a brutal shock wave of force. The blow not only deals twice as much damage from my boost, it also leaves the StoneTower temporarily stunned.

This gives Chiroptera a window to trigger her Creature ultimate, *Selfless Tank*. It does exactly what it sounds like, charging Chiroptera right into the StoneTower's face and swiping away with her customized talons. She strikes so fast, it looks like she becomes a melee tornado. The move is measured to deal damage in a proportionate percentage to what an enemy has doled. This deep into the boss fight, that damage is massive. The StoneTower's health meter takes its biggest blow yet . . .

But channeling an ultimate this strong also takes a toll on Chiroptera. With her own health meter blown, she vanishes from sight—transported to the UndeRealm to be respawned by UnderTee. Which means Chiroptera is effectively out of this fight, given how long that takes.

Hopefully our final heaviest ranged hitter will be enough to finish this and render Chiroptera's sacrifice worthwhile. Apollix flies in front of the StoneTower and triggers his Bender ultimate, *Spell Storm*. In his customized case, this means something spectacular . . .

Pulling a blast from the literal sun in the sky. This blast of fire and light beams down on the StoneTower like a reckoning from the heavens above. The damage dealt is *massive*.

But this also knocks the StoneTower free from sMOte's stun—and it retaliates by punching Apollix out of the sky. Apollix vanishes too, bottoming out to join Chiroptera in the UndeRealm.

"No!" I startle, seeing the StoneTower still standing.

Are we going to lose this battle in the last few seconds?

"It's on critical health," Mo says. "Hit it with anything you have left!"

I don't think, I just react. I have another weapon ability ready, so I execute my gravity sword pulse again. This knocks the StoneTower back, opening it to a follow-up attack from sMOte. Apparently she has an ability attack ready too, her *Arsenal Call*.

sMOte spins, sending her chosen arsenal—her braids—shimmering with energy. Weapons fly from these braids at the StoneTower, crystal shards and beaded bombs riddling its stone body . . .

Which finally falls to the ground with one. Epic. *Thud!*

"Yes!" Britni shouts, now standing behind Mo's chair. "You did it!"

"*We* did it," I correct.

"Wait, everyone," Mo interrupts. "Look."

As the boss's body crumbles apart, the imbued RunedGod energy is returned in an enormous cloud. At the same time, a crystalline energy bird emerges from the very top of the steeple peak above—a sign we've done our part to reclaim this realm. However, this isn't one of the typical winged aspects we're used to.

Instead, this much larger bird shines with red light, taking the unique shape of a firebird. This red firebird is clearly a more potent aspect of the Source Wing—one that also directly references the creation myth origins I suspected earlier. Hovering before us in all its magnificent splendor, this rare bird produces a speech bubble that leaves me breathless once again.

"The Source Wing is held in the Stoneruned Horde Nerve Center found in the Techno Classic earth realm."

I finally exhale.

Because we did it. We finished round one and uncovered the earth realm location needed to finally free the Source Wing.

Now we just have to see if we're among the first five teams to unlock this achievement.

Back in the physical Revelatory Shrine meeting room, we don't have to wait very long to learn the results. All the teams gather before the stage, where the flat-screen displays the leaderboard for round one. Each advancing team is written upon a golden pillar:

Fifth Place: Effing Divas

Fourth Place: Epic Hearts

Third Place: One4All Seasons

Second Place: Ann Apolis

First Place: Mythic Goats

These are the five teams who cleared round one and brought the revealed Nerve Center realm location to TravelGee the fastest. I'm sure we'll have a field day discussing the good, like the Apolis coming in second . . .

And the bad, like the Goats coming in first as expected.

And the ugly, like the Divas barely surviving.

But for now, us Epic Hearts all look to one another, shining with pride. Not only did we survive the first cut, we took fourth place.

Maybe we really can hold our own in this tournament?

I lock eyes with Alix, who looks at me in a way I don't quite recognize. Is it . . . admiration? No, I realize—it's much more like relief. I obviously need to check in with him, but for now I send a warm smile back his way. Besides, any excuse to get to look at Alix, I'll take.

A hush falls over the room as the two eliminated teams walk forward to the stage where Dahlia stands and begins to shake each of their hands. First is the WeReap WhatYouSows, a team we barely got to meet. Which is a shame, because they all seem like kindred spirits based on their avatar builds—loosely inspired by more Eastern mythological figures like Xi Wangmu, Vishnu, the Rakshasas, and the Baba Yaga.

Though I can't say I have any sadness about the other eliminated team . . .

The Heroic Heirs.

The feeling seems mutual, as they currently send death glares at the Effing Divas for slowing them down—and at me for doing the same.

Thankfully I'm not feeling much guilt about this.

I suppose if we all can learn any lesson from their elimination, it's that pride does indeed go before the fall.

CHAPTER TWENTY

TONIGHT, TO THE VICTORS GO THE SPOILS OF A HOTEL room pizza party. At least that's how our pantheon has decided to celebrate our first tournament win. We've all gathered in Mo and Britni's room to gorge on the finest slices in the realm and revel in the conquests of the day.

Currently, that means huddling around Britni's laptop to go over today's streaming coverage posted by *Pantheonic* earlier this evening. We watch another cutscene animation of round one's story being etched into the official Pantheonic Texts. It reminds me, I need to carve out some time later to do the same in my personal mythology journal.

"I cannot believe our avatars are now added to the official game mythology," I gush.

"We're getting to live out our very own K.Odyssey!" Alix replies.

Thankfully he seems way more himself tonight. I still want to ask him if something was up earlier, but I don't want to ruin the mood. I'll ask him when we're back in our room, alone, and I'm totally not wanting to do lots of other things . . .

"Seeing our own post-round interviews was way more surreal," Mo says. "Thankfully some of us are literal camera-ready models."

Mo winks at Britni, who appears even more natural and glowing onscreen than in person. As for me, once the adrenaline wore off, that unprecedented burst of chronic pain while gaming became top of my mind. I wasn't feeling very chatty, but thankfully Britni and Mo took the lead answering our interview questions. Especially Britni, who is already great at talking into a camera for her social media influencing.

"I'm just so glad we decided to wear your team T-shirt designs," Britni says to Alix. "It's such a great first step to expose your brand."

"Thank you," Alix replies. "But I was way more concerned with watching the exit interviews from the other teams. Anyone else worried how pissed the Effing Divas seem at us?"

Indeed, our *allies* were very vocal in their exit interviews about how angry they were to see us run by their battle in-game with the Heirs. That said, in the gaming coverage, we saw that our hunch was correct—the Divas did indeed attack the Heirs first. Soon after we advanced past their battle, the Divas abandoned their efforts in stalemate. They rushed to the boss gate first . . .

Which didn't even end up mattering a ton. It turns out the Heirs hadn't paid attention to the color-coded coordinates and had to run back to the labyrinth. By the time they returned and defeated the boss, it was too late. So all that sabotage and ambushing wasn't even what ultimately took them out.

"If anything, the Divas showed everyone why attacking another pantheon unnecessarily during this tournament is a terrible idea," Mo says. "I mean, the Divas barely managed to beat the boss in that weakened state."

"As long as the Apolis are good with us, I'm happy," Britni adds. "With allies who play like the Divas, who needs enemies?"

"Can I get an omen?" Alix replies, his catchphrase perfectly timed as usual.

"Honestly, I'm more worried about the other two teams," I jump in. "Obviously the Goats are dominating as expected. But the Seasons also decided to call us out."

The Seasons' interview package replays in my head, their words ringing in my ears . . .

"Who would we say is our biggest competition?" Mia—their team leader—furrowed her brow and turned to her teammates.

As she did, a little chyron displayed her name and the pronouns she/they. We learned after watching the One4All Seasons' team package that this team of teens all met in a local neurodivergent support group in Kansas. They all wore T-shirts with their support group name: *The Neurodivergents*, in the style of *The Avengers*. They've also been very vocal about wanting to take their team pro in esports, even though they formed somewhat recently.

A teen with dark brown skin spoke up next, her chyron reading *Qymana, she/her*. "I know the other teams are probably all saying the Mythic Goats. But we think there's a dark horse pantheon to watch."

"Especially because, with the lowest levels now left in the tournament, they're our fellow underdog undergods," Shae, another teammate, concluded. "We think the Epic Hearts are a team to keep our eyes on."

Hearing our team mentioned in this context was a bit of an honor, obviously. But it's also a huge red flag to be on anyone's radar in this way.

"I think it's a good thing," Mo says. "Everyone loves a healthy rivalry. And as long as the one brewing between our teams remains friendly, it'll just add story drama to the tournament. I say we lean into the rival-dark-horse-team thing against the Seasons even more. Especially since they're the only single-pillar team in the tournament. Everyone is curious how an all-Bender team can continue keeping up, since it's such a rare composition."

"Of course you know how to write the best storyline for us," I reply, feeling my perspective shift. "We have a budding reality TV rivalry in our midst! Mo, you're a genius."

"Oh, I'd tell you to stop, but when you're right, you're right!" Mo beams. "Storytelling is just in my soul. Though let me tell you, one plot twist I didn't see coming was the Goats coming up to apologize to us. I just wish they had done so in front of the cameras."

"It was a nice gesture," Britni says. "But I agree, I wish they had spoken up earlier. Not privately, only *after* the Heirs were eliminated. But it's progress, I guess."

Indeed, the Goats approached us to apologize to our team—and specifically to Britni—for not standing up to the Heirs. Jim, leader of the Goats, claimed that the Heirs glommed onto them from the start. The Goats didn't know what to do, feeling afraid to make enemies or put a bigger target on their backs. But now he said their entire team was happy to see the Heirs eliminated.

"Well, a win is a win," Mo replies. "And speaking of wins, it looks like the streaming numbers for the first day of tournament coverage are already huge. So we need to keep putting on a good show to ensure Dahlia's future for the game continues to launch well."

Britni and I nod along, but I notice Alix has gone quiet again. Okay, something about the tournament is definitely bothering him—maybe it has to do with the coverage?

"And on that note, I'd like to raise another toast," Mo declares. "To the first in-person victory of the Epic Hearts!"

Putting aside my worries, we all grab our plastic cups and cheer. It also gives me a chance to see how excellent our four brand-new matching badges look pinned to our tops. The twenty players who won the first round all got the same one: an enamel pin of a red firebird set against a stone pillar.

Looking at these badges, I seriously hope we can add to our collection in round two.

CHAPTER TWENTY-ONE

BACK IN OUR ROOM, I TRY TO KEEP MY EYES OFF ALIX emerging once again from the shower. Instead, I focus on the incredible clothes hanging in his closet. They're all exposed on hangers, save for one set still stored in a closed garment bag.

"Something special tucked away there?" I ask, pointing.

Alix glances over while pulling on his concert pajama sweater.

"Oh, that's just the outfit I hope to wear if we make the final round," he answers. "It's a project I devoted some extra time to making once we got the invitation to be here."

"That's certainly extra incentive to make sure we keep advancing," I say, taking a deep breath. I really shouldn't delay bringing this up any longer. "Speaking of, I didn't want to make it a thing in front of the others. And I might be imagining things. But you maybe seemed a little . . . stressed today at the tournament."

"It was definitely stressful," Alix says. "You didn't feel it?"

"A little, of course. But I was also enjoying a lot about the whole experience."

"Me too!" Alix replies, but it sounds more like he is trying to convince himself. "Well, I mean . . . I just don't want this experience to end yet. Today everything was so new, I guess I was a little terrified. And I couldn't stop thinking about how many people might end up watching every little thing we did."

Alix's expression darkens, that stress seeming to overwhelm him again. But then he works to brighten back up.

"That all makes total sense," I offer. "But you were great, for the record."

"Aw, thanks. You too," Alix says. "Okay, want to get a *Project Runway* episode in before lights out?"

I do—but I also can't help but feel like Alix just swept all that under the rug a little too quickly. Then again, a fresh ache in my piriformis reminds me I'm maybe doing exactly the same thing. So I nod, ready to try to let all of this go for tonight.

Soon we arrange ourselves against the headboard wall with Alix's laptop perched on a pillow between us. I try to brace my back with another pillow in the right position, but the pain in my lower right side suddenly progresses from relentless to alarming. I try not to groan out of frustration. All I want to do is relax and unwind in comfort, but that feels impossible as I keep shifting to try to find a tolerable position.

"Hey, Keegan, you okay?" Alix asks, pulling me back to the present.

"Yep," I lie—and probably not particularly well given my current state.

"It's just, you seem squirmy," Alix follows up. "And I could tell last night you got pretty restless sleeping, even off the cot. But maybe I'm just imagining things?"

I sigh. "No, you're not."

Alix waits a few seconds for me to elaborate.

When I don't, he says, "You don't have to tell me if you don't want to. It's okay."

I sigh again. I really don't want to talk about this. But then my gaze lands on my journal, which I pulled out to craft an entry about round one. I didn't end up writing anything because I felt stumped over how to translate the mythology *Pantheonic* adapted to my own life. But suddenly an idea pops into my head. If round one's moral was that good things come from sharing and not keeping to oneself . . .

I may have a way to start answering my question about building equally genuine friendships IRL. Besides, right now the pain feels so consuming, I don't think I can keep ignoring it. Maybe if I tell Alix, I can find some positions other than sitting up that are more comfortable without seeming like a total weirdo? And more importantly, maybe I can actually apply the lesson from round one?

"It's just a really long story," I finally begin. "But basically I have this chronic pain in my right hip and tailbone area that hurts whenever I put pressure on it sitting or lying down. No one has been able to figure out what's causing it, but best guesses are something affecting the muscles and nerves that connect there. The pain seems to shift and evolve and have a mind of its own. Usually playing *Pantheonic* is the only time I can sit without it bothering me. But today the pain has been . . . rough. I didn't want it to impact this experience at all, but that's not exactly working out."

Once I finish, Alix takes a moment to let this sink in.

Meanwhile, I feel . . . strange. I've never really explained any of this to anyone outside of a medical visit. And certainly not to someone I consider a friend . . . or more.

It's terrifying.

What if Alix doesn't believe me, or brushes it off, or doesn't understand?

"I'm so sorry to hear that," he finally responds. "Is that why you're always stretching? And why you seemed so hesitant about coming here at first?"

"I wish I could say otherwise," I admit. "But yes."

"Well, if it makes you feel any better, I was equally worried about us sharing a room," Alix offers. "My transition is still pretty ongoing, and I'm always adjusting. Don't get me wrong, I'm finally starting to feel at home in my body. But forever home or not, it feels like I'm still moving in. So I know a thing or two about not feeling at peace with your body."

"Oh, jeez," I react. "Here I am complaining when your gender affirmations must be ten times harder."

"It's not a contest, Keegan," Alix says with a gentle look. "Sure, it's been uncomfortable, but at least I know what's causing it and the expected recovery window. And it's for such a joyful reason. It must be really hard to have pain you don't understand, from the sound of it."

"Well, thank you for that," I reply. "I just really didn't want to make a whole thing of it. This issue has eaten up enough of my last year as it is."

"I get that, trust me," Alix adds. "You don't want to magnify this physical thing to feel othered. But it's still your whole reality. I mean, my entire teenage experience has basically been puberty: the double jeopardy round."

I laugh, and so does Alix.

"That sounds taxing," I say. "But if you ever need to express something, or need to take a minute to make yourself comfortable, I hope you know you can tell me."

"You took the words right out of my mouth," Alix replies.

I hold his warm gaze. I should have known Alix would handle this exactly the right way. It feels like a current of connection suddenly opens between us, full of understanding and support. Could Alix be feeling the same way?

As if that wasn't enough, looking at Alix up close again, I am reminded just how beautiful he is. I can't help but wonder what it would be like to lean in and kiss those soft, full lips. What would Alix taste like? Should I just dive in and find out?

Right now, nothing else feels as important as taking another risk to reveal myself. Screw our friend or team or roommate relationship getting awkward. Doesn't Alix deserve to know the truth about how I feel? Don't I owe it to myself to tell him?

No, a voice then screams in my head. *You can't ruin everything before it even has a chance to begin.*

So I turn away, breaking our silent spell.

"Well, do you mind if we watched lying on our stomachs instead?" I ask. "I think it'll help shift the pressure a ton."

"Of course," Alix replies. "And for what it's worth, I'm very jealous of your butt, pain or no pain. It's way bigger and better than mine."

"Oh, I'd trade you in a heartbeat," I laugh.

Alix laughs too and hits me lightly with the pillow he pulls from behind him. Then he shifts the laptop down farther on the bed and flops onto his stomach. It all makes my heart flip around in my chest as well. Why can't Alix see me as more than his cuddly teddy bear friend? Why can't I be more than *cute* or *sturdy* to him?

I take a breath, forcing myself to remember to be grateful for what a good friend Alix is proving to be in person. And how pushing myself to open up really was the right move. Both mean the world.

So then why does it also still feel like not nearly enough?

CHAPTER TWENTY-TWO

ROUND TWO ISN'T SCHEDULED TO BEGIN UNTIL EARLY afternoon. Mo and I decided to spend our free morning visiting one of the NYC comic stores she has always wanted to explore. Britni and Alix planned to spend their morning visiting the garment district, since Britni is all fired up about helping Alix grow his design brand. In turn, Alix offered to show off his favorite fabric stores so Britni could scout for some content to justify a future trip back to New York.

Those two have quickly become besties—and I'd be lying if I said I wasn't still a little jealous. Not just because I feel disconnected from Britni the most on our team, but because I find myself wanting to be included in everything Alix does. I wonder what he's doing right now, what he wanted to show Britni, what he is saying and laughing at and—

"Oh, I so have to get this for Cary."

Hearing Mo's voice snaps me out of my mini daydream. How did this go from an online crush to a full-blown obsession in a matter of days? I don't quite know what to do with myself. I've never really reacted this way to anyone before.

I just try to return to the present moment I get to spend with Mo. After all, my new friendship with her is another one I care deeply about. Not to mention she also happens to be in a successful queer teen relationship. So maybe I can drift off her experience a bit and hit two of my journal intentions with one stone: bonding IRL and handling my feelings for Alix.

Mo currently holds up a pin of Link from *Zelda* waving the gender pride flag. We've been in Union Square's Forbidden Planet for fifteen minutes, but it feels like we've barely scratched the surface of the treasures this place holds.

"You simply must!" I reply. "By the way, have I told you how encouraging it is to see a successful queer relationship between two fellow teens? I feel like a lot of the media we're fed about ourselves makes it look like the definition of gay pride is sleeping around or nonstop partying. Not to shame anyone who does enjoy that, but . . ."

"No, I get what you mean," Mo says. "Though the opposite stereotype of queer women only entering serious relationships is just as strong, I guess."

"Can I ask you something, on that front?"

"That depends on the question," Mo replies, walking forward along the clothing and accessories section. We started back with the new comics, combed the graphic novel shelves, and are now working our way through collectibles and action figures.

"Fair point," I say. "It's just, on our first day here you mentioned how Cary's gender identity factored into your own understanding of your queerness . . ."

"Damn! That's quite the prompt, Professor Keegan!"

"Oh! Sorry if I—"

"No, it's totally cool. You just sound so academic sometimes, I love it," Mo replies. "It's a good question. So many people seem to think being queer is some organized revolution threatening to take over, when really we're a small minority of very different people *just now* getting the wiggle room to understand and express ourselves. Case in point, since I was really young I had always thought of myself as only attracted to other women. It wasn't until I met Cary in a local gaymer group that I realized I was even *more* attracted to a certain nonbinary energy. I identify as pansexual out of respect for Cary's own identity. And because it's a truer definition. But really, I fell for Cary specifically. I don't know yet if that needs to extend to my entire sexual identity, but we do our best with the labels we have."

"I love that," I reply. "And I guess that's the real revolution."

"What do you mean?" Mo asks.

"Freeing everyone in general from the rules society tells us to follow about gender and sexuality limitations. Even if by trial and error, we're still leading by example. Well, not me yet. I haven't had much personal experience being gay outside of coming out. But it's liberating to see two people figure out how to define their queerness on their own terms."

Mo stops walking and browsing to turn and give me a long look. It's almost like I'm a puzzle piece she is excited to place.

"You do continue to surprise me, oh fearless leader," Mo says, smiling bright. "Now it's my turn to ask—could there be a particular reason you're curious about gender-nonconforming romance?"

I try not to react too visibly, but Mo's very-leading question makes me want to run and hide.

"Not yet," I answer, figuring it's an honest enough answer. "So what do you think of this store?"

Mo eyes me like she wants to keep pushing. Instead, she accepts my deflection question.

"It's great. It reminds me a lot of Third Eye Comics back home. And how spoiled we are. New York has some of the biggest and best comic stores in the country, but Third Eye is still like five times the size and scope."

We move into the action figure aisle, and I marvel at all the colorful boxes of articulated plastic. Maybe someday they'll make some *Pantheonic* figures, since I see they've already done so for *Overwatch* and *League of Legends*.

"Does it give you any inspiration for your own store?" I ask.

"A little," Mo replies. "But what I have in mind is more like a boutique department store. Whether you're a collecting expert or a complete newbie, we'd curate a profile of products around your area of interest and budget. Think like a stylist putting together a head-to-toe outfit. We'd set you up with new monthly comics, graphic novel collections, novels and books, games to play, collectibles to display, merch to wear, music to accompany—and most importantly, a community to enjoy and explore it all with. I envision the physical store being like a gallery hub, but mostly we'd custom order product bundles. And all of it could live online at the same time, like a social media shop paired with a Discord community."

"That honestly sounds like heaven," I say.

I would love for Mo to build the perfect *Pantheonic* bundle for me. With all the content and merch out there, who couldn't use a pop culture coach to help maximize their precious free time? Imagine wasting no time searching or scrolling and only spending time *enjoying*?

"We'd be like stylists or glam squads, but for fandoms," Mo says. "Taking all the guesswork out of your geekery."

"That is truly genius."

"I know!" Mo exclaims. "If I were a nepo baby, I'd have it up and running already. Sometimes young people don't need some big growth arc to kick-start our dreams. Sometimes we just need the right people with money and power to believe in us."

"To quote Alix—can I get an omen?" I reply. "But hey, sometimes that *does* happen. I mean, our team fought our way into this tournament, right? That's some preparation-meeting-opportunity magic right there!"

"Right you are again, Professor Keegan. And I think we have as good a shot as anyone of making it to the final round."

I nod back. However, I still have no idea how we're going to beat a team like the Mythic Goats. Then again, if we've learned anything from round one, it's to expect the unexpected—especially in the physical challenges.

Just then, my eye catches on something. It's a tray of beaded bracelets representing lots of different characters and brands. But I focus on one in particular at the corner of the pile: a bracelet with hearts-suit beads.

"Oh, I need to get this for Alix," I exclaim, scooping up the bracelet.

Mo then hits me with another curious look.

"Because of hearts?" she asks. "Why not get one for everyone on the team, then?"

My cheeks flush the same crimson of the bracelet I hold, caught red-handed.

"Right. Yes. Of course," I say, rooting through the tray for more.

"Keegan, I could be totally off here," Mo begins. "But is it possible you have a crush on Alix?"

My insides freeze, along with my limbs.

I'm not sure I can wiggle my way out of this. More importantly . . .

I'm not sure I even want to?

"It's . . . possible." I sigh. "Am I that obvious?"

"I knew it!" Mo squeals.

I groan.

Until I think—wait, could Mo be so excited because she already talked to Alix about the same thing? Hope expands in my chest like a balloon.

"Wait, how? Do you think Alix does too?"

"It's subtle, but there's a little twinkle in your eye when it comes to Alix," Mo answers. "And Alix is harder to read, so I don't know. But I could certainly ask him for you."

The balloon in my chest promptly bursts.

"No," I reply. "I mean, I don't want things to be awkward if he doesn't think of me that way. For the team. And for sharing a room. And a bed."

"Oh. Right." Mo looks about as deflated as I currently feel, processing this reality.

"Seriously, team leader mode now taking over," I add. "I don't think Alix sees me that way. And on the off chance he does, it can wait until after the tournament. I mean, I'm moving here soon. I want to focus on keeping Alix as a friend first and foremost."

"Roger that. Your secret is safe with me," Mo promises. "But for the record, I think you two would be so cute together. And imagine the double dates we could go on!"

I hit Mo with my very best *I'm Serious* stare, because I cannot go there. Even though I desperately want to.

Instead, I clutch the sole hearts bracelet I plan to buy for Alix now that my cover is blown. Knowing how much this sign means to him beyond the game, I can't wait to give it to him.

CHAPTER TWENTY-THREE

LATER THAT AFTERNOON I STAND BESIDE MO, BRITNI, AND Alix as round two begins in our Revelatory Shrine. We are gathered to watch the second illuminating *Pantheonic* mythology cutscene. I can't wait to experience another of these firsthand, for so many reasons.

Once again, on a large screen before us, an animation begins. Back in the Divine Realm we now know was created by the Source Wing, UnderTee and TravelGee use seven golden apples from their brand-new orchard to create our first deities. We watch as these original seven pillared figures are born as fully formed adults, inspired by archetypes found to be universally true across earth realms.

We then witness the seven archetypes being given a home to develop—in an early version of Mount Pantheonic. Each deity is allotted a plot of land in a ring, with one central divider in the form of a seven-sided pyramid. These founding deities are then left to their own devices with one mission: to spawn an entire race to watch over the many earth realms.

It turns out that in striving to do just that, some serious drama ensues. I watch in awe as the animation text weaves a twisting tale of deity drama . . .

First, the regal Ruler and the armored Warrior discovered they could impregnate each other, as ageless beings representing all genders. When the first generation of Rulers and Warriors was spawned, the other archetypes were inspired. The pale Reaper and the beastly Creature paired off next, followed by the eclectic Traverser and the woodsy Bender.

Feeling jealous and unwanted as a seventh wheel, the cloaked Trickster snuck through the shadows cast by the pyramid to murder the Traverser. Then the Trickster changed shape to take the Traverser's place, spawning with the unwitting Bender.

One night when the Bender came upon the Trickster in their true form, the Bender cast the Trickster back to their own sector. The Bender then transformed their wind into the breath of life to revive the Traverser.

But the Traverser had not died, being immortal. Instead, they were temporarily exiled down to the farthest known earth realms, where they traveled among the most fantastical and rare species to exist, teaching them the Traverser ways. Until the Bender's wind of life carried the newly fantastical Traverser home . . .

Where the Creature fell madly in love with this new Traverser. As they spawned, the Creature vowed to defend their new beloved Traverser from the jealousies of the Bender and the Trickster.

Devasted to be forsaken by their beloved Creature, the Reaper banished themself from the Divine Realm. Instead, feeling lifeless, the Reaper became consumed with the affairs of the afterlife—for the giving and taking of life reminded them of the giving and taking of love.

Meanwhile, the Warrior was so greatly offended by the Trickster's deceptions, the Warrior made it their mission to bring forth justice. Trapped in a game of cat and mouse, to match the Trickster's perpetual evasions, the Warrior had to grow all the more formidable—and barbaric—to complete their quest.

The Ruler, now left alone by the Warrior's questing, had only time to bear witness. The Ruler built a throne atop the central pyramid, from where they could watch the drama of the archetypes—and their multiplying generations of adult deity spawn. The Ruler watched as Mount Pantheonic grew into seven distinct city sectors, each home to a community of deities inspired by the deeds of their archetypes—and spreading their mythos into the earth realms as they saw fit. And the Ruler came to one conclusion . . .

The seven archetypes had become seven principles—and principles always served better as ideals. So the Ruler destroyed the central pyramid. From its rubble, they built instead seven pillars stretching from each of the seven sectors. These pillars elevated the archetypes themselves above the homes they spawned, where they all made a pact—to become the pillars themselves, inspiring their deities for all time as immortal tributes.

As their final act, the seven archetypes erected the Revelatory Shrine, a central meeting place for all seven sectors. Then they retreated to embody the pillars of their sectors, holding up this central shrine in equal measure.

I turn to Alix, Mo, and Britni with my jaw dropped. I wish I could burn that text into my memory and dissect every detail with them. But instead, the moment this explosive animation ends, all of the remaining five teams are told to select one of seven quest objective envelopes at random.

Then we are quite promptly told to race to a brand-new space and open them—only moments before the start buzzer sounds.

Feeling a bit of whiplash, I follow my team as we begin to race through a series of hallways to reach a new room. I cannot believe our round two physical challenge has begun already. Feeling frantic and overwhelmed, I take a second to try to reground myself.

Stories and images from the animation we just watched light up my mind like a whirring computer. If round one was about creation myths, then round two will clearly be about another trope existing across all mythology—deity drama. We've always been presented with the seven pillar archetypes as idealized icons to aspire to . . . but it turns out they're way more like parental figures—just as flawed as we are.

"Keegan, got any unique mythical influences for us?" Mo asks as we run.

"Total system overload," I answer. "But the first thing that springs to mind is the ancient Egyptian myth of the King's Murder. It's about the jealous Set murdering his beloved king brother, Osiris, then contending with the fallout in the form of the mighty wife, Isis, the birdlike heir, Horus, and the sun and moon gods, Ra and Thoth."

"That makes sense," Britni replies as we finally run through the entrance. "I mean, it doesn't get more ancient Egyptian than *that.*"

Entering this new space, we all stop short. It's a vast open hall with a replica of early Mount Pantheonic's unique seven-sided pyramid in the middle. It might not be four-sided like the classic pyramids, but this sight definitely gives distinct Egyptian vibes.

However, our attention is immediately drawn to the crowd milling about this pyramid replica. They're all cosplayers dressed as different deity spawns from the seven pillars. I'm tempted to stop and stare at all the incredible and intricate sights, but we need to focus on our mission—which deity needle to pick out of this crowded haystack.

Mo rips open the envelope we randomly picked, which depicts UnderTee speaking. Mo then reads the clue out loud.

"Find my dramatic deity who represents many realms traveled."

"Okay, that's obviously the Traverser archetype," Britni responds. "But it can't be that simple, can it?"

"Probably not," I agree. "Let's just start looking?"

Our team breaks forward into the crowd of roaming deities, trailed by camera people. I try not to get too distracted separating the spawned deities from potential archetypes, but I can't help marveling at the elaborate costumes. I spot a Bender in a dress made entirely of sun discs, a fully mummified Reaper, and a very muscled Hercules-style Warrior. Until my eyes finally land on a lone figure standing still, fully cloaked.

"Everyone, over there," I whisper, trying to point subtly.

We all turn and as we approach, I see the figure's cloak has a unique figure printed on it: a human body with the head of a falcon, armored wings, and eyes that are the sun and the moon.

"That's a typical depiction of the Egyptian god Horus," I explain. "We're obviously right on the money guessing Egyptian mythology is the inspiration here."

"And all of that symbology covers the seven pillars in different ways," Britni adds. "That cloak has to be hiding an archetype for sure."

I'm feeling very confident until, before we can reach the cloaked figure . . .

Another team cuts in front of us. They don't physically push us or anything, but the way they run directly into our path feels very pointed. Which suddenly makes sense as I realize who this team is.

It's the Effing Divas who reach the cloaked figure we found first.

My jaw drops open. Are they really so mad at us that we're their next target for subtle sabotage? The Heroic Heirs might have sucked up front, but the Divas are turning out to be downright petty. Way to live up to our gay stan stereotype, boys.

"I'm going to drop-kick those flops," Britni nearly growls.

"Those stunt queens aren't even worth our time," Mo cuts in. "Look."

As the cloaked figure removes its veil for the Divas, we see it is a person dressed in stone-colored robes with their skin painted a matching shade of pillar gray. They wear a headdress with a crown and throne—the seal of the Ruler.

Okay, so that's not even our quest's archetype. Which means more useless sabotage on the part of the Divas.

Except their leader calls out to the One4All Seasons to let them know they found the Ruler. Judging from how quickly the Seasons rush over, this must have been their quest's archetype. And it becomes obvious these two teams have formed a new alliance. If the Seasons want to lean into a rivalry with us, teaming up with the Divas is one surefire way to go about it.

"Let's just keep moving," I say, trying to ignore the pit that opens up in my stomach.

One that doubles in size as I turn to find the Mythic Goats already pushing themselves to the exit, heading back toward the gaming hub. They're still moving faster than anyone, despite seeming to work totally solo.

This leaves just the Divas versus us and our own alliance, the Ann Apolis—who I turn to find have also located their archetype, the scythe and angelwing-sealed Reaper. Panic erupts like a geyser in my system. An accompanying bolt of pain bursts open in my right piriformis. I don't know what's worse—the fact that we're already falling behind, or the fact that this pain is somehow finding me in the usual safety of standing and moving?

Trying to get a grip, I scan the crowd. But all that stands out is a Creature hybrid sporting a fully prosthetic horse face, then a very drag-eleganza Ruler. This can't be happening. What if we fall too far behind to recover, like the Heirs last round?

"There's one!" Mo shouts, already running.

I exhale sharply and follow. Thank Hel *someone* is acting like our leader right now. Why does it feel like I'm totally choking?

I banish that thought as we reach this next cloaked figure, who remains veiled. Before they reveal themselves, I realize the sun and moon eyes are different on their Horus cloak. While the sun is more geometric, the moon is in a crescent shape. I send a little mental *thank you* Annie's way for helping me to notice this altered detail in the first place.

Then my eyes connect with Alix's again. There's an added layer of meaning this time, the way this crescent moon complements Apollix's sun symbology. It's like this makes us our own secretly balanced pair. It also makes me want to pull out the hearts bracelet stored in my pocket and give it to Alix right now.

But then I see that despite his best intentions, Alix looks just as stressed and tense as yesterday. And I realize he hasn't spoken a word since we started. So I try to offer him a reassuring smile before moving on.

The figure's cloak comes off, and we all audibly exhale as a portal and chariot-sealed headdress is revealed. This feels extra special, since we now finally know why the mythical fantasy genre species like elves and faeries are considered travelers in *Pantheonic* lore—thanks to the Traverser's original betrayal and exile.

Our Traverser cosplayer finally takes off their headdress and hands it to Mo.

"Our full gaming hub code is inside," Mo says. "Time to traverse!"

I feel a simultaneous flush of relief and fear. We're now only a few steps behind our competitors—I just hope we can keep this up in the gaming quest.

Sprinting back alongside the others, I look to Alix again. Instead of finding him stressed, he now appears *sullen*—and he actively avoids my gaze. Which is definitely new.

Then another thought hits me like a lightning strike.

Is it possible Mo already told him about my crush since this morning?

Does he now feel uncomfortable around me?

Could we have possibly unleashed some deity drama in our own pantheon?

I try to banish these thoughts from my brain. I really doubt Mo would ever do that, even with good intentions. Maybe Alix just doesn't want to show me his stress is getting the better of him again today? Whatever the reason, I vow to focus on the quest before us as we run back to the gaming hub.

Right now, I hope we can all leave our anxious worries behind in this physical realm.

CHAPTER TWENTY-FOUR

BACK IN THE VIRTUAL GAMING WORLD OF *PANTHEONIC*, WE find ourselves in another familiar earth realm map: the Temple Ruins. It's inspired by coastal West Africa, except the multiversal tournament twist is that nature's colors are different from what we'd expect. The ocean beyond shines deep orange, while the earth beneath us is a brilliant blue, and the plants are all shades of purple. The effect is as pretty as it is jarring, but I'll take this visual change over the usual enhanced environmental hazards any day.

UnderTee's debrief informed us that this is a race event, which means we have to battle as fast as we can through the Stoneruned Horde to a hidden endpoint that will help dismantle their stronghold. The fifth pantheon to reach their secret endpoint will be eliminated from the tournament.

After that, we emerged from one of the seven gates alone, knowing we have to reach the middle of the map to begin searching for our endpoint. The Epic Hearts have already battled through several Stoneruned battalions. And I'm glad the environmental automatons aren't enhanced today. They're already deadly enough, able to animate the crumbling artifacts and shrines of the Temple Ruins. These include statues of enormous serpents and warrior women—a nod to this region's Dahomey mythology, which includes the cosmic serpent Aido-Hwedo and an infamous female Amazon army.

So far we have cleared three Temple Ruins sectors, but we have yet to run into any other teams, for better or worse. I dread it's for the worse, because we are having more trouble clearing the Stoneruned than usual. If our team gaming yesterday felt seamless, today it feels like we aren't gelling. We're out of the usual pocket rhythm, and we all know it. Alix in particular feels like his heart really isn't in it. Apollix has mistimed several of his usually foolproof sun-fire attacks and taken way more damage than average. I'm dying to stop and regroup and figure out what's up, but if we stand any chance of surviving this round, we have no time for that.

To make matters worse, my entire lower right side feels like a lightning rod in my chair. I'm distressed that my preemptive measures—the Aleve pills I swallowed and the Icy Hot I applied before the round started—aren't working at all. I feel just about as uncomfortable and hopeless as I have in a very long time, but right now the only way out is battling through.

As the last of the Stoneruned battalion automatons crumble, we finally spot UnderTee waiting for us just up ahead. She must be here to tell us how to find this quest's secret endpoint. Our avatars rush up to her, but there still aren't any other teams in sight. Are we really about to lose this round? I expect more anxiety to wash over me . . .

But instead I feel an unlikely wave of peace arrive. If this really is the end, I have to ultimately be thankful for the experience. And hey, maybe losing now would even give me the freedom to finally tell Alix about my crush? I could see what's up with him and how he feels, with all the pressure removed. I'm sure I'll hear Alix just thinks of me as a friend, but at least I could gift him the hearts bracelet as a sign we'll still stay friends when I move for college.

Embracing this new state of semi-calm, we approach UnderTee. She stands at the nexus of seven paths, all leading up into clouds that shroud the endpoints we race to. Just then, a second team approaches from around a bend at the same pace as us . . .

The Ann Apolis.

It's certainly the one team we would rather not defeat. But at least this means we're still in the competition.

"Ah, I see there's a booger convention in town today."

UnderTee's speech bubble appears, and I know the Apolis are getting identical engagement on their own monitors.

"To find the dismantling points of this realm's stronghold, you must ascend these clouded paths. But beware! Only one path is meant for each pantheon. Be sure you choose the right one, or it'll be a long journey back to try to choose again. And mother doesn't have all day, children!"

Looking at the seven paths, I see a cloaked figure standing beside each—just like the cloaked archetypes from our physical challenge. Except standing in a row this way, it's clear the mythical symbols depicted on their cloaks are different.

Instead of Horus, these cloaks are inspired by another Dahomey deity: Mawu-Lisa, a goddess with the composite faces of Mawu of the earth and moon, then Lisa of the sky and sun. But just like physical cloaks, the moons and suns across these virtual cloaks are all slightly different. And thankfully, in this round, I kept my eyes open for details like this.

"We're the cloak with the geometric sun and crescent moon," I say. "I know for sure."

"How did I miss that detail?" Mo cries. "sMOte, forgive me!"

"Well, we forgive you," Britni says. "Let's—"

Before she can finish, a voice chat invitation pops up from the Ann Apolis. We all accept a new inter-team call.

"We don't know which path is ours," Laura begins, sounding frantic.

"Ours is path three," Mo replies. "Anyone remember any other details?"

"The Ruler cloak for the Seasons had a sun with straight beams and a halo moon," I add. "That's path seven."

"I got nothing," Britni says.

"Same here," Alix follows up, adding two to the grand total of words he has spoken this round.

"Damn." Mo sighs. "You've got a one-in-five shot. That's gotta be faster than returning to the cosplay pyramid. Get moving!"

"Thank you, love!" Cary replies.

The call disengages and we watch as the Ann Apolis run toward path five. If they're wrong, they'll have to waste lots of time running blind up and down these other probably long paths. That kind of slowdown could cost them the round, and the odds are not in their favor. We might have just gotten our luck back—but none of us are thrilled if it comes at the cost of our closest allies.

Just then, in the corner of my range of vision, I spot movement. I spin my point of view behind K.Odyssia's body to find a new environmental Stoneruned battalion ambushing us, fronted by a giant animated stone serpent . . .

One that will hit the Ann Apolis first.

My first instinct: Do we make a run for it and let them deal with this attack on their own?

In the same moment, Alix triggers his ultimate ability. A devastating beam of sun shoots through the clouds to decimate the stone serpent before it can strike.

What a guy. While I hesitated, Alix chose to defend our allies without a second thought. The gesture makes my heart flush and ache.

"Let's help them take this horde out fast," I say. "There could still be another team behind us, for all we know."

"Thank you," Mo says as she sends sMOte running at the horde, her dagger blasters unsheathed.

As Chiroptera and I follow, the Ann Apolis also spring into action. Cary's Traverser elf jumps into the air and fires several energized arrows from their crossbow. Beside them, Laura's Reaper assassin—an *X-Men* meets *Fortnite* ninja—slashes and shoots with a rapier-blaster. Natalie's dragon-hybrid Creature blasts deadly breaths of fire, while their final member, Jessie, doles out kicks of fury with their *Street Fighter*-style Warrior.

With support from our own team, the remainder of this horde is taken out in record time. Which means we've now done all we can do to help the Ann Apolis.

As we begin our own trek up into the clouds, I don't even ask Mo to use some short-jump portal items to get us there faster. She must already be beating herself up for not somehow memorizing the cloak suns and moons for both of our teams.

And if we really are about to take out Cary's team, Mo shouldn't have to be the one to put the final nail in their coffin.

I sit with the Epic Hearts in the physical Revelatory Shrine meeting room, anxiously awaiting the results of round two.

Back in the virtual Temple Ruins realm, we reached the correct designated endpoint. Doing our part to reclaim the realm and dismantle the stronghold, this victory released another special energy bird aspect from our stronghold section. This new rare bird was a green hawk . . .

Which I realized was also likely inspired by ancient Egyptian spirituality—where a person's ka, their life force, could be reunited with their ba, their soul, if they were properly mummified. The ba was often depicted having the head of the deceased atop a winged hawk body, one that could fly and reunite with the source. If this round two hawk really was inspired by the Egyptian ba, it's another potent metaphor for us returning aspects to the Source Wing.

Still, I was left wondering how all of this related to our core mystery for this round: *How is this vital force being contained and tapped by the Stoneruned Horde?* It turns out that was the shocking answer the green hawk was waiting to give each team:

"To entrap the Source Wing, the Stoneruned Horde stole its most precious possession. Which means the Source Wing has chosen to remain contained at the Stoneruned Nerve Center of its own free will. Just like it has chosen to willingly fuel the Horde along with all other life . . . at least until its most valuable possession is safely reclaimed."

I can tell everyone in this room is trying to absorb this twist while we anxiously await the results. It's certainly puzzling, even to a mythological expert like me. What could be so valuable to an energetic life source, one that isn't even supposed to be sentient like the rest of us? Despite all the mythological context, I find myself at a loss for any specific inspirations or references offhand. Which I'm sure is by design. After all, rounds three and four will no doubt continue unfurling this mythical mystery we're in the middle of solving.

Learning all this, I have never wanted to stay here in the tournament more.

I've also never been less sure we've done enough to pull that off.

Cary told Mo that the Ann Apolis managed to find their endpoint on their second path try. It stands to reason we still managed to finish faster—unless they somehow won this race using Cary's Traverser short-portal jumps? Or could it be possible a different team fell behind both of us, or didn't remember their own sun and moon symbols?

Looking beside me in our team's row of chairs, everyone seems as uneasy as I feel—especially Alix. So when Dahlia takes the stage to reveal the results, I'm quite glad the wait is over.

"You battled bravely and uncovered much, my pantheons," Dahlia begins. "Which is why tomorrow, you have earned a day of rest. Our quest will continue for the final four the day after. But right now, a more *eternal* rest awaits one pantheon among you."

With that, Dahlia pivots to the flat-screen onstage above her. The results animation sequence begins to play, populating the screen with four golden pillars—and one in the fifth position turned to stone.

The lowest pillar soon reveals the name of the team in first place, as the green energy hawk flies across it . . .

First Place: Mythic Goats

I barely have time to react to this expected-yet-intimidating news before the next two teams are revealed . . .

Second Place: Effing Divas

Third Place: One4All Seasons

So this elimination will indeed come down to us or our closest allies, the Ann Apolis. I turn to Mo at the end of our row and find her holding hands with Cary. My heart breaks for them in this moment.

But is it about to be shattered entirely by our own elimination?

Finally, the fourth golden pillar reads . . .

Fourth Place: Epic Hearts

Which means the Ann Apolis have been cut in fifth place.

I feel a flush of relief.

But I can't say I feel particularly victorious, given the way we've won. We didn't perform at our best, instead barely creeping past the only other team we can trust. Our team has also yet to clear fourth place. Is that where we're destined to finish in round three? Especially if our vibe stays as . . . *off* as it felt today?

I force these doubts from my mind, trying to lock into Ruler mode. Right now it doesn't matter how we did it, because we still get the privilege of experiencing another round. We have a day tomorrow to recover and regroup. I will take the time I've neglected to get my chronic pain back into manageable shape with my own items and elixirs. And most importantly, I'll help get our team mojo back—and hopefully find out what's really up with Alix.

Right now, I need to focus on giving the Ann Apolis a proper send-off. And making sure that Mo is okay, since her partner just got cut. Round two might now be set in mythological stone, but there is still so much work left to do in its wake.

CHAPTER TWENTY-FIVE

HOURS AFTER ALL OF OUR POST-ROUND DUTIES ARE COM-plete, I walk down the hotel hallway with Alix toward Mo and Britni's room for a team meeting. I should be focused on strategizing and planning, but all I seem capable of registering is the smell of citrus and sandalwood soap wafting off Alix's warm skin. Or how adorable he looks currently wearing an oversized T-shirt half tucked into jean shorts. A green hawk badge from round two is also fastened to his chest beside round one's matching red firebird. My eyes lift to the perfect curve of Alix's lips and the set of his jaw before he notices me staring.

"Hey, you okay?" I ask, trying to cover. "You seemed pretty off again today."

"I do feel off, but I'm okay," Alix answers. "How are you? How's the pain level?"

"Not great," I reply—also not loving this deflection, thoughtful as it may be. "But I'm glad we have a day off to get back on track."

Alix offers a tight smile and nods. I wait a second for him to maybe say more, but he doesn't seem in the mood. Something is definitely bothering him, but I can't make him tell me. I just pray it has nothing to do with my ever-expanding crush. The only downside of staying in the tournament is that it extends the reasons I can't profess my feelings for Alix . . . assuming he doesn't already know.

"Alix!" Britni says, opening the door after we knock. "I need to show you something in this novel. Mind if I steal him away quickly, Keegan?"

"Be my guest," I say.

Usually I'd feel a pang of jealousy over their separate connection, but right now this means I can pull Mo aside for a little private chat. Once our pairs are situated in opposite corners, the question practically leaps from my lips.

"You didn't tell either of those two about what I confessed at Forbidden Planet, right?"

"Of course not!" Mo almost shouts. "I'd never!"

I exhale a breath of relief. But now I also feel like a jerk.

"I know, I'm sorry." I sigh. "Alix just seemed really off today, and he's not telling me why. My paranoia got the best of me."

"It's okay, I noticed it too," Mo replies. "Alix is taking Cary and me thrift store shopping tomorrow morning before Cary's train back to Annapolis. I can try asking Alix if something's still up then after he's had a night to sleep on it?"

"I'm so dumb, leading with that question," I say. "I know we said plenty of goodbyes to the Ann Apolis earlier, but how are you doing?"

"I'm sad, but Cary and I knew the chances that both our teams would make the finals were slim. The Ann Apolis are having one final team dinner tonight before checking out tomorrow morning. Britni was so sweet, she offered to let Cary stay here in our room. But Cary wants to head home. It's probably too painful to go from a contender to a cheerleader, but really now they have to take less time off work. Cary will be rooting for us and calling in with tips. Honestly, even with all the tips and tricks in the world, I don't know how we're going to survive round three."

"I know, me too," I reply. "At least now we have some time to prepare. And you know, I was thinking—if the Divas and the Seasons are still working together . . ."

"I was thinking the same thing. Should we approach the Mythic Goats about teaming up in round three?"

"If you can't beat 'em, join 'em?" I try.

"I hear you," Mo says. "As enticing as that seems, I'm afraid it would put an unnecessary target on us. What if the other two teams go all in on sabotaging the Goats next round, and that leaves us the room we need to wiggle by? The Divas seem just as likely to turn on the Seasons too, eventually. Maybe if it feels organic in round three to work with the Goats, we go for it. But I don't think we should make any promises. Especially to the one team no one seems able to beat."

"You know, you really could be our leader if you wanted," I say, in awe of Mo as usual.

"But I don't want to be," Mo replies. "I'm the information specialist—recon and espionage action are my first loves. You're way better at thinking globally and setting each of us up to shine best with our strengths."

"Well, I don't know if that's true," I reply. "But I'll take the compliment all the same."

Mo and I share one last private smile before Britni calls across the room.

"Okay, we're ready to talk game."

She and Alix settle on her bed while Mo walks to sit on her own bed. I opt for standing at the edge to give my butt a break.

"So my head has been swimming with all this revealed lore and connected world mythology inspiration," Britni kicks us off. "I'm not an expert like Keegan, but I think we must be due for some kind of midpoint shift. Tomorrow's day off feels like an intermission between acts. I mean, we've learned all about *Pantheonic*'s secret past origins in this first half. I bet the second half is going to be about its present and future, maybe pushing us into even more unexpected territory?"

I smile big at Britni—I've rarely gotten to see this side of her, the literary analysis brain. Maybe we have some things to connect on just her and me, after all? It reminds me that I've been neglecting my journal, but I'll have some time to unpack and apply the lessons from round two tomorrow.

"Agreed," Mo jumps in. "We also haven't had an 'escort something important' event yet. Given that round three's mystery is about what weapon can defeat the strongest Stoneruned, I bet that's next."

"That's a very good point," I reply. "Should we practice an escort event quest? Though I did want to mention: Did anyone else feel like we weren't gaming as seamlessly today as we did yesterday?"

"I definitely felt it," Britni replies.

"I did too, but I honestly don't know why," Mo says. "We could get some practice runs in tonight and see how we feel?"

"Hey, you know what, I hate to say this, but I'm feeling really run ragged," Alix finally says. "I'd hate to push myself and get sick on everyone. Do you think I could take the night off and we can regroup tomorrow after lunch? We can spend the whole afternoon practicing, totally fresh. I think tonight I just . . . need a break from all the pressure?"

The tone in Alix's voice once again makes my heart feel heavy. Something is obviously weighing on him. I'm worried it's potentially about his transition or gender dysphoria, but I already promised not to push or other him there. He knows I'm here to listen when he is ready.

I wish Alix knew all the things I'm here for, if he is ever ready.

All that aside, Alix's instinct is probably correct. Maybe today we were off because of all the pressure we're putting on ourselves, several days in a row. Maybe some time away is exactly what we need to refill our tanks—not more time drilling away. I know I could certainly use some precious time with my massage gun and stretching routine. Alix is right, as usual . . .

Until another thought occurs to me.

The only thing Alix might *not* be right about is keeping whatever is bothering him to himself. But how can I expect Alix to open up if I'm not doing the very same thing—still hiding my pain issues from Mo and Britni? It's like all my intentions to be a brave friend and leader align, making it clear what I need to do next.

"Alix, I think you're totally right," I reply. "But if it's okay, before you go, I have something I want to share."

And then I take the plunge.

I tell Mo and Britni *everything* I told Alix about my chronic pain last night.

I can't say doing so feels as good as I want it to, but I do feel ready.

When I'm done, Mo and Britni both look nothing but sympathetic.

"Keegan, I'm so sorry to hear you've been struggling with this," Mo responds first. "If it's any consolation, you put on quite the brave face. I had no idea."

"Yes, same," Britni adds. "But we're here for you, whatever you need. And don't feel like you need to push yourself for us."

"Thank you both," I say. "Mostly, I just didn't want this to even be a factor in the first place. But like I told Alix last night, I'll speak up if I need to, now that you all know. It was bothering me a lot during our gaming today, but a day of resetting will get us back in order."

"On that note," Alix begins, "mind if I head back to our room?"

"I'll come with you," I say, relieved. It's so nice getting this thing off my chest, even if it's still somewhat literally on my back.

I walk with Alix out into the hall, but before we get too far, Britni follows.

"Hey, Keegan, can we talk a second?" she asks.

I stop, letting Alix walk ahead. Standing with Britni, I realize this is the first time we've gotten to chat one-on-one since we've been here.

"Hey, I don't mean to overstep, but I had this back pain burst in LA and found this book," Britni explains. "It really helped me. It might not be the same for you at all, but I figured it can't hurt."

Britni then hands me a well-worn paperback. I look down at the title: *Healing Back Pain: The Mind-Body Connection* by John E. Sarno, MD.

"I know, it probably seems like woo-woo LA nonsense," Britni adds. "But this book came out decades ago and has thousands of positive reviews online. It's an . . . alternative perspective. But it helped me deal with some pretty nasty lower back spasms. Like I said, it can't hurt, when you have some time to read."

"Oh, well thank you so much," I say. "I'm open to everything at this point, since no one else has had any answers."

"Let me know if anything rings true," Britni replies. "Okay, have a good night."

As she turns away, I find myself a little shocked that someone like Britni could suffer from anything. She seems so . . . effortless. But I suppose that's exactly the kind of bias someone might have against me as an outwardly able-bodied, young, white, cis guy. It's also, come to think of it, the clearest moral from our round two mythology: that everyone, even mighty archetypal gods, suffers—and that means we all have more in common than not. Putting this together for my journal, I hope it might be a touchpoint for Britni and me to bond a little more, whether the book helps or not.

I resolve to start reading back in the room. I love the idea of cozying up with a book in bed beside Alix like we're an old married couple. The hearts bracelet I want to give him still feels like it burns a hole in my pocket, but now I'm saving gifting it for a special moment.

I'm hoping I'll know when the time is right.

CHAPTER TWENTY-SIX

"BRITNI, I THINK YOU JUST CHANGED MY WHOLE LIFE."

I sit at a coffee shop down the street from our hotel with Britni. I texted her last night before I finally fell asleep to arrange this breakfast, because I stayed up super late to read the book she gave me. And not just read—I finished the entire thing in one sitting.

I feel like I practically vibrate, and not because of the coffee I've started sipping.

But rather because for the first night in many months, I was able to sleep pain-free . . . Thanks entirely to this seemingly magical book Britni gave me.

Hearing my response, Britni's whole face lights up above her own latte.

"I hoped it would help," she replies.

"Help is an understatement," I say. "I don't even know where to begin. I feel like I was just reborn from the UndeRealm myself."

My Professor Keegan brain continues to buzz with the details. I know Britni is obviously already acquainted with the basics of this medical theory, but I can't help reviewing the details in my mind like a book report. I just want the whole thing crystallized forever, this curative diagnosis I have *finally* found after nearly a year of relentless searching.

The radical thesis is that neck and back pain has had a big rise in the past century—and that the cause is not physical from our spines or nerves, but rather from our minds coping with repressed emotions.

To begin, the doctor who wrote the book outlines the type of person who is prone to what he calls Tension Myoneural Syndrome, or TMS for short. First you have to rule out any specific traumatic injury, which obviously applies in my own case. From there, the general personality type most prone to TMS is competitive and high-achieving as a source of validation. That's definitely me, between my school performance, college admissions, and *Pantheonic* playing. I mean, even confronting this pain, I put a ton of pressure on myself and never felt like I was doing enough.

Us overachievers or people-pleaser types are trained to repress any unlikable or "selfish" behavior, because we fear it won't be accepted. But where does that repressed emotion go? The answer is that it creates pain in the body to draw focus and keep repression working. There are plenty other stress-related expressions of this—like IBS, headaches, skin rashes, and ear-ringing. But the most insidious expression of TMS is when it leads to spasms that lock up muscles in our necks and backs.

How does it do this? The theory is that the brain sends slightly lessened blood flow to a specific muscle, causing mild oxygen deprivation that is actually harmless in the long term.

However, the physical reaction is super painful and very scary—especially if it cramps muscles, creates knots, or throws out your whole back.

Then the vicious cycle begins. Once the initial pain episode does recede, we become terrified of that awful pain recurring. So we take precautions with physical treatments and often seek out medical diagnoses. And then our preoccupation with physical treatment becomes complete—a very effective distraction from the emotional or mental pain we are repressing.

I mean, our whole modern culture is built around this fear of back pain: rituals about sitting too long, weak cores, industries of ergonomics and physical therapy, or spinal disc shots and procedures. When in actuality, our backs are designed to be among the strongest muscles in our bodies. Yet we have *so many* different medical diagnoses and treatments for back pain, so few of which seem to cure anything.

So the vicious physical-focused cycle continues. These diagnoses and practices create more fear and anxiety—which, when repressed, continue to cause the pain. I experienced this *exactly* myself after getting that surgical joint injection. I was terrified by the experience and then felt weak when it didn't work, so I internalized it all. I didn't want to be the one who can't sit or walk or travel as easily as everyone else. I hid that pain—bringing me right back to the repression and fear that keep the pain going.

Since the proposed pain comes from a lack of blood flow directed by the brain, anything that does stimulate blood flow temporarily provides relief. Things like applying heat, massage, foam rolling, exercise, and acupuncture work for a little while. But these methods aren't curative, because the physical pain is a *symptom*, not the cause. And the central zones cited in the book for this kind of TMS pain? The shoulders connecting to the neck, both sides of the lower back—and the *outer part of the butt.*

Reading that, I nearly fell out of bed.

All of this just sounded so hauntingly *familiar.* Obviously, the more I read, I was dying to know what the cure was.

It ended up being so simple I could cry.

The cure for TMS pain is possessing the *knowledge* of how that pain works—then convincing yourself that you are not injured, the physical pain is harmless, and you need to focus instead on your emotions. Once this camouflage of pain misdirection becomes useless, our brains eventually stop using it. Apparently in most cases, within two to six weeks the subconscious mind will stop.

To kick-start this process, when pain recurs you're supposed to process any anxiety or anger, then tell your mind you don't need an accompanying physical pain response. Instead of feeling like a helpless victim of the pain, you simply dismiss it. Then, once any spasms subside enough, you have to stop all physical treatments and resume normal bodily activity. Of course, exercise, proper form, and stretching still matter, as do other treatments like massage and physical therapy for actual injuries. But the feeling of muscles being sore from exercise is quite different from the deeply persistent cramping of TMS, as I know all too well.

Finally, we must remember it's impossible to remove anger and anxiety from our lives entirely. Mental health awareness has come a long way since this book was written, but now in the age of toxic positivity, we're told to pretend negative thoughts shouldn't even exist. However, the key is to not think of having negative emotions as a sign of weakness.

Really, facing our emotions head-on is a sign of *strength.*

"You don't understand. This felt like reading a history of my last year," I say to Britni. "After I finished reading, I didn't do my usual before-bed stretches. I didn't get up every thirty minutes. I didn't use any numbing creams or ice packs or heat pads. I didn't pull out my massage gun or foam roller. I didn't track my exact positions sitting or lying down. I didn't use my sleep support pillows.

"Instead, I just lay down like an average freaking human—and when the pain would flare up, I told my brain I didn't need a physical response to anxiety. Then I took some deep breaths. *And the pain would calm down.* It kept coming back, but the mental approach worked every time until I fell asleep—for the entire night. It was . . . unbelievable."

"Oh, Keegan, I'm so happy for you." Britni beams. "But you don't need to tell me how magical it feels. I had terrible lower back pain when I first moved to LA. I'd throw out my whole back like an old lady and have to lie flat on the floor for hours. An orthopedist almost convinced me I needed a spinal procedure. But then I saw my favorite YouTube yoga teacher talk about this book, and it helped so much."

"And you don't have back pain anymore?" I ask.

"It will start to cramp and seize up if I'm stressed out about something in particular, but now I can talk it down before it gets too bad. It took a couple months, and then the pain started flaring up as a stiff neck instead. But I applied the same mental process, and it worked there as well. There's so much about the mind-body connection we don't understand. TMS obviously doesn't apply to everyone, but I think in general we overlook that our brains regulate our bodies and tend to treat the body in isolation."

"Totally," I agree. "Why do you think this book isn't more widely known? I mean, it feels revolutionary."

"Lots of reasons," Britni begins. "Think of all the industries devoted to back pain. They all mean well, but so many places would go out of business if everyone knew about TMS. But honestly, I think it's just because it's so antithetical to the American or Western way of thinking. Any time I try to tell someone about TMS without giving them the book, they think I'm silly. Or even if they do have pain and read the book, a lot of people still think it's nonsense."

I turn these thoughts over, and it all makes sense. Honestly, I don't think I would have believed this myself if I hadn't spent the previous year walking down every other available avenue to cope with the pain.

"I get it," I say. "It really is kind of unbelievable. I don't know how I'd even explain this to someone. I'm so used to doctors not understanding the pain—if I told them about TMS they'd probably think I was a total loon. But I always suspected there was some broader connection—it didn't make sense why I wouldn't feel the pain in certain situations, or why it would shift around, or react to treatments only sometimes. It's like the pain didn't want me to relax, which makes sense now—because relaxing would mean time to focus on my emotions. I think that whether I knew it or not, the pain gave me an excuse to hide away and control things and feel safe."

"I get it," Britni says. "My back thing started when I moved to LA. I was so lonely and overwhelmed. I told myself I had to be strong and succeed, but everything gave me anxiety. The way I look has defined my whole life. I was terrified my body was betraying me once the back spasms started.

"Although honestly, I think the real key for me is anger. Girls aren't supposed to be angry if we want to be liked. But so much about our world makes me furious. The way I'm treated like an object. The environment crumbling. Otherwise loving people using religion as an excuse to hate. People in power stoking culture wars to make money. Genocides and natural disasters and mass shootings and pandemics and rights bans—all the things I can do seemingly nothing about. I feel so angry and helpless all the time, and we're told no one likes an angry woman. But want to know where I get to be brutal and strong and fight to feel like I can save the world?"

"*Pantheonic*," I answer. "That makes so much sense. I don't really think it's about anger for me . . . but there is a lot of it just built into being queer. And if we express that anger in the wrong place, speaking up can get us killed. At least as K.Odyssia, I can be as loud and strong and fearless as I want."

"Exactly," Britni says. "Do you mind if I ask when the pain started for you?"

Thinking this over, I know exactly when. But that's not as important as realizing *why*.

"It seemed to come out of nowhere at the time. But now, I realize it was right in the middle of filling out college applications. And then . . ."

The next realization hits me like a brick in the head, illuminating my typical pattern.

"A few months after the pain started, a new friend I made died suddenly. And I didn't think I deserved to grieve her, because we had really just met. So I swallowed it down . . ."

"More repressed emotion." Britni sighs. "I'm so sorry, Keegan. For your loss, and for the pain it caused. But you're allowed to give yourself some grace. And to grieve a loss, no matter the size."

Tears spring into my eyes. Not just for Annie, but also for myself—for all the treatments and procedures and copays I put my whole family through. For all the time I spent spiraling and spinning out focusing on the only pain I knew how to feel.

Britni reaches out to place her hand on mine. I flip it over to grasp her hand.

"I can't tell you how much this means to me," I say. "How much I think it's going to help change my entire life."

"I know how much it means to be believed, to be seen," Britni says. "You've always done that for me in the game. I'm just glad you finally spoke up."

To think I might never have found this answer if I had stayed silent. If I had never come to this tournament, keeping myself a willing captive at home.

"I'm so glad you trusted us enough to finally share the real you," I say. "Though I like to think Chiroptera has been a big part of the real Britni all along."

"Can I get an omen?" Britni says, coining Alix's catchphrase.

We both laugh.

"By the way, it's obvious how much you love books," I say. "And how good you are at recommending them. I'd sign up for the Britni Book Club in a heartbeat, for what it's worth."

Britni's face lights up once again.

"That means more than you know. Thanks, Keegan."

"No, thank *you*," I reply. "Seriously."

In this moment, I can tell Britni and I have just bonded in a real way. Maybe even deeper than with the others. No, not deeper—just differently. I'm so grateful Britni was put in my life, along with Mo and Alix. Maybe I've been on a painful path to get here . . .

But now in hindsight, it's starting to feel somehow worth it.

I still have lots of work ahead of me—and I'll need to be patient about allowing the time for healing. But I'm obviously not afraid of putting in time and work, even if it's mental instead of physical. Now that work can *actually* start to pay off, with a specific diagnosis that explains literally every little detail of my chronic pain—and that shouldn't cost another dime.

Britni has no idea how indebted I truly feel.

I only hope I can find ways to make it up to her in this tournament and beyond. And now that I've solved two of my own core questions—conquering my chronic pain and bonding with everyone IRL—maybe I can focus on another big intention:

Leading my teammates to victory.

CHAPTER TWENTY-SEVEN

WE SPEND THE REST OF THE AFTERNOON PRACTICE-GAMING in Mo and Britni's room. As planned, we focus on escort events and even a few boss battles.

The only part that doesn't go to plan? Alix decided to skip out. Mo relayed that after their morning of thrift shopping, Alix said he needed more time to decompress alone in our room. When I asked Mo whether Alix opened up about what was bothering him, she just said he dodged the subject. Again.

Even though I'm disappointed by Alix's sudden guardedness and absence, I try to understand. My own pain crept into our usually escapist *Pantheonic* gaming yesterday once it became about pressure and performing. Now I understand why. It feels like I have a new outlook on this brain-driven chronic pain in every single way. The pain is definitely still present, but now it's so much less consuming. I'm not constantly poking at myself. And even more importantly, I'm no longer *terrified* of the pain.

It's gotten so much easier to dismiss it, even over the course of just one day. It makes me feel powerful and back in control.

Now I just need time for my body to catch up with my mind.

This is the primary thought that consumes me as I walk back toward our room, knowing I'll find Alix there. I so desperately want him to share what's bothering him. I want to keep connecting. But I remind myself I have to be patient about that too.

Repeating this thought like a mantra in my mind, I open the door to our room . . .

And I freeze in shock.

Alix stands in front of the bed wearing a blazer, his hair all done, smelling like amber and oak cologne. He looks nervous while he lingers there holding a . . . Barbie doll? I pause with the door still open, trying to process what the Hel is going on. Alix seems like he was waiting there for me to enter, but how did he even know I was coming back now?

"Keegan," Alix says, his nervous eyes lighting up.

I want to say something, but my throat has gone dry.

"I . . . have been practicing what to say all day, and I still have no clue," Alix starts. "So I guess I'm going to wing it. I was talking to Mo this morning on our thrifting trip, and I told her how I really feel about you. She told me she thought a big romantic gesture might work out in my favor? Since this might be one of our last nights here together . . ."

Alix pauses, taking a breath.

I wish I could, but I feel entirely breathless.

"Would you want to have dinner with me?" Alix asks. "Like, as a date?"

My heart leaps into my throat.

My vision blurs.

I try to steady myself against the still-open door.

Is this really happening?

Then I look closer at the doll in Alix's hand and see he has customized it to look like K.Odyssia. She wears her signature red fringe leather skirt with gold metallic armor—all of which Alix must have cut and created himself. Is that why he skipped practice? To make this for me?

"Is that K.Odyssia?" I ask, still feeling an overwhelming rush of everything all at once.

"It is," Alix answers. "I was going to get you flowers, but this felt way more . . . I don't know, meaningful?"

I blink back tears. Another surge of emotion cascades through me.

Then, at the tail end of this tsunami of reactions, I feel one thing wash over me . . .

Elation.

Finally, I spot a detail sewn into K.Odyssia's belt that sends me right over the blissful edge: a crescent moon design.

Alix sees me.

He cares.

He . . .

Feels the same way I do about him?

"It's okay if you want to say no," Alix adds, his face falling. "I promise nothing will be awkward between us if Mo was wrong. Or if you changed your mind."

That's when I realize I haven't said yes yet. I haven't said nearly anything.

Well, that's okay.

I can do better than words.

I reach into my pocket and pull out the hearts bracelet I've been hiding there. Then I walk into the room and right up to Alix. I take his empty hand and slide the bracelet onto his wrist.

Alix looks down and lets out a little gasp once he sees what I've given him. Then, when his eyes look back up to connect with mine . . .

I take his face in my hands.

And I kiss Alix for the first time.

I expect him to be tense and surprised, but instead it's like he melts right into me. His mouth opens a little against mine, and his lips feel softer than anything I've ever experienced. As far as first kisses go . . .

I don't think it could get any better than this.

Then I suddenly hear squealing and cheering coming from behind us. Alix pulls away, and I turn to look at the door . . .

Where Mo and Britni stand, clapping like giddy schoolgirls.

"How did—"

"Did I maybe text Alix to warn him when you were coming back?" Mo replies. "Then did we maybe secretly follow you and hold the door open behind you like total creepers to witness this moment?"

"We absolutely did," Britni adds, actual tears in her eyes.

"I hope you don't mind my meddling," Mo says, looking a little worried.

But I just turn to Alix, beaming at his beautiful face.

"I don't mind one bit," I answer.

Then I lean in and kiss Alix again, like it's the most normal and wonderful thing in the entire world.

After that, I turn back to Mo.

"But you're not also crashing our first date, right?"

CHAPTER TWENTY-EIGHT

ONE QUICK CHANGE LATER, I SIT ACROSS FROM ALIX UPSTAIRS at the hotel restaurant. The skyline of the west side feels like the most romantic backdrop possible. Then again, sitting across from Alix, a cardboard box would probably seem just as romantic.

And it's not lost on me how little my pain is bothering me right now. I mean, could this day possibly get any better?

I look at Alix and realize I must have the dopiest grin on my face.

Good thing his own grin looks just as deliriously goofy.

"Were you ever going to tell me you had a crush on me?" Alix asks.

"I guess I could ask you the same thing!" I reply, still feeling like I'm sitting in a dream.

"I *did* finally tell you." Alix laughs.

"It sounds like we have our own cupid, Mo, to thank for making that happen," I say.

"It took quite a lot of pushing. Mo said you were worried she told me yesterday. So she still wouldn't confirm anything. Instead, she just kept saying I needed to go for it."

"I'm so glad she did," I reply. "By the way, I was worried that was why you seemed so off yesterday. That you could sense my crush and didn't know how to let me down easy."

"Not at all," Alix insists. "I have wanted to ask you out since the second I caught you outside the Vessel. I've been dying to touch you again ever since. I mean, you're the one who made a whole thing about not wanting to share a bed."

It feels like Alix's words light a fire inside me. But I try to ignore the urge to jump across this table and kiss him again.

"Because my crush on you doubled when we met in person!" I explain. "I didn't want you to feel weird that I was so attracted to you in the same bed. Plus, the whole chronic pain thing."

"Oh, yes. By the way, Britni told me you had some kind of breakthrough on that front?"

"Yes, thanks 100 percent to her. But we can talk about that later. I still can't believe you actually . . . like me back."

"Why?" Alix replies. "You're smart as hell and twice as thoughtful. Plus I've always had a soft spot for Irish guys. Honestly, I tried not to openly stare every time you changed clothes."

"What?" I respond, bewildered. "I was doing the same for you. And you're the one with the six-pack abs."

Alix blushes.

"Sure, but Keegan, have you seen your arms and your ass? I mean, thick in the best possible way. I kept trying to drop hints."

Now it's my turn to blush.

Thinking back, Alix did compliment me *a lot* this way. But I obviously never recognized that as flirting. The qualities Alix was complimenting aren't the ones I'm attracted to in other guys, so I never thought of them as being potentially attractive. But who says I have to be the things I'm attracted to in another guy? Being queer really is a constant revelation, sometimes . . .

"Plus I'm not totally . . . settled, transition-wise," Alix continues. "I didn't know if that would matter to you."

Alix tries to minimize this last statement, but I know the question he really means to ask is: Am I okay being with a transman the same way I would be with a cis-man?

So I answer the bigger question without hesitation.

"You are exactly who I want to be with, in every single way," I say, knowing I mean every word. I just hope Alix can feel how sincere I am.

"Really?" he asks, now holding back tears in his eyes. "I mean, are you sure you really know what—"

"Alix, I am a teenage guy with hormones who didn't get out much and has access to the internet," I interject. "Not to be gross, but it's not hard to find the . . . intimacies of every kind of queer relationship. I don't have a lot of experience in real life. But just like with *Pantheonic*, trust me—I know what I'm into. And I'm into *you*."

Alix looks like his heart might explode, hearing this. I know the feeling.

"I'm still shocked you're into me," I add. "That's very new for me."

"I, too, have the internet," Alix replies. "Plus my own studio apartment in New York City. I also know what I'm into, both virtually and in real life. But I've never . . . *felt* this way about anyone before."

Now it's my turn to hold back tears.

Thankfully, the server arrives to take our order. It gives me a moment to try to collect my exploding emotions and racing mind—and surging hormones, after that conversation.

"Not to switch topics," I begin once the server leaves, "but I still want to know what was up with you yesterday, if you're ready to talk about it?"

"I'm still not sure I should say anything," Alix begins. "But I guess if today has taught us anything, it's the value of speaking up."

Alix forces a deep breath before going on.

"Playing *Pantheonic*, and with our team specifically, has always been a really important escape for me. Given all I've been going through personally and everything in the world these past couple years, *Pantheonic* is one place I can always go to have fun and blow off steam and turn off my practical brain. I didn't expect how much coming here for this tournament would change all of that for me. The pressure was really messing with one of the few safe spaces I can rely on. But I pushed so hard for us all to be here, and we all want the money. So I didn't want to say anything.

"Still, I just felt so *awful*, especially in round two. Making this hobby into a cutthroat competition really rattled me more than I thought it could. I even thought about quitting yesterday . . . until I came across a jack of hearts card on top of a deck, left behind on a hotel lobby table. I felt like it was a sign to stick it out. Especially because I'd never want to let our team down. But all that said, I don't know if I'm cut out for this competition thing. Keeping *Pantheonic* as a purely fun safe space feels more valuable for my mental health than any amount of money. Am I making any sense?"

Listening to Alix, he makes all the sense in the world.

And suddenly it hits me crystal clear why our team efforts felt so off yesterday. We were *forcing* ourselves through a space where we can usually just *float*.

"As team leader, I'm making an official call," I say with resolve in my voice. "We need to stop pressuring ourselves to keep up and survive. Instead, we need to focus only on enjoying this experience and having *fun* together. If that means we get eliminated in round three, that's a price I am willing to pay."

Alix looks back at me in a way I've never seen before. It's like he is seeing something in me no one else ever has.

Well, if I'm shining like the moon to him, he shines like the sun to me.

And I think he knows.

"There's only one thing left to say, after that," Alix replies. "Can I get an omen?"

After what is easily the best dinner of my life—not that I really even remember the actual food—Alix and I head back down to our room. Emerging from the elevator, we turn down the hall.

"So this gives a whole new meaning to *walking each other home*, huh?" I joke.

"Speaking of, do you think we should set some ground rules?" Alix asks. "Call me old-fashioned, but I don't think we should jump all the way in on our first night."

"May I remind you this is far from our first night," I contend. "But I don't want to rush things, either."

"I mean, have I lain awake these past few nights wishing I could roll across the bed and . . ."

Alix doesn't finish that sentence—but the possibilities get me excited, to say the least.

I can't help myself. I grab Alix and pull him against me, my back to the nearest wall. And I kiss him like I really mean it.

This kiss is different. It's not sweet and surprised like our first. This one is deep and . . . insistent. This time our bodies connect. I can feel Alix's muscled torso press against me. My hands reach around his shoulders just as his hands find their way down the curve of my back and . . . even lower.

"Okay," Alix suddenly says, stepping back. "If we get in the same bed tonight, I will not be capable of keeping my hands to myself."

"As tempting as that sounds," I reply, "I agree."

I want Alix's hands all over me. I want to soak in every inch of his skin.

But then I remind myself that I'm moving back here to live in his city in a matter of weeks. There's no rush. And the only thing I want more than Alix's body right now?

To build the foundation for something real and lasting.

So when we do get fully physical, I want to be prepared in every way. Especially since for me, it will involve many firsts . . . like, my first time being with *anyone*. Let alone someone I might fall all the way for.

"Should we ask if Mo will switch rooms with one of us for the night?" I ask.

"She helped create this beast." Alix laughs. "It's the least she can do, right? Besides, Britni and I talked about having a slumber party one of these nights."

"Okay, it's settled then. We text Mo and ask her to swap rooms for sleeping," I say. "But first, I think we can make out for another few minutes in the semi-public decency of this hallway, right?"

Alix smiles back at me, looking devastatingly hot.

"I think that can be arranged."

CHAPTER TWENTY-NINE

THE NEXT MORNING I WAIT WITH MO IN THE KING-BED hotel room for Britni and Alix to meet us. Alix texted the group chat first thing to request a mini team meeting before dressing for round three.

I feel both bleary and bright, since I was barely able to sleep last night. I was up super late filling Mo in on every detail of my first date with Alix. Then, still buzzing, I cracked open my personal mythology journal to record this momentous day. One where I answered *three* of the core questions I asked at the beginning of this experience. Which feels fitting after a gaming round built around the theme of deity drama—which is really just about deity connection.

First I wrote about my own connections: *building genuine friendships IRL* with Mo and Britni. Then I spent way too much space writing about my fantasies becoming a reality with Alix. Though I guess my question about him still stands—*how to handle my feelings for Alix and embrace new emotions*—just now with a way brighter context.

After that, I finally worked my way to processing the TMS *pain-coping revolution* gifted to me by Britni. My chronic pain still popped up plenty last night even while journaling, but I didn't let it control me the way it always did before. The pain might still be more persistent than I'd like, but I know my body will take time to adjust. After all, it's only been a day.

This left me dwelling on my fourth and final question: *How can I lead my teammates to victory?* I had the start of an answer from my date with Alix . . .

But our morning team meeting is where we can set this intention for round three, maybe even shifting our idea of what victory really means for us.

The door opens and Britni and Alix walk in. I feel a beam of light wash over me at the sight, and my face breaks into a wide grin. I don't waste any time crossing the room to kiss Alix good morning.

Because I can do that now.

Who knew after so much time spent alone that I'd be such an affectionate . . . boyfriend? Is that what I'm about to become to Alix?

Mo and Britni clap and swoon once again. It's like all four of us have suddenly melted into giddy kids.

"Okay, as much as I could do that all morning," Alix says, breaking away. "We have some important team business to attend to."

Squeezing Alix's hand, I follow him as the four of us arrange ourselves around the end of the bed. After Alix's very reserved round two, it's so nice to see him excited and engaged about *Pantheonic* again.

"I know Keegan filled Mo in on the goal we discussed last night, like I did with Britni," Alix begins. "It sounds like we're all on the same page: going back to basics by focusing on having *fun*."

"Hel yes!" I reply.

"Here, here!" Britni affirms.

"Spoken like a true champion," Mo agrees.

"Okay, then if we're at peace with today's round potentially being our last day here," Alix continues, "I just want to focus on *enjoying* it together. In that spirit, I'd like to give everyone something now that I was saving for our last guaranteed day, one way or another."

Alix walks over to our closet and points at the secret, sealed garment bag there.

"I may or may not have made us all outfits based on our avatars," Alix announces with a huge grin.

"Stop!" Mo practically shouts. "You didn't."

"Oh, yes he did," Britni answers. "I even helped him add some finishing touches during our shopping trip. He needed to make some alterations after we all finally met in person."

"If you're all willing," Alix finishes, "I think we have to wear them today."

"I couldn't agree more," I say, smiling even wider, if it's possible.

Looking around, it feels like this tiny hotel room contains many realms of my own life. Between the K.Odyssia Barbie on the nightstand, the cosplay garments waiting to be revealed, friends like Mo and Britni, and a guy like—*my* guy—Alix wearing the hearts bracelet I bought him . . .

After what felt like a long year, it feels richly deserved. Like the end of an odyssey.

So if this really will be our last round here, there's no way finishing in fourth could feel like losing.

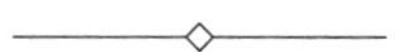

Not long after, we stand waiting for round three to start. Except we're not inside a convention center meeting room as usual.

Instead, we find ourselves a few blocks away on a Hudson River pier, one left empty to be transformed for different events. We all stand gathered in front of a wall that blocks our view behind it, beyond which lies our next physical challenge. This wall has a stage and screen for Dahlia's usual intro, but I see it also holds a special adornment: a slim gilded dragon with the scales of a snake, the claws of an eagle, the legs of a lion, and the stinger of a scorpion.

"I'm pretty sure that wall is inspired by the Ishtar Gate, which stood outside ancient Babylon," I whisper to my teammates. "And given where we are, it looks like Britni was right about things switching up in the second half."

"Professors Keegan and Britni for the win," Mo replies. "Also, it's definitely going to storm."

I look up to confirm that there are clouds rolling ominously across the sky. They threaten to unleash a summer rain shower at any moment.

"Good thing Alix made our outfits to be all-purpose," Britni adds.

She is completely right. I look down at my own, which exists somewhere between cosplay and athleisure. The outfits

Alix designed feel like a brand partnership between *Pantheonic* and Supreme. Mine is a lightweight track jacket and a pair of joggers in white with a golden metallic stripe up either side. Our team name is written in red across the back, while the upper right chest has K.Odyssia's crest—a shield over a guarded heart—positioned like a logo.

I'm feeling ready to weather any storm, wearing this custom armor on the outside.

But on the inside?

I must admit, if only to myself, I'm feeling thrown off by this unexpected outdoor twist. Along with a burst of nerves, I experience a fresh shot of pain in my piriformis area. But instead of letting it freak me out, I run my finger along the ripped-out journal page I have stashed in my pocket. I wrote it out last night, as a way to clear away doubts—just like the ones I experience now, with the signals in my body insisting that something is physically wrong with me.

Going it over in my head, I know how the page reads:

REMEDY REMINDERS

- When pain flares up, must think psychologically and not physically.
- The pain is due to my mind triggering mild oxygen deprivation, not a structural injury.
- This pain, while alarming, is harmless and not a sign of something wrong.
- Since there is nothing to fear, take deep breaths and focus on remembering I don't need a pain signal to process my emotions.
- I must resume all normal physical activity. I will not be intimidated by the pain anymore.

I go through these steps, quieting my mind. And once again, the deep stinging ache begins to recede. It feels like a magic spell or a miracle. And it's not the only miracle I think, looking over at Britni. And then Mo. And Alix.

How did I get so lucky?

We all turn our attention to the stage as Dahlia walks up, wearing another resplendent suit. This one is pastel pink and cut to perfection.

"Come rain or come shine, our quest to end this war continues with our fearsome final four pantheons," Dahlia begins. "After an exhaustive investigation conducted during our recent conflict, the Pantheonic War Council has confirmed that *our physical earth realm* here contains the secrets needed to chart a course to the Stoneruned Horde Nerve Center.

"But why is *our* realm the key to ending this war? It turns out our earth serves as one of several origin points for the entire multiverse of realms, including the Divine Realm. This means our own mythological source material contains the details that are able to answer the final questions of our war. So the final two rounds will tour facets of our *own* earth mythology!"

I experience another wave of chills. All my teammates turn to me—because touring our physical world mythology to solve *Pantheonic*'s final virtual mysteries? Hel yes.

The screen beside Dahlia comes to life with another animation. Yet this time, instead of the usual mythological story, we are shown a block of stone being slowly chiseled away. Above it reads *The Epic of Gilgamesh.* The animation shows the sped-up carving of a stone relief of Gilgamesh. He strikes a victorious pose, standing over a defeated bull and dragon.

I feel another rush of excitement as our third core mythological trope is obviously revealed: the heroic epic, told in world-spanning poems and myths—just like *The Odyssey.*

The epic of Gilgamesh goes that he was the tyrant king of Uruk, a city just south of Babylon. He became great friends with his first rival sent by the gods, Enkidu. Together they overcame all the godly trials: killing a fire-breathing monster, Humbaba, slaying the Bull of Heaven, resisting the seductions of Ishtar, and accepting the inevitability of death from a failed quest for immortality. There are many general heroic epic themes here, but the focus in the animated stone relief is on the *monsters* Gilgamesh most famously slayed.

Our pantheons also have monsters to slay—monsters made of stone. Does this mean we're all about to be featured in our very own *Pantheonic* heroic epics?

As the short animation finishes, Dahlia continues her speech.

"The War Council has confirmed that here in our own earth realm, your task will be to assemble the pieces of ancient weapon artifacts. We believe these weapons will prove most effective against even the strongest Stoneruned defending the Source Wing. Once assembled, these artifact weapon pieces will also provide your team with your unique gaming hub code . . . and a new experience in the virtual realms."

As Dahlia finishes her dramatic introduction, each team is handed a smartphone by the production staff. Once activated, we all lean in to see the screens open to a custom augmented reality app. Mostly it just shows a camera view, likely primed to reveal hidden secrets and artifact fragments galore beyond that wall.

I want to take a moment to process this deeply cool reality and fill my team in on the epic of Gilgamesh. But the time to do so vanishes as the usual start buzzer blares across the pier.

It's obviously time to *Pantheonic* go.

CHAPTER THIRTY

WE RUN FORWARD WITH THE OTHER THREE TEAMS—EXCEPT for the Mythic Goats, who roll in wheelchairs or hustle on supports just as quickly. It reminds me that we didn't speak a word to the other teams between rounds. We decided to let go of building any rivalry with the One4All Seasons or feeding into the feud with the Effing Divas. The Epic Hearts are just ready to leave it all on the field and run this round for ourselves.

Coming around the dragon wall, we see that the pier has been transformed into another mazelike course. As I guessed, this space is clearly inspired by ancient Babylon. It features hanging plant gardens and ziggurat stair sculptures that appear to be purely decorative, since there will be accessible ramps in all necessary cases.

Upon first glance, it feels like we're standing at the mouth to my ideal mythical playground—one with three paths leading further inside. The Goats rush to the left path, while the Divas and the Seasons run together to the right path. That leaves us with the middle path, I suppose. Moving as one, I lead our team down the center path. As we wind along its curves and turns, I wonder if we'll be experiencing the different story points of the epic of Gilgamesh.

We eventually come to a kind of shrine-like dead end. So this won't be a traditional maze—it's instead three stations, with each team likely needing to visit each one. At this station, we stand before a ziggurat sculpture displaying three stone tableaus.

"Okay, ancient Mesopotamians placed carved stone reliefs in their temples and homes for protection and ownership," I share. "Which tracks with Gilgamesh and Babylon. Except these don't show specifically Mesopotamian deities."

Instead, each stone relief depicts an epic hero from world-spanning poems and myths. Each one stands victorious over two of the most infamous beasts they defeated. Then I realize that the three separate stone reliefs seem to create one connecting portrait, with the details from one spilling into another.

"Everyone, gather around," Mo says, reminding me we are indeed in the middle of a race. As our recon specialist, she has pointed our smartphone camera at the stone reliefs.

On the screen, new digital descriptions float above each physical stone relief.

Epic Hero Crossover: The Ever Clever

Odysseus: Greek. Odyssey Lost Journeyer. Slays Cyclops & Scylla.

Ananse: African Ashanti. Cunning Spider Weaver. Slays Hornet & Python.

Monkey King: Chinese. Intelligent, Mischievous Rogue. Slays Heaven & Hell.

Reading this, especially the Odysseus reference, my K.Odyssia heart overflows. This obviously symbolizes heroic icons from different world mythologies joining together for some seriously epic crossovers—forming brand-new pantheons.

"It says to solve the puzzle designated for our team," Mo reads, once again snapping me back to the present. "Then to use the answer provided to open the chest below. This will uncover a weapon fragment."

Looking underneath the stone relief altar, we see four separate puzzle stations marked with each team name. These stations are also all under a protected roof, clearly in case of a storm—which is feeling more and more likely as the air charges with that pre-rain bluster.

We run up to our designated station to examine it. There's a puzzle board that stands over a chest, which has a keypad lock attached. The puzzle we face is a graphic design image with several overlapping squares that are filled with the mythological figures from the stone tableau. The instructions below say to count the number of squares present. Immediately, my eyes cross and my brain buzzes, especially since the squares are filled with battling heroes and monsters.

"I love these puzzles," Mo says. "I got addicted to them after they showed up on *Survivor* and *The Challenge*. I can take lead, but double-check my work?"

I am very happy to let Mo do so—this kind of puzzle is so not my strong suit. I try to keep count, but I realize halfway through that I didn't necessarily differentiate between squares and rectangles.

Instead, I find myself marveling at Mo, especially in her Alix-designed outfit. She wears the same lightweight track jacket and pair of joggers with a side-stripe, but colored flat black to match sMOte's design. Our team name is written in metallic silver across her back, and her crest is displayed in the same place on her chest like a logo: a changing heart half vanishing. Mo looks every bit as badass as her avatar.

"I counted thirty-six," she says.

"I counted thirty-eight," Britni replies.

"Should we just punch numbers around there until we get the right one?" Alix asks.

"No, I recognize those keypads," I interject. "They lock you out for a minute if you punch the wrong code."

"I trust Mo's eyes over mine," Britni says. "Let's do it."

Mo reaches down and enters her number with the pound sign after it . . .

And the chest door unlocks, swinging open.

"sMOte, puzzle slayer!" Mo shouts as we all crouch down to look inside the chest.

There's nothing inside, but Mo grabs the gaming phone and points the camera. On the screen we see a glowing blade hilt inside the chest. This virtual hilt is clearly the bottom part of a sword broken in three. This fragment also has our first gaming-room code number printed on it.

Mo taps the screen to claim the weapon fragment virtually. Which means we're not assembling this weapon in the real world, but rather within *Pantheonic*. This connects our physical realm to the tournament's virtual gaming realm most directly so far.

It feels . . . mythical, in all the right ways.

"Okay, we must need to visit the puzzle station at the end of each of the three paths to assemble the virtual sword," I say out loud, just in case everyone hasn't also put this together. "Let's head back to the start and pick our next path."

Moving together, we do exactly that.

On our way to the left path, we pass the Goats as they swap with us to head down the middle. We purposely don't exchange a single word. We're focusing on ourselves, as promised. And I must admit, I'm having a *blast* with this challenge. It's truly like a reality game show has sprung to life all around us, like Mo pointed out.

We soon reach the next station. It looks exactly like the last, except this one is themed with hanging pots spilling over with leafy vines. Mo points the smartphone camera at the stone reliefs nestled between cascading plants. In the virtual view, descriptions once again float above each relief.

Epic Hero Crossover: The Hell Raisers

Ghesar Khan: Tibetan. Destined Savior Defender. Slays Demons.

Hercules: Greek. Twelve Impossible Tasker. Slays Hydra & Cerberus.

Rustum: Persian. Shahnameh Doomed Defender. Slays White Demon & Dragon.

Once again, I resist the urge to stop and absorb how cool this round's trope is. I mean, it's like *The Avengers* for a Classics nerd like me—which I suppose is another way to think about *Pantheonic* itself.

Filing this revelation away for later, I follow the team as we run up to our next station. It's a slide puzzle, with squares once again depicting this station's heroes and monsters—except for one solid gold piece. Once this piece is in the upper left corner, it can be removed to give us our chest keypad code.

"I am a slide puzzle queen," Britni says, surprising the rest of us.

"Good because I am definitely not a puzzle queen," I reply, looking at the others.

"Go for it, girl," Alix reinforces.

I step back once again to watch as Britni flies through the slide puzzle. As usual she is the perfect mix of elegance and brute strength, enhanced by her Alix-designed outfit. Her track set is deep purple with a metallic black side-stripe to match Chiroptera's design. Our team name is written in that same metallic black across her back, while her chest logo bears Chiroptera's signature crest: a broken heart being sliced by a claw.

Speaking of slicing, it's only a matter of seconds before Britni finishes the puzzle, releasing our chest code. We crouch again to retrieve our next virtual weapon fragment: the glowing sword middle with another number on it.

In the span of another racing blur, we all breathe heavily as we run to our third and final station. We haven't seen the Divas or the Seasons, but that doesn't matter.

Instead, I focus on enjoying the final stone relief setup. It's nestled under another roof and between more hanging pots of colorful flowers.

Epic Hero Crossover: The Inner Beasts

Arjuna: Indian. Mahabharata Humble Archer. Slays Kinsmen & Blind Fish.

Kintaro: Japanese. Golden Boy Samurai. Slays Tsuchigumo Spider & Giant Fish.

Wawalag Sisters: Australian. Aboriginal Duality Bringers. Slays Rainbow Snake & Ants.

It turns out the last puzzle is a sudoku, with a different epic hero figure wrapped around each number. Once all the missing numbers are filled in, there will be a highlighted portion that reveals our final chest code.

"I can take lead on this one too," Britni says.

"I also love sudoku," Mo adds.

I turn to Alix—I guess we are indeed not the puzzle queens of our team.

So while Mo and Britni once again set to work, I take this moment to soak in Alix in his own outfit. His is deep red, with orange metallic striping. Our team name is written in yellow-gold metallic writing, while his chest logo bears Apollix's crest: an open heart set ablaze.

I feel similarly ablaze, smelling the mix of sweat and cologne that wafts off Alix's skin. It makes my knees feel weak.

But soon enough, Mo and Britni have solved for the correct code solution.

"Okay, we're ready to rock," Mo says, crouching to claim the final sword piece for us.

I almost gasp again when I see it in the camera view. It's a glowing blade tip . . .

To a sword that is *quite literally* set in stone.

"How very King Arthur!" Britni exclaims, beating me to it. "Could that be where we're headed virtually?"

"We're ready to find out!" Mo says, now that all our virtual sword fragments are collected and assembled.

At that very same moment, the wind shifts and the light dims.

Then it's like the sky opens up all at once, pouring rain down in heavy bursting drops. The sound feels lyrical atop the tin-like roofs constructed over the puzzle station. We're able to stay dry under here . . .

But we're definitely not staying here for long.

Looking at one another with big smiles, we all sprint forward into the pouring rain. With our puzzles complete, now we only have to make our way back to the convention center for the gaming half. So the rain only makes everything feel even more epic, creating a big splash as we run through the downpour. It's a good thing they make phones and cameras waterproof these days.

It's actually the first time today I've even given these cameras a thought—which is a very good sign of where my focus has been. But once I do consider the cameras, something new occurs to me. We might not want to put on a big show of feuding with our competitors . . .

But what if we put on a show about our team coming together?

I mean, who wouldn't love a little nerdy romance storyline?

As we run, I reach out and grab Alix's hand. He turns to look at me, water dripping down his hair and across his gorgeous face. I slow down a little, leaning in toward him. I hesitate just long enough for Alix to wave me off if he wants, in case he is uncomfortable with this show of PDA.

But he seems to catch my drift, slowing down too.

We don't have much time to waste . . .

But we certainly make time to stop here in the middle of the puzzle path, with rain pouring down all around us.

And we give the camera a sweeping, epic, romantic kiss for the ages.

CHAPTER THIRTY-ONE

ONCE FINISHED WITH THE COURSE, WE ARE ESCORTED back to the gaming hub and given a grace period to dry off, timed equally for all teams. However, when the time comes to be escorted in the game from Mount Pantheonic to a new virtual earth realm, no one awaits us in the usual tournament gate hall our avatars populate into.

"Where's UnderTee?" Alix asks first.

It might be small, but the fact that Alix is engaged enough to speak first feels great.

"Well, that portal between the columns is already activated," Mo replies.

"We must need to go through," I decide. "Maybe UnderTee will be waiting for us on the other side."

Everyone agrees, so we move forward through the portal. After a lightning-fast load, we emerge into a completely unfamiliar realm—yet one that feels infinitely familiar at the same time. This map is an island with British estate vibes, since we stand at the base of a hill that holds a distant castle—one surrounded by glittering ocean cliffs and rolling apple orchards.

"This is a brand-new map," Mo reacts first. "Wait, is this supposed to be the Pantheonic War Council castle?"

"I think it's meant to invoke that," I reply. "But the island setting is different."

"I think it's also inspired by Avalon, the fruitful resting place of King Arthur," Britni adds. "I mean, we *did* just pull a sword out of stone."

"Um, wow," Alix jumps in. "UnderTee looks amazing over there."

Our avatars all turn to find UnderTee standing between exit paths blocked by two sets of heavy stone doors. She is dressed in flowing blue fabric that looks like rippling water. Then I spot a lake beside the doors, shimmering the same shade of blue.

"Oh my goddess, UnderTee is dressed like the Lady of the Lake," Britni says, looking mesmerized. "She was the one to gift King Arthur the legendary Excalibur sword."

"Let's hope Lady UnderTee is here to power up our own mythical sword," Mo responds, already running sMOte toward the doors. "I just hope her wolf fur doesn't smell when wet."

"Okay, I really hope we're about to become Knights of the Pantheonic Round Table," I also gush as we reach UnderTee, flashing Britni a private lit-geek smile.

"Never not looking run ragged, you lot," UnderTee begins. "Nevertheless, I have some updates from the War Council. This incursion point is located on a usually quite hidden earth realm, Orchard Isle—one rather close to the Stoneruned Horde's nasty little Nerve Center realm. That's why I'm out here in these castle pathways—because TravelGee could only open two entry gates instead of the usual seven. You'll be entering this new earth realm two by two, skipping to my Lou."

"I was half expecting something like this," Mo says. "Funneling the teams closer together for more direct interaction in these final rounds."

"And it sounds like we're going to be first to explore a brand-new map before public release," Alix adds. "How cool is that?"

I'm glad Alix is excited instead of freaked out by all this, finally. But I have to turn off the part of my brain that thinks about how many viewers this event coverage will likely draw. Instead, I focus as UnderTee continues her debrief.

"Your quest is to escort your assembled sword to the Stoneruned stronghold without this sword being destroyed or stolen. Once you have arrived, you must use this weapon to slash away an assigned fortification. This will be our first—and our final—test of how potent your wicked weapon truly will be against the strongest Stoneruned defenses. It will also unleash the Holy Grail of intel we seek: the pathway to infiltrate the Stoneruned Nerve Center on the Techno Classic realm.

"To be deemed worthy of this heroic quest, you have pulled a sword from stunning stone. Now, to aid you in this epic journey, I have been empowered to upgrade your sword to an Excalibur Class. This has also unlocked a new ability for you, so keep an eye out for it, yeah?

"Please enter through the first gate. And don't muck it up. I'm in no mood to ferry your sorry behinds from the UndeRealm and muddy this gorgeous gown."

"A new map and a new ability?" I say. "Britni was totally right about this second half being about the present and future of *Pantheonic.*"

"You're welcome," Britni replies. "But we're moving."

With that, a new item appears jointly in all our inventories—the Excalibur Class Sword, grayed from use for now. Then we are ushered by UnderTee through gate one, so the Epic Hearts run down to a field below.

There's a small village ahead surrounded by orange groves. There's also a Stoneruned battalion descending another hill to attack this valley village. It occurs to me that we have no idea what the environmental Stoneruned can do here in this new Orchard Isle map. But then I see something potentially even more intimidating . . .

The Mythic Goats running ahead of our team.

"The Goats must have entered through this same gate right before us," Britni says.

"Does that mean the Divas and the Seasons will have to enter through gate two?" Alix asks. "Assuming they're behind us and not ahead?"

"I'm more concerned with whether the Goats will want to work with or *against* us," Mo replies.

Indeed, this is a question that races through my own mind as the Goats turn back toward us. I can't help but stare at their imposing deities—some of the most leveled-up in the entire game. My eyes fall on Freyjathena first. A thick braid swings across her crimson skin and blood-stained war armor as she wields a deadly Warrior axe. Could K.Odyssia ever hope to take on this fellow goddess of war?

Then again, K.Odyssia would more likely match up against Odinzeus as a rival Ruler. I take in this pale-skinned male elder wearing chunky battle armor and many scars on his bearded face. I don't feel any less intimidated.

I'm sure sMOte feels the same way facing their Trickster, Lokihermes, a starkly white-skinned, gender-fluid royal dressed in flowing robes of deception. And same for Apollix facing their Bender, Thorares, a pale-skinned male prince with mostly exposed muscle underneath a lighting bolt strap.

Seeing the top-ranked team in *Pantheonic* in the virtual flesh, I quickly understand our position.

"We could never take them one-on-one," I offer. "The only shot we'd have is sticking tight and working as a team. We can't let them separate us for individual face-offs."

Before anyone can respond, a chat invitation from the Goats pops up at the bottom of our screens. I hold my breath while accepting.

> **ODINZEUS:** We know the other teams are still behind us and probably working together. If we team up, maybe we can stay ahead and force them to turn on each other?

Relief pours through my body.

"They're right," Mo says first. "Those desperate Divas will probably turn on the Seasons the moment they feel endangered."

"Sure, but this is better for us," Britni says. "Like Keegan says, I don't think we could take the Goats head-on and survive."

"Not to mention," Alix adds, "if we're looking to go epic and have some fun, battling alongside the Goats is a sure bet."

"Remember our code," I reply, knowing this repetition of our battle cry will be perfectly timed. "Battle efficiency and Horde kills always win the day. We don't aggravate our fellow deities, but we will defend ourselves to the death should any seek provocation!"

In return, I can only hear my teammates cheer their approval.

> **K.ODYSSIA:** We're 100% in. It will be an honor to battle alongside you.

I take a moment to worry whether the Goats are good for their word—but I realize that doesn't really matter when they have the upper hand. What *does* matter is how loyal we proved our own team to be, remaining true to the Ann Apolis. This must be why the Goats even made the offer in the first place, knowing they can trust us to keep our word.

This vote of confidence carries us directly into battle.

We all start by using our standard attacks, blocks, and dodges against these first Stoneruned battalions, knowing we probably should save our best abilities for the bigger threats to come. Though one such threat presents itself as I watch an environmental Stoneruned pick an orange and eat it. Suddenly it glows like a magma automaton.

"The fruit can power them up," I say. "Maybe into versions from different maps, like that lava-powered Stoneruned over there?"

The Goats must pick up on this too, since Thorares strikes the magma Stoneruned with a bolt of lightning, breaking it apart. I then see Odinzeus slightly separated, taking on a few automatons on his own. I run to help out—and as I do, a new ability suddenly appears on my list: *Pillar Pair.*

"Wait, anyone else see this new ability option?" I ask as I keep K.Odyssia battling beside Odinzeus. "It only appears when I get close to Odinzeus, a fellow Ruler."

"Whoa, I see it when I get close to their Trickster," Mo replies.

"Me too, with their Bender," Alix adds.

"Damn it, why don't they have a Creature?" Britni cries, sending Chiroptera into an even more feral display of rage. "I want to try a new move!"

"That sucks," I say. "But this must be why we were shown all those epic hero crossovers in the physical challenge. Maybe that's the moral here—rival heroes putting aside their egos to team up, forming new pantheons across team lines?"

"Except some teams have pillar duplicates," Mo replies as sMOte continues smiting. "With some obvious exceptions in this tournament, one-pillar teams usually don't work as well. But maybe if they can access this *Pillar Pair* combo, it'll change what compositions are most popular across the entire game?"

"*Pantheonic* future," Britni adds. "Except in the present, won't an ability like this power up both the Divas and the Seasons?"

The Divas *do* have three Traversers, while the Seasons are all Benders.

"Britni is right," I begin, "but this new ability might also encourage teams to become mightier by working together instead of sabotaging. Let's hope this is the first sign of the next *Pantheonic* gaming era to come?"

"Um, anyone else dying to find out?" Alix calls out. "Let's do it!"

Agreeing with Alix, I trigger this new *Pillar Pair* ability. It takes a few seconds to engage, probably needing Odinzeus to do the same. What follows is a display that leaves me breathless as I spring into action as K.Odyssia.

I automatically run beside Odinzeus, who begins to imbue me with his mighty strength. Once I shine like an invulnerable beacon, Odinzeus literally *picks me up* and throws me like a human shield. I crash through the Stoneruned hordes as an immortal wrecking ball.

While this is happening, I manage to catch sight of one other *Pillar Pair.* Thorares has turned himself into a shade of buzzing, human-shaped energy. Apollix then casts Thorares like a spell, using his energized form to blast away more Stoneruned.

"Lokihermes just transformed into a cloak and dagger for me to sneak attack with!" Mo exclaims.

"I want to see what the Creature pairing is even more now!" Britni gasps. "Because you all just cleared this entire battalion with those abilities."

"And we got to be the first teams to test it out!" Alix gushes. "Every single *Pantheonic* player on the planet is going to want to see this."

Soaking all of this in, I'm glad Alix is now excited by this prospect instead of terrified. But it's also absolutely time to move on in the game.

There's only one path forward through the town, so we all begin running. Villagers cheer us on like famous heroes as we run, gifting us oranges and bonus Worship Points. It's rare to see NPCs not hiding away in these events, but obviously the residents of this Orchard Isle realm are bolder than usual.

Moving through, I glimpse a central town square with monuments to magical goddesses I don't recognize. But I see that this Orchard Isle must have its own moon goddess as we pass a statue of one cradling an orange crescent moon.

In the physical world, I look over toward Alix. He has tears in his eyes, just like me.

It makes me feel like we're exactly where we're meant to be.

As our realm battling continues, we seem to play as well and in sync as we ever have. Maybe it's because the pressure is off and we're just focused on having fun? Or maybe because we're working with the Goats? Whatever the reason, we have been in an epic flow of play. I feel like I lose all sense of time, at one with K.Odyssia and our team.

In a wild blur, we battle through a grapevine-rowed village alongside the Goats, with grapes that turn the environmental Stoneruned into spirit channelers. Then we battle through cranberry bog and banana leaf villages that turn the environmental Stoneruned into laser-beaming and boomerang-throwing automatons. Through it all, both our pantheons are able to protect our team Excalibur Class Swords from being stolen or destroyed.

From there, the paths split in four, each one designated for a specific pantheon team. Knowing this will be the final run to our escort endpoint, we bid the Goats farewell and go on our way. Then we have to clear three more fruitful villages besieged by Stoneruned battalions.

Now we reach another apple orchard. Our health bars hang dangerously low, and our abilities are mostly on cooldown, so I am quite relieved to find this orchard glowing with golden apples. Not only is it a nice nod to the round one creation myth, but it also signifies the end of our escort quest . . .

Because one of the fortifications holding up this realm's Stoneruned stronghold stands ready for destroying: another golden pillar.

"I guess it's time to test out our Excalibur Class Sword?" I ask.

"Let's do it fast," Britni replies. "I think we actually have a shot at surviving this round."

We still have no idea where the Divas and the Seasons are on this map. For all we know, they could have already finished before us and the Goats, since they can use the *Pillar Pair* within their own teams.

We gather before the pillar. As we do, the option to use our escorted weapon finally turns to full color on all our screens. Without hesitation, we each engage it.

Our assembled Excalibur Class Sword—now much more elaborately bejeweled, gilded, and glowing than the original—appears between us. Then this ornate blade slashes forward on its own, destroying the stone pillar in one profound strike.

So, yeah . . . the weapon works like a charm.

Next, a new energy bird emerges from this destroyed pillar. It's a yellowish-orange, dragonlike bird, one partially inspired by Babylon's Ishtar Gate dragon from the physical challenge. In fact, all three of these revelatory birds have reflected the physical challenge locations specifically. It's a nice way to once again merge the virtual with the physical realms.

This dragon-bird does not provide us with a speech bubble explanation, however. Instead, it turns and flies out of a gate that opens in the back of this lush, golden orchard. We automatically follow as the released bird flies up to a new peak . . .

Where TravelGee awaits, dressed in flowing robes and a pointy hat—to emulate the great wizard Merlin. I can hear Britni gasp with delight across the cubicle.

I can't blame her. As the released dragon-bird settles on TravelGee's robed shoulder, it's quite the mythical sight to behold.

"I am so pleased you've survived your heroic epic quest to join me here," TravelGee begins. "As you have just proven for yourselves, the Excalibur Class Swords you unearthed are strong enough to infiltrate the Stoneruned Horde Nerve Center.

"However, merely one sword won't be enough to defeat our fiercest foes in the heart of their stronghold. For that, we will require a Holy Trinity of Excalibur Classes, wielded by a Holy Trinity of Heroic Pantheons. This means that the three pantheons who have proven themselves most worthy today must form the final Knights of the Pantheonic Round Table, equipped with the Holy Grail Trinity Sword.

"The key to our ultimate victory will be how well this trinity works together as equals. I await word from the Pantheonic War Council about which teams I am cleared to transport to our final war frontier. But again, I applaud you for making it to this rare peak."

As TravelGee's speech bubbles finish, I feel awestruck. Obviously there are still new maps, moves, and mysteries to uncover in this final round. Now we can only hope we've done enough to be among the final trinity that gets to be there.

CHAPTER THIRTY-TWO

LATER THAT NIGHT, WE SIT OVER A FEAST OF KOREAN BAR-becue, buzzing over the results from round three. We've also watched the streaming coverage of everyone's gameplay and exit interviews, so there's much to discuss.

The results animation from earlier remains burned in my retinas, like lingering bright spots after glancing at the sun. I can practically still see the golden pillar revealing third place, right below the stone pillar memorializing the fourth-place elimination:

Fourth Place: Effing Divas

Third Place: One4All Seasons

Given how we were prepared for today's gaming to go—for us to be the team eliminated—these results still feel deeply surreal. The latest team cut was the Effing Divas.

"Most of me is happy the Seasons won out over the deceitful Divas," Mo speaks between forkfuls of kimchi. "But if we're sizing up our rivalries, the Seasons are going to be way harder to beat. They want the win and the prize to go pro pretty badly. And this new *Pillar Pair* ability is obviously big for them, being four Benders."

"Maybe," I pick up. "But we saw how the Divas attacked their 'allies' the Seasons the moment they realized they were in last place. Since it's looking like we're meant to find new ways to team up in the final round, I think it's a good thing we don't have to worry about those Divas."

"Plus TravelGee seemed to emphasize how the final three teams will battle as equals," Britni adds. "Who knows, maybe we'll all be graded on a curve or something for the final win?"

"Maybe. But we're also still facing the Mythic Goats, the odds-on favorite to win from the start," Mo counters.

"Yep, but guess who is no longer undefeated?" A grin widens across Alix's face as he speaks.

This brings me back to the best part of the results, the final gilded pillars:

Second Place: Mythic Goats

First Place: Epic Hearts

"Unseated from their throne, thanks to us!" Mo declares.

We may still have one round to go, but this still feels resoundingly like our victory dinner. Not only because we defied all the odds to make it to the final three—we did so by ranking *first*. We ended up finishing our escort quest just seconds before the Goats. Sure, we might have gotten there by working alongside this mighty team—but it's becoming clear that the capacity for cross-pantheon teamwork counts as a strength, not a weakness.

By embracing this strength—which was clearly the mythological moral of round three—we became the only team in this tournament to unseat the Goats from first place. If there was ever a way for the heroic poem of the Epic Hearts to be written into the Pantheonic Texts mythology, I can't think of a better one.

And as for my journal, I don't know if any entry will capture this day more elegantly than the round three badge I now proudly wear. I run my fingers over the enamel depiction of the yellowish-orange dragon-bird set against a stone pillar, feeling it practically course with power and meaning. I know that this badge will always represent so many things to me . . .

The time when we bested a top-ranked team in *Pantheonic*. When we decided to stop pressuring ourselves to win and enjoy the experience instead. When Britni, my dear new friend, helped me understand my chronic pain in the most unexpected way. When Mo, my other dear old friend, broke the wall between me and Alix. When I got to go on my first real date . . . with the potential first love of my life.

Now and forevermore, this badge will stand for all the things I care about most in one sacred symbol. It can remind me that the power I feel playing as K.Odyssia is also available to me in this physical realm as myself. I am infinitely capable of leaping into the things that scare me, letting go of old habits that no longer serve me, and opening up my interior life to learn things I never would have otherwise.

Because it turns out the safe and silent cave I built to avoid pain was much more like a gilded cage, trapping me in a cycle.

"I just have to say, whether we win or lose tomorrow," I begin, feeling quite stirred to speak, "right now I can't think of asking for anything more than what I have with all of you, here at this table. I'm so proud of us."

"Stop, you're going to make me cry," Mo replies.

"Too late," Britni says, wiping at her eyes with a napkin.

"You're so right, Keegan," Alix adds, squeezing my hand across the table.

He looks like he wants to say more, but he fights back some tears of his own. We all take a moment together to try to absorb how meaningful this experience has been. It feels like we've forged the kind of friendships here that will last our entire lives.

And Alix and I are standing at the start of something that could be just as beautiful.

"Not to shift gears from this magical, mushy moment," Mo then says, "but can we maybe take a second to daydream about the *possibility* we might win? I mean, I don't want to lay the pressure back on. But if today proved anything, it's that we *can* win."

Mo is right. Before today, it felt like a foregone conclusion we wouldn't win the entire tournament. Our only focus was surviving, then still thriving if we lost. But after today? Anything feels possible. And this does happen to be my final question intention: leading my teammates to victory—however that is now defined. And that includes the victory of this tournament experiment in general, to secure Dahlia's vision for our favorite game.

"You're right," I reply. "We'd be doing ourselves a disservice if we didn't go into tomorrow believing we are good enough to win. As long as we remember that winning isn't the only goal. We have to focus again on enjoying the experience, right?"

"Couldn't have said it better myself," Alix adds.

"Of course winning isn't everything," Britni follows up. "And I know money isn't everything either. But I think our *dreams* are everything. So let's aim for the big prize, knowing all the good we can do with it. But let's also remember that if we don't win, it doesn't mean our dreams are over."

"Can I get an omen?" Alix replies. "Listen, $200K each—or whatever that ends up being after taxes—would definitely give me the nest egg I need to focus on kick-starting my career as a fashion designer. But right now the exposure we've been getting within the *Pantheonic* community online feels important too. My social media following has grown a ton. And I have more DMs than I've had time to open, asking if I can design new avatar cosplay outfits. If I think it through properly, I might have a fashion-related business model right there."

"Hell yes, you do," Britni affirms. "And listen, I wasn't going to say anything, but yesterday people finally connected me as a gamer to my influencer account. All the new followers and messages from fellow closeted nerds coming through—I think I might actually be able to pivot my account away from LA model lifestyle stuff and into gaming and books instead. It's a risk, and I'd have to plan the transition very carefully. But this tournament might have been the spark I needed, even without winning the final prize. Though I certainly could use that money if I want to move to New York . . ."

"Oh my god!" Alix yells. "Are you really thinking of doing that?"

Britni nods, looking both sheepish and assured at the same time.

"I'd be leaving nothing behind in LA and gaining two friends here I love," Britni says. "Besides, NYC is as viable as LA in terms of influencing. If I can figure out how to afford it."

"My studio is a shoebox, but you're welcome to crash there as long as you need to get on your feet," Alix offers without a second thought.

Again, what a guy.

"I wish I could say the same, but I'll be living in an NYU dorm with a roommate," I sigh. "But I'll be here for you too."

"Yes! And thank you so much, Alix," Britni says, looking like she might very well take him up on his offer. "Plus, I'd be way closer to Mo in Annapolis. Which is important, because if I can pivot my account successfully to gaming and books and cosplay fashion, I'd want to use it to help promote Alix's designs and open Mo's store. Even if we need to start virtually, I can use my experience as an advisor and my platform as a signal boost."

Now it's Mo's turn to fight back tears. She looks struck speechless by Britni's show of support—and speechless is not usually Mo's vibe.

"Look at us, turning our virtual fortune into physical reality," Mo says. "We really are augmented reality queens. Who needs the powers that be to invest in us when we have each other?"

Looking around the table, my heart couldn't be fuller. This feels like the start of a beautiful partnership that extends outside—but also expands upon—our gaming synergy. And if we've learned anything, it's that this team can accomplish just about anything when we put our minds together.

At the same time, I've hardly been opening my socials, so I have no idea what's going on with my own following. It makes me grateful that my dreams remain on the quiet professor track—and that there are systems in place to get me there through my own hard work and my parents' connections. I don't necessarily need to engage in all this public-facing brand-building and entrepreneurial spirit. My dream is to have a cozy and stable life teaching others—but also to have love in my life. It finally feels like I'm firmly set upon that path. And how awesome is it to have cool friends who want to work together to create incredible things in the world?

But even as I settle into this familiar pattern, a new consideration tugs at me. What if my final intention for round four is to remain open to new lessons for the future? If I'm starting a bold new chapter in my life, maybe I should leave room for my dreams to evolve—just like my favorite game.

With this new thought in mind, I raise my glass. "To the Epic Hearts, the ultimate pantheon team."

Mo raises her own mug. "To the Epic Hearts, who could win it all."

Britni follows suit. "To the Epic Hearts, who fight together on every front."

Then it's Alix's turn. "To the Epic Hearts. As long as we stay together, there's no such thing as losing."

One more time, we toast together to our big night—and our even bigger tomorrow.

CHAPTER THIRTY-THREE

I STAND IN THE HOTEL ROOM BATHROOM GETTING READY for bed. Sleep feels both essential and impossible at the same time. I can't believe that, on top of everything else, tomorrow we will also finally solve the greatest mysteries of my beloved mythological game. The answers to more questions I've daydreamed about for years are about to be unearthed . . . by us.

Then, in my bleary state, something else pings in my brain. A brooding doubt I can't seem to avoid considering: What if the answers we reveal are somehow unsatisfying? What if the new era Dahlia is planning for *Pantheonic* isn't as good and ends up flopping? What if our own team disappoints in our performance as well?

Suddenly, a rocket of muscular pain accompanies these intrusive thoughts, clenching my body along with my brain. It's as awful a feeling as ever, aching through my hip and butt as usual.

But the good news?

Where I felt totally helpless before, I have now equipped upgrades to help me cope.

So I cut off this worry spiral before it can continue, telling myself these anxieties are *noted*—but unhelpful. Then I tell my brain that I don't need a pain response to these emotions, because I'll process and release them instead of suppressing them. There's no need to roll into that old vicious cycle anymore.

Now I understand this chronic pain isn't some foreign enemy—it's a part of me. There will likely be good days and bad days, flare-ups and remissions. I'm not "cured" because there was nothing wrong with me to begin with. Now I just have the understanding to appreciate my body—and take care of it the best way I know how, without shame or fear.

To help me feel better, I pull out my phone to connect outside my own head. As expected, I find two messages on it that make me smile.

> **MOM:** Your dad and I watched all the coverage today. We're so proud! Call us when you can.

Still smiling, I write back that I'll call first thing in the morning. Then I read the next message from my physical therapist.

> **CHRIS:** I can't wait to hear all about this magical mental cure you mentioned! Hoping you can teach me your ways so I can help anyone else with mysterious pain.

I smile even wider.

Yes, I think Professor Keegan will be able to arrange that.

I also haven't fully processed what my social media now looks like, after chancing a peek on the way home. The new followers are cool I guess—and I definitely had to ignore or block my fair share of toxicity. But what really touched me was seeing so many other queer *Pantheonic* gamers cheering us on. It didn't even occur to me that this was possible, but it seems the thousands of players have rallied around their most representative pantheons like local sports teams. And I guess in a way that's what we are, dropping into this esports-adjacent world—especially featuring that big ol' gay kiss with Alix.

I just hope we can keep doing all our fellow gamers—and *gaymers*—proud tomorrow.

Walking out of the bathroom, I get ready to settle into bed. And I delight in the notion that I won't have to writhe in silent agony anymore. But looking there, I am surprised to find something equally delightful waiting . . .

Alix, instead of Mo.

"Okay, hear me out," Alix begins, a devilish grin on his gorgeous face. "I know Mo was supposed to swap sleeping rooms again. But I think we have earned ourselves a night of making out and cuddling. That said, I will only stay if you agree to two key terms."

"I'm listening," I reply, crossing my arms over my chest and smirking back.

"One, nothing below the belt," Alix says. "When we go *there*, I want us both to be comfortable. I want it to be really . . . special."

I smile. Taking things step-by-step physically is a term I can most definitely agree to.

"Deal," I say. "The second term?"

Alix hesitates just a moment, biting his lower lip.

It makes me want to pounce on him.

"Two, you agree to be my boyfriend when you move here next month."

Alix's words crash through me like a meteor, streaking with cosmic light and setting my insides ablaze. Still, I do my best not to visibly react yet.

"I'm afraid I can't agree to that term," I reply, pausing for a moment. "I will only get in that big bed if you agree to be my boyfriend *right now.*"

Alix's face turns from disappointed to beguiled to elated in rapid succession.

"Done deal," he says. "Now get the Hel over here."

CHAPTER THIRTY-FOUR

THE FOURTH AND FINAL ROUND OF THIS MYTHICAL *Pantheonic* tournament begins in a blur. Maybe because of my adrenaline, it feels like reality is on fast-forward—like I'm watching it on a screen instead of experiencing it. Which is somewhat fitting for our final augmented reality physical challenge. Not ideal, but fitting.

Much like round three, round four begins with a very simple animation. First, it repeats our final mystery to solve: *What will happen to our competing pantheons should peace be restored—and what unknown home will the Stoneruned Horde be banished to?* Clearly, the only way to find out is to dethrone the Stoneruned Horde by winning the Pantheonic Stoneruned War. Which rolls rather nicely into announcing our final mythological trope, this time without any bells or whistles:

A great war.

Sadly, nearly every world mythology possesses some version of this. So instead of recounting them, the animation depicts our own realm-spanning great war. The seven archetypes are shown clashing against the Stoneruned Horde. Below this, the twenty-eight avatars of the seven tournament teams begin to rise. But they also fall away one by one, until only the Mythic Goats, One4All Seasons, and Epic Hearts remain.

Seeing our avatars animated and immortalized again this way . . . it gets my heart beating double time, which I didn't think was physically possible. I barely have time to register this surreal sight or relish it with my teammates before the fast-forwarding feeling continues.

The theme of our final meeting room is inspired by ancient Mesoamerica. We stand before three shed-sized pyramids, each topped with a pillared temple and containing nine stair-like levels—likely representing the nine levels of the underworld believed in by both the Mayans and the Aztecs. Which makes sense, given our final challenge in this physical realm . . .

To complete nine levels in three identically outfitted underworld escape rooms.

My brain buzzes with questions about how this relates to our own *Pantheonic* UndeRealm, or to our great war trope. But I have no time to process these thoughts as our teams are separated to enter the escape room pyramids.

It still feels like I'm living in a dream state when we enter our escape room. The fact that we are promptly locked inside—with a safe phrase for emergency exit—does nothing to ease my racing nerves. Finishing a big cup of coffee before this round now feels like a huge mistake. I want to luxuriate in this experience, but my body feels intent on surging instead.

As the start buzzer sounds, I try to focus on our challenge goal: working together to unearth the key to our escape, which will also bear the final virtual gaming hub code. Before we entered, I expected to find our pyramid escape room filled with tasks inspired by the infamous Mayan and Aztec deities who escaped the nine underworld levels. However, I am thrilled to find the levels of our underworld escape room will take us on another tour across world mythology.

Each set of levels is sprawled across three walls, with one final wall holding the exit door. It will take three tokens—unlocked from three challenge walls, each holding three levels—to unearth our escape key. That's a whole lot of trinity energy we're dealing in.

"Should we split up to work on the walls?" Britni asks.

"No, the instructions say we need the token from wall one to access wall two," Mo replies. "We have to go level by level."

So that's what we start doing.

I wish it didn't feel like I was underwater, experiencing this challenge through a thin film. Even the others' voices sound muted. I'm obviously having some kind of heightened physical reaction to this final round. But instead of panicking, I try to focus all this energy into the escape room tasks before us.

Level One requires us to escape the Slavic underworld, which is represented as the tangled roots of a world oak tree. Their god of the underworld, Veles the dragon serpent, is coiled among these roots in rope form. We have to undo the braided ropes under a raised sculpture of the world oak until all brown strands are separated from the green. Once this is done, the brown-rooted rope becomes long enough to reach an acrylic lockbox near the floor. Using the key attached to this undone rope, we access the next challenge.

Level Two requires us to escape the Japanese underworld of Yomi, which is ruled by the goddess Izanami. She descended to Yomi after being badly burned giving birth to fire. So on a tablet attached to the wall, we have to complete a *Temple Run*-style mini game where we all sprint to evade various fireballs. Once this course is complete, the tablet gives us a code to open a locker embedded in the wall for our next challenge.

Level Three requires us to escape the Chinese-Buddhist underworld, presided over by Yama, the king and judge of the dead. Inside the locker we find four human-shaped flat metallic "coins" that need to be inserted into a slot in the correct order. Each coin is numbered and shaded a different color, but we notice each also seems to represent an eliminated tournament team. So we decide to insert them in placement order.

Once we do, a plastic bubble rolls out of a slot, like from a grocery store toy machine. Opening it up, we find a golden token—with a red firebird on it. If I were feeling more myself, I'd probably note how our first wall token references round one's freed bird aspect. Or how all three of these initial underworlds reference the world mythologies that inspired round one, adding in another from the same general continental area. But I'm not feeling like myself, so those thoughts slip through my mind like sand through fingertips.

Except, I *did* still make these observations—so a new thought occurs to me. Maybe this isn't me in a state of panic . . .

Maybe this is me totally in the zone as a competitor?

What do athletes call it—flow state?

Deciding to embrace the flow instead of forcing anything, I follow as our team uses the firebird token to access the second wall. Once placed in a decorative slot facing out, a closet door in this next wall opens.

Level Four requires us to escape the Egyptian underworld, this time by entering a closet-sized tomb. Inside we must properly prepare a mummified doll to meet Osiris by reuniting its ka with its ba. This means searching around the floor of this dark room to find a replica of the headdress from the round two scavenger hunt. Once we find it, we exit the closet and place the headdress into a slot atop a clear bin, unlocking the lid.

Level Five requires us to escape the Hindu-Indian underworld of Patala, ruled by Vasuki, king of serpents. Patala is said to be filled with splendorous jewels and lovely lakes, so we must root through a bin of plastic gemstones to find the Vasuki crown jewel. Once we do, depositing this gemstone in a slot uncovers a new puzzle in the wall.

Level Six requires us to escape the Mesopotamian underworld, ruled over by Ereshkigal, the goddess of darkness and twin sister to Inanna. There are two near-identical depictions of the twins on this puzzle portrait, and we must point out nine key differences. Once these details are removed from the puzzle, it reveals a code. We use it to unclip the next token from a typical bike lock.

Then we place this second token—depicting a green hawk—to access our third and final wall.

Level Seven requires us to escape the Norse underworld, ruled over by Hel—my very own chosen deity to curse in vain. Hel is depicted on a mural with her usual beautiful face and rotting body. We need to click open little doors on this body to find a miniaturized representation of Hel's crown. Once we do, we discover it is also a laser pointer. We must then use this to point at a trigger spot near the top of the wall, which is trickier than we expect. Once we get the angle just right, a curtain drops to reveal another mural.

Level Eight requires us to escape the Greek underworld, ruled over by Hades. Though it's his partner, Hecate, the queen of ghosts, who we'll need to rely on. This mural has dozens of spirits following Hecate, and we need to *Where's Waldo* search for the one holding a moon—since Hecate is also a moon goddess.

That's when I feel Alix's hand on my shoulder again, firm and warm as always. I turn to him and we lock eyes. Staring back into his face, with this moon sign now before us . . .

It's like I finally sink back down into my body. I feel time catching up with me, like some internal video has finally finished buffering.

Alix nods at me, and I nod back.

Hel, is he always going to have this effect on me, either calming me down or exciting me? It's a thought that's as enticing as it is terrifying—for someone else to have that kind of power over me. Especially since it's power I don't always even seem to have over myself.

Still, I let the grounded feeling take root as we unveil the final level.

"Of course the ninth level is the Aztec underworld," I speak out loud, for the first time since we started. "Its deepest layer was believed to be ruled by Mictlantecuhtli, the father of Quetzalcoatl."

"And there our fearless leader is!" Mo replies. "I thought we lost you to zombie mode for a moment."

"I'm good," I say. "Was just in a bit of an overfocused daze. What do we need to do?"

"Actually, I think we're done," Britni says, opening this final Aztec chest using the Hecate moon code.

This chest, of course, also has a yellowish-orange dragon-bird token on its seal. Britni reaches inside and turns to us, holding up a key . . .

One that is ornately shaped with a depiction of Quetzalcoatl, the plumed serpent. This Aztec snake-bird once famously escaped the underworld—and now it will help us do the same.

At least, that's what I think when we run to the exit door in wall four. Britni inserts and turns the key, but instead of opening the door . . .

A large screen on this wall lights up. On it, another animation begins to play. We all gather to watch.

This animation shows the horizontal row of earths we are used to seeing, a representation of the multiverse of alternate realm dimensions stacked beside one another. The three energy bird aspects of the Source Wing we released during this tournament begin to fly around the stacks, streaking red and green and yellowish-orange. Their flights tilt our perspective, turning the horizontal earth realms into a *vertical* stack. Then the birds all converge—and fly directly out toward us.

As the birds swoosh out of sight, the scope of our view onscreen also begins to push back and expand. We can see more and more of the now-vertical stack of earth realms, which as far as we've been told stretches on forever. However, we've never been shown this much of the multiversal stack before, as our view of realms goes from hundreds to thousands rather quickly. As it does, a portion of the stack begins to glow with the prism-refracted light of the Source Wing. A name appears beside this portion of the stack:

The Human Wing.

Then, directly below this glowing wing, a new portion begins to reveal itself. This section of the earth realm stack glows with grayish-brown light, feeling watery like the depths of the ocean. And this section suddenly takes on a new name:

The Stoneruned Depths.

My mouth drops open.

Part of our final mystery has just been solved by the *Pantheonic* powers that be. *What unknown home will the Stoneruned Horde be banished to?*

It turns out this unknown home can be found in an entirely different section of alternate earth realms—one directly below our own set of human-dominated worlds.

From a set of literal *underworlds.*

CHAPTER THIRTY-FIVE

I STILL FEEL BREATHLESS MINUTES LATER, EVEN AS THE EPIC Hearts have taken our seats in the gaming cube. Once the final revelatory animation ended, the exit door to the escape room clicked open. We grabbed our Quetzalcoatl key, which contained our last gaming hub entry code, and made our way in here.

The Stoneruned Horde comes from a different section of earth realms, the Depths beneath our Wing.

This revelation spins off so many additional questions. Does this mean their under-section of realms represents a more divergent set of earths, one where the Stoneruned evolved to become the dominant species instead of humans? If so, it sets a precedent that other, even more divergent earth realm portions with different dominant species should also exist. Plus, if the Source Wing only enlightens our own human-centric section, does that mean there other prime sources out there?

And even though we now know where the Stoneruned Horde comes from, we still don't know *why* they came to our section. Could it be as simple as colonization conquering, or are there deeper motivations yet to be discovered?

I suppose that's what we've been assembled to learn next.

Right now, our Epic Hearts avatars stand on a floating platform high above Mount Pantheonic. We're not sure exactly why we're here, but I try to enjoy the view all the same. The seven city sectors bristle below with divine life, and I can even spot our unofficial team fountain in Creature Town. When we checked on it during our team practice sessions, we found our fountain had become a place for our fellow deity fans to meet and cheer us on. It's another nice little footprint we've left on *Pantheonic* for now.

Soon after we arrive, the One4All Seasons appear on an identical platform. But after a few minutes, it's still just us.

"I know it's only been a minute or two," Alix finally says, "but we're probably waiting for the Mythic Goats to finish their escape room, right?"

"I think so," Mo replies. "Which means this last round must not be a race like the others. I bet they'll grade our overall performances so they can do an extra-suspenseful final ceremony."

"And probably to encourage us to work together?" I add.

Our time to ponder ends as a third platform suddenly appears, populating with the Mythic Goats. Then it's only a few seconds before we all begin to fade out—and reappear in the now-familiar tournament column gate hall. There's no sign of UnderTee again, so we all walk through the portal gate like last time.

We emerge into another new earth realm map—the one we've already been told is named Techno Classic. We enter what feels like the ruins of an ancient Greek temple, at least at first glance. We stand among crumbling columns and pillars, but each reveals frayed wiring and circuitry inside. The sky is a brilliant blue, but a shade so vivid it seems artificial. It does feel fitting, though—this iconic setting where the mythological meets the technological.

It also feels fitting we've reached a realm where Alix probably feels most at home, since his whole fashion identity is future-meets-classic. I give him a quick wink and elevator eyes, noting this. He winks back at me, not needing to speak a word to understand.

Our collective attention is then drawn as UnderTee appears before us in this circuitry coliseum. I resist the urge to react out loud seeing that she is dressed up in an outfit serving Hermes meets Charon—a cross between the Greek messenger deity and its own underworld usher. But I also react because UnderTee is joined by TravelGee, dressed in a matching outfit. Come to think of it, we rarely get to see these NPCs together in the game. Knowing now that they're kind of like our divine ancestors, it's a surprisingly moving sight.

UnderTee steps forward first to start our debriefing.

"Oh, it's you again. Not the Knights of the Pantheonic Round Table I'd have chosen, but . . . I kid! For once, I'll give you deity ditties some kudos. You've overcome quite a bit to be here, so we are proud to send you into battle. I don't expect many of you to survive, but I'm proud nonetheless! Take it or lump it.

"Now, your final quest in this war is clear. You must battle as one force across this Techno Classic realm ravaged by the very first Stoneruned occupation. Your goal? Work together to reach the Parsenon, where you will face the most menacing boss yet . . .

"The One True RunedGod, who guards the Source Wing.

"Now I'm afraid that, in this specially protected earth, I don't have access to the UndeRealm—my best costume for the day notwithstanding. If any of you deities require rebirth, I will be able to bring you back—just not here to this particular realm.

"Clocking this, my bestie, TravelGee, and I have used our divine orchard to craft something special—a super-rare, one-time bushel of items for our Holy Trinity of pantheons. Not only will these organic yummies bring each of you to the same max level, they will also grant you four rebirths before being banished to the UndeRealm."

UnderTee pauses as she gifts each player an identical item: an apple-shaped pendant adorned with symbols for the earth, sky, sun, and moon. Of course, it feels fitting to see one final crescent moon appear at the end of this experience. It reminds me of the person who gave me the strength to start this journey in the first place. Sure, that strength might have always been my own, but it was also boosted by Annie's memory.

Feeling this, I find Alix's eyes once again. Because it's quite nice to always have a new sun shining right beside this old, familiar moon.

"Once you—hopefully—reach the Parsenon, facing this ultimate RunedGod threat will require our Holy Trinity of pantheons working together to weaken this monotheistic monolith. Then, when the critical moment comes, you must combine your Excaliburs into the Trinity Sword for one final strike. And if that isn't motivation enough for you glory mongers . . .

"Should you succeed, the single pantheon who is deemed most vital during this final quest will be written into the

Pantheonic Texts as the mightiest team of the Pantheonic Stoneruned War. If you should succeed in this final quest, you will all uncover the secrets that have eluded the War Council and the Pantheonic Pillars from the dawn of this conflict.

"So do me a favor? Don't muck it up. After all, our worlds are watching."

Inside our gaming cube, my eyes shift to connect with Mo's. This confirms our theory that the tournament's final three rankings—and its big winner—will be determined by our performances across this entire final round, not simply who finishes the fastest.

TravelGee then steps up to deliver one final message:

"I shall meet you at the base of the Parsenon mountain to escort you to its peak. As always, we *believe* in you."

As both of our divine ushers finish our final debrief, I feel the adrenaline surge back into my body. But unlike before, I now feel grounded enough to harness it. And despite feeling a shot of pain in my piriformis, I now know enough to acknowledge and dismiss it.

It's time to embark upon the honor of our gaming lifetime.

And I can think of only one way to get us moving.

"Remember our code," I say, pivoting in person to look at each one of my teammates. "Battle efficiency and Horde kills always win the day. We don't aggravate our fellow deities, but we will defend ourselves to the death should any seek provocation!"

Finishing our usual battle cry, I smile as Mo, Britni, and Alix all pump their fists in the air inside our gaming cube.

The moment UnderTee and TravelGee fade from sight, two things happen. First, several Stoneruned battalions begin to close in from every direction. Second, an inter-team chat invitation appears—one I quickly accept.

ODINZEUS: Made a chat for just the three leaders, so we can coordinate cleanly.

LUMINUSHUE: Smart.

K.ODYSSIA: Agreed.

ODINZEUS: I'm gonna scout forward to see what we're up against.

K.ODYSSIA: I'll ask our Creature tank to do the same.

"Britni, can you scout out to test the environmental Stoneruned with—"

Before I can finish, we all witness exactly what we're up against in this new earth realm. An environmental Stoneruned hardwires itself to a nearby column and downloads an electrical upgrade—one it promptly unloads to electrocute Odinzeus, plummeting his health bar down to just about zero. All around us, similar Stoneruned start to buzz with techno-chainsaws or crackle with wire whips. Which means these techno-environmental Stoneruned are going to be stronger and more unpredictable than any we've ever encountered before.

The only reason we aren't immediately overrun, suffering the same near-death fate as Odinzeus, is because the One4All Seasons spring into action. Without hesitation, they trigger the *Pillar Pair* abilities between the two Bender pairs on their team.

The standard move looks just like it did between Apollix and Thorares—one deity turning into energy for the other to attack-cast with. The first pair to do so from the Seasons is AeroWynd, a wind Bender visually themed after the Aquarius flowing jug, and BobbyUndying, an earth Bender visually themed after the Capricorn goat. Not literally, though, since both look more like sorcerers adorned with unique accents that nod to their secondary specializations in Reaper healing and Trickster fighting.

The second pair is J0J0, a water Bender themed after the Scorpio scorpion, and LuminusHue, a fire Bender themed after the Sagittarius archer. These two specialize in Trickster fighting and Traverser travel, and both look like genderqueer sorcerers, making the entire team feel even more like a cohesive unit.

Witnessing the Seasons' quick instincts, it's clear why they have made it to the finals with us. Even though we didn't actively lean into our proposed rivalry with them, the fans following the tournament have been rooting for them just as hard given their neurodivergent gamer status, unique single-pillar composition, and pro esports aspirations.

Thanks to the Seasons' counterattack, enough space is cleared that we aren't immediately besieged by battalions. It probably helps that their levels—along with our own—have been temporarily raised to match the Goats. The Seasons may have bought us a few seconds, but we'd better start mounting a wicked counteroffensive. Quickly.

Because it's clear we're in for the toughest Stoneruned battalion run to ever exist.

CHAPTER THIRTY-SIX

BY THE TIME WE REACH THE BASE OF THE MOUNTAIN THAT holds the Parsenon peak, we've been run ragged. All three teams managed to make it here intact, but we're down lots of rebirths. Plus, all of our abilities have been used and need to recharge.

"How are we going to face the strongest boss there is in this shape?" Alix asks.

"TravelGee is supposed to meet us here," Mo replies. "Maybe they will have something extra special for us kiddos? Pretty please?"

"Let's hope so," I say, nerves rattling in my system. It would be pretty embarrassing for all three of our teams to be wiped out at this final boss battle, losing this great war for everyone watching and rooting us on.

"Look, over there," Britni says, pivoting Chiroptera.

Just ahead, the stone gate to a mountain path begins to glow. As we approach, the glow shakes loose and takes the form of another energy bird aspect. As expected, this final aspect of the

Source Wing is a blue serpent-bird, inspired by Quetzalcoatl from our physical challenge. However, this final bird does not offer us any speech prompts. Instead, just like last round's dragon-bird, it flies toward the mountain path beyond . . .

Where it once again settles on the shoulder of TravelGee.

"I knew you'd make it here. But we also knew your battle would be hard-fought. So before I escort you up to the Parsenon peak, please consume the potions hidden in your pendants."

As TravelGee finishes, a new item appears in our inventories—replicating the elemental apple pendants UnderTee and TravelGee made for us. All around, we open the secret lids on our pendants and drink the potion contents. Once the last drop is finished, my health is restored to full, and all my abilities are recharged.

Thank you very much, fruits of the Divine Realm orchard.

"I'm fully reset," Mo shares. "But I didn't get any new rebirths."

A quick round confirms this is the same for everyone. Which means that while our strength is restored, we're going to have to make do with whatever lives we have left.

"The time has come for the final battle to commence. I believe in you, our Holy Trinity."

With that, TravelGee spreads their wings to create one final portal gate . . .

Which deposits us at the Parsenon peak of this final Techno Classic realm mountain.

I expect a grander version of our usual boss-level steepled spires, but instead our setting is shockingly simple. We stand in a large open-air courtyard—an arena, really. Pillars of familiar stone and gold line the perimeter, splayed with circuits and frayed with wires. Scrawled across the pillar faces are ones, zeroes, dashes, and brackets—illuminated code runes.

Something about this arena instantly feels vast and intimidating. Like we've come to the place where the earth meets the sky, where the mythological meets the technological . . .

Where the Source Wing meets the One True RunedGod.

I also still somehow expected the Source Wing to be kept in some kind of cage. Instead, it just floats beyond the arena courtyard, settled atop a set of crumbling stairs. The Source Wing looks like the large energy bird we are used to seeing, but also somehow different "in person." Every color courses through its energy form all at once, like it is a being made purely of light—or maybe even of thoughts and feelings, like a collective consciousness.

It's clearly true that the Source Wing remains here of its free will, uncaged—and bound instead by whatever the Stoneruned Horde stole. Or perhaps the Source Wing is uncaged because, at the base of the steps, the One True RunedGod stands guard.

The RunedGod is smaller than the imbued bosses we're used to facing. It stands only slightly taller than the average automaton, but its stone-stacked body glows with multicolored light between its seams. And it has a singular rune glowing in its chest: the alpha symbol.

"Is it just me, or is there actually something . . . similar about the Source Wing and the One True RunedGod?" Britni asks. "Not in their appearances, but in their . . . vibes?"

"I totally get what you mean," I reply. "Like, is the One True RunedGod meant to be a sourcing entity like the Source Wing? Or is it just the strongest deity of the Stoneruned Horde, like our own trinity of pantheons?"

Either way, there's an eerie sense of calm on this mountain peak, a kind of . . . understanding that feels settled between the Source Wing and the One True RunedGod. A new thought then strikes me like a thunderclap.

Could it be possible that the invaluable thing the One True RunedGod stole from the Source Wing is its . . . heart?

"Okay, my beautiful literary minds, time to focus," Mo says. "That boss is gearing up."

Sure enough, the One True RunedGod speaks the phrase all bosses eventually utter:

"YOU WILL FALL UNDER OUR SINGULAR MIGHT, FALSE GODS."

Here we go.

We coordinate attack after attack.

We dodge powerful beams of focused elemental energy, which the One True RunedGod can fire from its alpha rune.

We lose more rebirths, eventually bringing each of us down to our last lives.

We execute every *Pillar Pair* we have between six Benders, two Rulers, and two Tricksters.

We time our ultimate abilities to smash the RunedGod in precise succession.

And yet . . .

None of it has been enough to knock the RunedGod down to critical health, where it must be for us to activate our final *Trinity Sword* finisher.

"What are we supposed to do now?" Mo asks, sounding frayed herself. "This thing is too strong for us, even with maxed levels."

"I guess we have to just stay alive long enough for our abilities to restore?" I reply, barely able to convince myself this is possible.

"I don't think most of us will survive that long," Britni admits. "Between the RunedGod's short-range fist strength and the accuracy of those blasts, there's nowhere to hide."

"Do the other teams have any ideas?" Alix asks.

Glancing at the leader chat, everyone there seems just as exasperated. We're running out of options as quickly as we're running out of lives. We need something big to knock the RunedGod down one last health peg . . . but we're out of big moves.

At least that's what I think until Freyjathena lands a very heavy axe blow, rolling under a force beam with expert precision. As the RunedGod's health bar drops from green to yellow—*finally*—something happens on my screen.

The apple pendant icon, which was grayed out after we consumed our potions, suddenly becomes available again—but this time in our abilities list. When I hover over it, a new name appears:

Pantheon Primer.

"Is everyone else seeing this?" Mo asks before I can speak. "I was starting to lose hope there'd be any new eleventh hour abilities, but . . ."

"Oh my goddess, is that what I think it is?" Britni adds.

"If you think it sounds like a new team combo, I'm right there with you," Alix replies.

"The other teams have the same new ability," I relay, glancing at the leader chat. "And we're all going to try it at the same time. After the next RunedGod blast, we gather at that right pillar marked with the bracket rune. Once everyone is there, we engage. Got it?"

"I don't know if I'm more nervous or excited," Mo responds. "But got it."

"Copy that," Britni adds. "Time to end this."

"Can I get an omen?" Alix quips one last time . . .

Then our moment arrives. Once the RunedGod rattles off another elemental force beam—one that Apollix and AeroWynd both just narrowly manage to dodge in midair—all three pantheons rush to the designated pillar. Once there, we seize the tiny window of opportunity we have as the RunedGod turns its heavy body.

"Now!" I shout, as all the leaders give their go-ahead.

I engage the *Pantheon Primer* pendant ability.

And I hold my breath.

As the move engages, it becomes clear what *Pantheon Primer* really means: all four members of a team engaging in one super combo. Our three teams break apart in a row, executing the same sequence simultaneously and separately.

Three shining orbs appear before each team, coursing with the same rainbow-streaming energy as the Source Wing. Then, one by one, we begin jumping into these orbs . . .

Until all that remains are three glowing masses, three super-dense stars shining down on the RunedGod.

Then the orbs burst apart in a dazzling display of explosive light.

The Epic Hearts drop to the ground encased in shimmering, translucent armor. I know this is happening to the other teams as well, but now my full focus stays on the divinely charged visage of K.Odyssia. Standing in line with Apollix, sMOte, and Chiroptera, we look like the brightest and most badass pantheon to ever live.

Then we all streak forward like godly comets, a deadly blur of pantheon force . . .

That smashes into the One True RunedGod like a meteor, like a hammer, like a bolt of lightning, like . . .

Divine intervention.

For a moment, everything washes with blinding and brilliant light.

When it clears, only a misty haze lingers, settling down across the Parsenon like smoke. This reveals all our pantheons standing as we were before, except now with the *Pantheon Primer* ability grayed out.

My eyes dart to the RunedGod. I am very dismayed to find it still standing . . .

Until I see that its health bar has finally dropped into the critical red.

K.ODYSSIA: Sword time!

LUMINUSHUE: Trinity move!

ODINZEUS: This is it!

All three messages send at once.

And then all three teams act as one yet again, for hopefully this last time.

That's when it occurs to me—not for one single second did it seem that our final three teams might sabotage each other for solo glory. Somehow, we all believed we needed to work together for any of us to be able to win. Given these new game-changing abilities, we were right. If the mission statement of *Pantheonic* is to bring people together from different worlds, across physical and virtual space . . .

It has certainly succeeded in that, especially here in this tournament.

The Trinity Sword assembly is a very straightforward process. We all look to the sky as our collective ultimate weapons combine—a three-pronged blade, tripled in size and three times as ornate. For several shining seconds, it also glows with the same spectrum of light as the Source Wing . . .

Before the Trinity Sword shoots forward to pierce the alpha heart of the One True RunedGod.

And with that . . .

The RunedGod finally falls.

The Source Wing will soon be freed.

The war is over.

I expect to feel pure elation and satisfaction. Instead, I suddenly experience a . . . bittersweet flood of emotions. Which makes sense. No one likes when things end, even if that ending is hard-earned and triumphant. Looking from Mo to Britni to Alix, I can tell they're all feeling exactly the same way. But it's Mo who speaks first.

"Congratulations, you bunch of winners. But this isn't over yet."

She is right. We may have just beaten our ultimate foe, but victory isn't our only reward. We are still due so many mythological answers—and to see how the final rankings fall. After all, it's not just the grand prize and title still on the line.

It's also the very future of our beloved game.

CHAPTER THIRTY-SEVEN

ONCE THE ONE TRUE RUNEDGOD FALLS ONSCREEN, I EXPECT it to crumble apart into the usual pile of stones. And it does . . .

Except no energy bird aspect emerges, as we are used to seeing. Instead, something entirely different happens. The leftover RunedGod *stones* become light . . .

And float to become one with the Source Wing, absorbing into the depths of its infinite being.

Once this happens, a beam of projection emanates from the Source Wing's eyes. It feels like some kind of translation system, a way to communicate its multi-realm insights in a way our semi-mortal minds will comprehend.

My stomach flips over.

This is it—the answers we've been waiting years to hear are about to be provided by the Source Wing itself. I go to turn to the others, until I realize they've already gathered around my monitor. I exhale, happy to know whatever we've earned next, we'll experience it together.

"My pantheons, We thank you for climbing to this perilous peak. For reaching this sacred summit, you have earned the right to learn a truth We have known from the dark dawn of this war."

The Source Wing's voice sounds harmonic, like a choir speaks each word in a heavenly reverberating chord.

"The Stoneruned Horde did indeed invade Our earth realm portion from its own divergent section. The existence of these sections was beyond even Our knowledge before this incursion. It . . . startled Us, in Our understanding of the way of all realms.

"But why did the Stoneruned Horde embark upon this treacherous travel to begin with?

"Because their own Source Depth has been corrupted and monopolized by a foul conglomerate, bottomless in its greed. The Stoneruned found the means to cross realm section divides out of dire need—as refugees. The moment the Stoneruned crossed Our border, they began drawing from Our source, as is the right of all life under Our Wing.

"But this unprecedented sourcing, at first, proved incompatible. The Stoneruned reverted to simpler versions of their once-evolved state in order to adjust to Our sourcing. This reduced them to automatons in a state of pure fear, fleeing their own conquerors. To self-protect, they also resorted to the same base instinct to conquer, perpetuating the vicious cycle that stole their home and corrupted their source. The Stoneruned Horde, led by their singular RunedGod pantheon, set out to spread and build as strong a refuge as they could.

"For one reality remained clear . . . If the Stoneruned refugees could find a way to traverse realm section boundaries, so eventually could the foul conglomerate seeking to monopolize all life. Armed with this terrible knowledge, We understood three holy truths. First, a defense must be mounted. Second, the Stoneruned Horde needed time to adjust and evolve. And third, Our own realms needed to grow much mightier.

"So We, the Source Wing, were justly robbed of Our most precious thing . . . Our sense of peace. Thus, We willingly came here to the Stoneruned Nerve Center to help them evolve more rapidly. Then We allowed the Pantheonic Stoneruned War to begin to strengthen and unify the countless inter-warring pantheons of Our own realms. We allowed the creation and drama and heroic challenges of a great war to prepare all We hold dear for what comes next:

"An even unholier war, between the core forces of peaceful source and ravenous greed.

"Now We have fostered a divine alliance We hope will prove capable of facing the mysterious, ungodly monopoly gathering in the distance. Forever and always, this mountain you've been climbing remains a grain of sand in the face of what's to come. However, reaching any peak is still a feat worthy of worship."

As the Source Wing's revelatory speech draws to a close, there is only one thing to do.

I look back at Alix, who returns my look of awestruck reverence. Our conversation—the one where we broke through to each other in person—floods back into my mind. About being spiritual beings dropped into physical bodies to learn through struggle and connection. About universal signs helping us along the way. About how nothing is what it seems when it comes to victory and hardship and good and evil. About how everything is a matter of perspective, like the elusive and ever-changing crescent moon.

Our perspectives—and the stories we tell ourselves—are so often limited by what we see. And as a result, sometimes the pain and struggle and trials we face are also of our own creation. Especially when we play great games, which always tend to teach us something . . .

I think back to Dahlia's opening question at the invitation event, asking why humans are drawn to games in general. And my mind races to put these new pieces together.

The Stoneruned Horde isn't evil—they're frightened refugees adjusting to a foreign land.

They aren't some kind of mindless hivemind—they just need time to return to their higher selves after a chaotic change.

And this great war wasn't a curse—it was a challenge to prepare us for what comes next.

Part of me is angry we didn't know all this from the start. Couldn't we, the pantheon players, have been trusted to do the right thing, to strengthen and unite ourselves without all this conflict? Then I think about Britni and her magical pain-changing book and how I never would have believed in it a year ago without experiencing all I did. I might not have *deserved* that pain . . . but I suppose the human spirit proves that good can come from anywhere, if we're willing to look for it. And some battles need to be fought to help us evolve.

Alix blinks back wordless tears. So do I.

If all this subtext has been baked into *Pantheonic* from the very start . . .

No wonder we were both drawn to this game.

Before I can summon any words, something shifts onscreen. The Source Wing returns the imbued stones of the

RunedGod. From them, four new bodies are built before our eyes.

Then the Source Wing speaks again.

"In their humbling defeat, the Stoneruned Horde will come to grow beyond their base urge to conquer. They will be gifted new earth realms to inhabit and expand across, now fueled by Our source. In short, they will become part of Our worlds, together and apart."

Then something especially beautiful happens.

The four forms don't become human, nor do they merge into one being. Instead, they each *evolve* before our eyes. Their seams seal and their runes brighten. Then the notion of One True RunedGod splits into a new pantheon, one that still reflects its worshippers and serves the same source.

A source which, if monopolized, turns you into the evil you fear most.

A new pillar then emerges between these four new deities. They all bow their heads in ceremonial prayer, shifting the light in their animating runes. Then their eyes shine with a renewed self-awareness, taking on pupils and irises instead of just one glowing hue.

The Stoneruned automatons haven't been inhabited by mindless animating energy like we always thought. All along they've been inhabited by some kind of spiritual consciousness—by *souls*. And now those souls shine with a brand-new symbol above each of their heads:

A seal of Stone and Rune.

As this new pantheon stands beside its pillar, the Source Wing has one last say in the matter.

"Behold the Challenger Pillar, made of titans, centurions, and the ritualistic. Archetypal of the environmental trait, they will oversee their Stoneruned realms from the soon-to-be-added Challenger Square of Mount Pantheonic. As the era of the Pantheonic Stoneruned War ends, the age of the Eight Pillars begins . . .

"Along with the dark dawn of the Pantheonic Ravenous Crusade."

CHAPTER THIRTY-EIGHT

WE GATHER ONE LAST TIME BACK IN THE PHYSICAL Revelatory Shrine. We have already learned so much—enough layered mythological lore that it will likely take me weeks to unpack and process it all. But first, there are still two questions that remain unanswered.

What comes next for the game—and which team has won?

To answer both of these questions, Dahlia has once again taken the stage to address the *Pantheonic* legions. Behind her onscreen, the revelations of the Source Wing have already been etched into the animated stone of the Pantheonic Texts. Much like how the final three teams proudly wear our round four badges that depict the blue snake-bird set against a pillar of stone, a pairing that now takes on a whole new meaning post-war. Only twelve gamers on the entire planet possess this complete set of four badges—and we stand among them.

I try to remember what a win that is as Dahlia begins her final speech.

"You have all battled long and hard, so I will not take up too much more of your precious time. I must say this first—*thank you*. Thank you for your energy, your attention, your community, and your spirit. *Pantheonic* was made lovingly by many hands, but it only breathes life thanks to the efforts of you, our mighty players. And you players must be wondering what we developers have created for you next. As always, the answers will be revealed in time. But you already possess so many of the clues.

"You've glimpsed the base *Pillar Pair* and *Pantheon Prime* abilities—now prepare to master them. You've seen how powerful combo moves can be with your own kind—now prepare to someday cross pillars and pantheons. You've witnessed the birth of our eighth pillar—now prepare to harness the Challenger environmental titan trait. You've turned sworn enemies into close allies—now prepare to battle against an even more terrifying, ravenous army. You've valiantly defended the earth realms of our own section—now prepare to launch incursions into the unknown underworld depths. You've watched our evolutions into augmented reality gaming in this tournament—now prepare to have this experience extended at home.

"For now more than ever before, the new era of *Pantheonic* aims to bring players together across all realms, physical and virtual."

Dahlia's speech comes to a close, but I instantly want her to say more.

At least until I turn to Mo, as I always do at times like these. And her bright expression says it all: *We're going to have so much fun exploring this new mythology.*

I smile at Mo. And Britni. And finally Alix.

This tournament might be ready to end, but the Epic Hearts are just getting started writing our names in the history books.

And I think it's safe to say we've all done enough to make this tournament experiment a smashing success—and ensure that Dahlia's next era has also been secured.

"Now the time has come to reveal the final rankings in our grand tournament—hopefully the first of many," Dahlia continues, drawing all attention back to the stage.

Behind her, three pillars animate across the screen. Two are made of stone, while one remains gilded—the pillar belonging to the champion pantheon of this tournament.

First, the blue snake-bird flies across the top stone pillar, revealing . . .

Third Place: Mythic Goats

That's . . . definitely a shocking upset.

Then again, given the way these last two rounds went, it's not as shocking as it would have been before. With the playing field leveled, any one of us final three truly had a shot to win. Still, it's the spot where I expected our own team to finish.

I can't help but hold my breath for what comes next.

Reaching out, I also grasp the hands of Mo and Alix beside me, and Alix in turn grasps Britni's hand.

Whatever the outcome is, we will accept it together.

Second Place: Epic Hearts

CHAMPIONS: One4All Seasons

Cheers erupt from across the Revelatory Shrine.

I expect to feel some disappointment, but I find that's nowhere near what I experience. Instead, as I squeeze Mo and Alix's hands and they squeeze back, I feel something entirely different.

Pride at having come so far.

Justice for another underdog pantheon taking the ultimate win, especially knowing they'll use it to go pro.

Joy at the memory of our own unprecedented round three victory.

Gratitude for everything this experience has given me.

And pure excitement for what comes next.

In this moment, it's like I can see the future coming together. The vision feels so crystal clear, I know exactly what will happen.

Britni will use her savings to move to New York, and Alix will help her find a home here. She will shift her influencing to books and gaming. And she will help boost the ventures of both Alix and Mo.

Mo will open her fandom-curating shop. It will start virtually, but she will establish proof of concept. And once she does, the investors will come running to forge her shop into physical reality.

Alix will start his own fashion label with the money he generates from creating more *Pantheonic* cosplay outfits, maybe even sold through Mo's shop—and maybe even managed by Britni's experience. He will eventually become the kind of designer the next generation needs, fusing so many beautiful things together.

And I will move into my dorm at NYU and continue climbing toward my dream of becoming a tenured Classics professor. I will do so with a new awareness of the balanced connection between my body and my mind. Most importantly, I will do it all with Alix by my side.

And we will find out just how deep this current between us really runs.

Then another thought begins to glow, that same new spark from our round three victory dinner. I'll have lots of entries for my personal mythology journal to adapt these final mythical reveals, but one important theme solidifies: remaining open to new and unexpected perspectives.

If my intention for this final round was to expand my horizons, *Pantheonic* has certainly delivered that. As new realizations begin to burn bright in my brain, it also occurs to me that I should take to heart another lesson learned: sharing important things outside of my own head.

"I don't know about you all, but I feel really good about this," I begin, turning to my teammates while the room celebrates the Seasons' victory. "Sure, taking first place and the prize money would have been nice. Most rules we've been taught say that's what matters most—being the best and having the most. But reflecting on this experience, I think we've won what we really *need.*"

I see my teammates all begin to brighten one last time, hearing this.

"A found family," Alix adds, smiling between us.

"Some new purpose," Britni follows up.

"A community to share it all with," Mo says, beaming.

"And some hearts mended," I finish, letting that team-theme sentiment settle.

Although I do have one last realization to add at the end of this era for the Epic Hearts, one that nods to our own next chapter.

"And I have to say, now that the entire Stoneruned struggle has cast our war questions in a new light, it's done the same for another core question of mine: Why do I want to be a Classics professor—I mean, what is my mission statement?

"If it's to adapt mythology to bring deeper understanding to those I teach, that doesn't have to be limited to a classroom or by a degree. Sure, I still want those things. But why can't I start practicing that mission statement right now for all the new social media followers I've gained? Working with my very smart and savvy friends as you share your own gifts?"

"Welcome to the influencer club!" Britni says, giving me a little hug.

"I mean, that's what this experience has really been about," Mo adds, still beaming. "Finding a way to build things that will last beyond us."

"Couldn't have said it better myself," Alix says, looking over at me like the sun and the moon shine in both our eyes.

Looking back at Alix, and at Mo and Britni, I can only think:

K.Odyssia would be proud, ushering so many warriors to new homes.

Really, there's only one way I want to end this epic-hearted experience. I turn to give Alix one more kiss . . .

And I can't think of a better happily ever after.

CREDITS

Editors: Britny Perilli, Julie Matysik

Design: Mary Boyer, Sara Puppala

Production: Amber Morris, Duncan McHenry, Erica Lawrence, Doug Wolff, Jess Riordan, Charles Kaszytski

Marketing & Publicity: Becca Matheson, Kara Thornton, Elizabeth Parks, Betsy Hulsebosch

ACKNOWLEDGMENTS

I don't know if only authors do this, but whenever I pick up a new book, I always flip to read the acknowledgments first. Whether you're reading this to start or at the finish, all my thanks need to go to my agent, Moe Ferrara. This book only started and reached the finish line because of your support and guidance! Equal thanks are owed to editors Britny Perilli and Julie Matysik for overseeing the many versions of this novel—from its own start as a potential interactive Choices game-book to this clean novel finale. Your support of nerdy queer fiction is forever appreciated!

There are two author friends without whom this book would not exist. The first is M. K. England, my RPK imprint sibling, whose books *Roll for Love* and *Player vs. Player* taught me what this novel could be. I also owe M. K. endless thanks for all the support and talks, plus beta and blurb reads along the way! The same goes for Jason June, my pop-culture taste sibling, whose beta/blurb read restored my confidence in this novel and gave me some invaluable notes that helped the final draft really level up, especially the ending. There are dozens of other author friends who talked me through various stages of this one. You all know who you are, but special MVP status goes to Robbie Couch, Hannah V. Sawyerr, Kate Myers, and Julia Rubin. And of course Sylvia Nacey, who provided a crucial early sensitivity read for Alix's character.

You may not know this, but I'm a kind of game writer as well (my interactive novels always possess an RPG element to them), so it was trippy to write my first precontracted linear print novel ABOUT games. This presented all kinds of unique challenges, but I'd like to thank myself (lol) for pushing through all the obstacles on this one. I was out of my comfort zone in many ways, but I'm really proud of where this one landed—and all the ways I leveled up as a writer figuring it out.

I also would like to thank Annie Verderame and Krzysztof Pakula for helping me along my own personal odyssey with chronic pain, obviously reflected in this book!

There are way too many gaming and mythological inspirations to cite here in terms of my research for this project, but a special shoutout needs to go to the artist Yoshi Yoshitani, whose *Tarot of the Divine* and accompanying world folklore book kept me continuously inspired. I pulled a different card from Yoshi's deck and read a different accompanying tale of world mythology every morning while working on this novel. The fact that we actually got Yoshi to do our cover still blows my mind!

As always, there are some special readers I'd like to name for their unwavering support: Rosa Van Wie, Mia Van Matre, Qymana Botts, and Kathryn Empson. To all you readers, past and future, I can't thank you enough for being here!

Lastly, the final thanks always belongs with my immediate family. While I hope it'll someday change, being an author has remained an indie endeavor for me, and I could never do it without my village of support. To my parents, Anne and Steve, my brother, Louis, and his family, Amanda, Everly, and Grace, I give endless thanks. And none of this would be nearly as possible (or as fun) without my own nerdy epic-heart romance, my partner of eleven years and counting, my husband, Kyle.